Acclaim for Colleen Coble

"The tension, both suspenseful and romantic, is gripping, reflecting Coble's prowess with the genre."

—PUBLISHERS WEEKLY, STARRED REVIEW FOR
TWILIGHT AT BLUEBERRY BARRENS

"Incredible storytelling and intricately drawn characters. You won't want to miss *Twilight at Blueberry Barrens*!"

—BRENDA NOVAK, NEW YORK TIMES AND
USA TODAY BESTSELLING AUTHOR

"Coble has a gift for making a setting come to life. After reading *Twilight at Blueberry Barrens*, I feel like I've lived in Maine all my life. This plot kept me guessing until the end, and her characters seem like my friends. I don't want to let them go!

—TERRI BLACKSTOCK, USA TODAY
BESTSELLING AUTHOR OF IF I RUN

"I'm a long-time fan of Colleen Coble, and *Twilight at Blueberry Barrens* is the perfect example of why. Coble delivers riveting suspense, delicious romance, and carefully crafted characters, all with the deft hand of a veteran writer. If you love romantic suspense, pick this one up. You won't be disappointed!"

—DENISE HUNTER, AUTHOR OF THE GOODBYE BRIDE

"Colleen Coble, the queen of Christian romantic mysteries, is back with her best book yet. Filled with familiar characters, plot twists, and a confusion of antagonists, I couldn't keep the pages of this novel set in Maine turning fast enough. I reconnected with characters I love while taking a journey filled with murder, suspense, and the prospect of love. This truly is her best book to date, and perfect for readers who adore a page-turner laced with romance."

—CARA PUTMAN, AWARD-WINNING AUTHOR OF
SHADOWED BY GRACE AND WHERE TREETOPS
GLISTEN ON TWILIGHT AT BLUEBERRY BARRENS

"Gripping! Colleen Coble has again written a page-turning romantic suspense with *Twilight at Blueberry Barrens*! Not only did she keep me up nights racing through the pages to see what would happen next, I genuinely cared for her characters. Colleen sets the bar high for romantic suspense!"

—CARRIE STUART PARKS, AUTHOR OF *A CRY FROM THE DUST* AND *WHEN DEATH DRAWS NEAR*

"Colleen Coble thrills readers again with her newest novel, an addictive suspense trenched in family, betrayal, and . . . murder."

—DIANN MILLS, AUTHOR OF *DEADLY ENCOUNTER* ON *TWILIGHT AT BLUEBERRY BARRENS*

"Coble's latest, *Twilight at Blueberry Barrens*, is one of her best yet! With characters you want to know in person, a perfect setting, and a plot that had me holding my breath, laughing, and crying, this story will stay with the reader long after the book is closed. My highest recommendation."

—ROBIN CAROLL, BESTSELLING NOVELIST

"Colleen's *Twilight at Blueberry Barrens* is filled with a bevy of twists and surprises, a wonderful romance, and the warmth of family love. I couldn't have asked for more. This author has always been a five-star novelist, but I think it's time to up the ante with this book. It's on my keeping shelf!"

—HANNAH ALEXANDER, AUTHOR OF THE HALLOWED HALLS SERIES

"Second chances, old flames, and startling new revelations combine to form a story filled with faith, trial, forgiveness, and redemption. Crack the cover and step in, but beware—Mermaid Point is harboring secrets that will keep you guessing."

—LISA WINGATE, NATIONAL BESTSELLING AUTHOR OF THE SEA KEEPER'S DAUGHTERS, ON *MERMAID MOON*

"I burned through *The Inn at Ocean's Edge* in one sitting. An intricate plot by a master storyteller. Colleen Coble has done it again with this gripping opening to a new series. I can't wait to spend more time at Sunset Cove."

—HEATHER BURCH, BESTSELLING AUTHOR
OF *ONE LAVENDER RIBBON*

"Coble doesn't disappoint with her custom blend of suspense and romance."

—*PUBLISHERS WEEKLY* ON *THE INN AT OCEAN'S EDGE*

"Veteran author Coble has penned another winner. Filled with mystery and romance that are unpredictable until the last page, this novel will grip readers long past when they should put their books down. Recommended to readers of contemporary mysteries."

—*CBA RETAILERS + RESOURCES* REVIEW
OF *THE INN AT OCEAN'S EDGE*

"Coble truly shines when she's penning a mystery, and this tale will really keep the reader guessing . . . Mystery lovers will definitely want to put this book on their purchase list."

—*ROMANTIC TIMES* REVIEW OF *THE INN AT OCEAN'S EDGE*

"Master storyteller Colleen Coble has done it again. *The Inn at Ocean's Edge* is an intricately woven, well-crafted story of romance, suspense, family secrets, and a decades-old mystery. Needless to say, it had me hooked from page one. I simply couldn't stop turning the pages. This one's going on my keeper shelf."

—LYNETTE EASON, AWARD-WINNING, BESTSELLING
AUTHOR OF THE HIDDEN IDENTITY SERIES

"Evocative and gripping, *The Inn at Ocean's Edge* will keep you flipping pages long into the night."

—DANI PETTREY, BESTSELLING AUTHOR OF
THE ALASKAN COURAGE SERIES

"Coble's atmospheric and suspenseful series launch should appeal to fans of Tracie Peterson and other authors of Christian romantic suspense."

—*LIBRARY JOURNAL* REVIEW OF *TIDEWATER INN*

"Romantically tense, but with just the right touch of danger, this cowboy love story is surprisingly clever—and pleasingly sweet."

—USAToday.com review of *Blue Moon Promise*

"[An] outstanding, completely engaging tale that will have you on the edge of your seat . . . A must-have for all fans of romantic suspense!"

—TheRomanceReadersConnection.com review of *Anathema*

"Colleen Coble lays an intricate trail in *Without a Trace* and draws the reader on like a hound with a scent."

—Romantic Times, 4½ stars

"Coble's historical series just keeps getting better with each entry."

—Library Journal starred review of *The Lightkeeper's Ball*

"Don't ever mistake [Coble's] for the fluffy romances with a little bit of suspense. She writes solid suspense, and she ties it all together beautifully with a wonderful message."

—LifeinReviewBlog.com review of *Lonestar Angel*

"Colleen is a master storyteller."

—Karen Kingsbury, bestselling author of *Unlocked* and *Learning*

Because
you're
Mine

Also by Colleen Coble

Because you're Mine

COLLEEN COBLE

THOMAS NELSON
Since 1798

Published in Nashville, Tennessee, by Thomas Nelson. Thomas Nelson is a registered trademark of HarperCollins Christian Publishing, Inc.

Thomas Nelson titles may be purchased in bulk for educational, business, fund-raising, or sales promotional use. For information, please e-mail SpecialMarkets@ThomasNelson.com.

Library of Congress Cataloging-in-Publication Data

CIP data is available upon request.

Printed in the United States of America

17 18 19 20 21 RRD 7 6 5 4 3 2 1

For my dear friend in heaven, Diann Hunt.
Because You're Mine *was her favorite of all the*
books I've written. I miss you every day, Di!

One

She'd never get through this final set.

Flinging her dark red hair away from her fiddle, Alanna Connolly swallowed down the soreness in her throat and danced across the polished wooden floor of the stage. She couldn't fail—not here at the great Hibernian Hall where Charleston had turned out in force for Ceol, the four-woman Celtic band she'd founded. Her fingers flew across the fingerboard, and her other hand manipulated the bow across the strings of her instrument.

Almost there. If her voice held out for one more song, she could rest. She turned slightly so she could see her husband, Liam, as he pounded out the beat on his bodhran. He twirled the double-headed tippers in his hand and nodded at her, the special sign between them. He was praying for her.

When the Irish jig ended, the applause rose in a crescendo. Alanna bowed, then stepped to the mic. Her throat thickened, and she knew not a note would clear her mouth with a true, pure sound. The pleading glance she sent Ciara caused the alto singer to step to Alanna's aid. Fiona and Ena joined them at the mic, and Ciara took the lead on the final song.

The audience fell silent as the melancholy Irish ballad "The Last Rose of Summer" wafted over the sold-out house. Alanna mouthed the words and prayed no one would miss her voice in the mix. Her face hurt from smiling, and she wanted to rush from the stage to the sanctuary of the dressing room. Her blood pounded with the thump of Liam's blows on the big bass drum behind her. *Run, run,* the drum said, but Alanna held her ground.

Just a few moments more.

The song ended and the four of them bowed, then Liam joined them. They bowed together one last time as the crowd roared its approval. Liam glanced at her, and she gave a slight shake of her head. There would be no encore tonight.

After their final bow, he led her out of the hot lights to the cool relief of backstage. "I shouldn't have let you sing tonight." Once they reached the seclusion of the curtains, he pulled her into his arms.

Fiddle at her side, she leaned into him and inhaled his beloved aroma, a mixture of Irish Tweed cologne and the pungent odor of the bodhran's goatskin. Weariness settled over her like a shroud. "I'll be needing tea."

He tucked her hand into the crook of his elbow. "You need some shut-eye."

She smiled at him. "That I do."

Jesse Hawthorne leaned against the doorjamb of the dressing room and watched his friend embrace his wife. Alanna should have been his—and would have been if not for Liam. He knew the precise moment when Alanna saw him, because she stiffened and pulled out of Liam's arms. Nothing would convince him she didn't still harbor some feelings for him. He approached the couple.

"Jesse, you made it!" Liam high-fived his friend and clapped him on the shoulder. "Weren't we on fire?"

"It was terrific." Jesse's gaze lingered on Fiona a moment. She'd given him a come-hither glance a time or two, but whenever Alanna was around, he found it hard to concentrate on another woman.

"Thanks." Alanna tucked a lock of burnished hair behind her ear.

Jesse stood close enough to catch a whiff of her sweet perfume. What would she do if he leaned in for a better sniff? "You should see my new Mustang. That convertible can fly! I'll take you on a ride sometime. Can't wait to get your husband out in it tonight."

She averted her glance and smiled. He took that to mean she'd like to go, and he let himself imagine a warm, sunny day with her long hair flying in the wind.

A suffocating blanket of depression settled over him. Liam had it all—beautiful wife, exciting career, and rich parents. Jesse's own life was going nowhere. If only he still had Alanna by his side. She had been his good-luck charm. When she was on his arm, he knew what it was like to ride the wave to better things.

Now he was nothing, and that was all he'd ever be.

There was something different about Jesse tonight, but Alanna couldn't put her finger on it. She'd dated him for a time, but his eyes wandered to other women. She had him to thank for introducing her to Liam, though.

The two men were very similar in appearance with their brown hair and eyes—both about six feet tall and broad in the shoulder. Their coloring was so close people sometimes mistook them for brothers. Liam often teased her that she'd never know the difference between them in a dark room, but she knew better. Liam was gentle and tender, while Jesse was someone who grabbed what he wanted and pushed his way to the front of the line as if it were his due. Tonight they looked even more alike in their identical black Ceol T-shirts. Liam had given one to Jesse last week.

Jesse gave Alanna a crooked smile but spoke to Liam. "I don't know how you play that bodhran."

She managed to smile at his light tone, but she wanted to run to the seclusion of the dressing room. Dealing with Jesse was one more pressure she didn't need tonight. Liam never seemed to notice the stares Jesse sent her way. Stares that made her uncomfortable.

"You could play it, too, if you just put in a little effort," Liam said. "I dare you to give it a try."

Jesse never took his gaze from Alanna. "I just might."

The wood-frame drum was surprisingly difficult to master, and no one played it like Liam. He was an artist of the top-end style and could vary the pitch of the thumps.

They stepped into the dressing room, and Alanna collapsed onto a silk-covered chair that had seen better days. The rest of the group filed in behind them and pushed through to the connecting room they shared—all except for Ciara. She was tuned to Alanna as if they were twins, though they couldn't be more different, both in looks and background. Ciara wore her black, kinky hair in cornrows that accentuated her strong cheekbones, while Alanna's red locks fell in a curtain of curls past her waist. Ciara never needed makeup on her beautiful dark skin, and Alanna was forever trying to cover the red splotches her fair skin developed when exposed to the smallest amount of sun.

"Sure, but I'm knackered. I'll be sleeping till noon." Ciara pointed her long finger at Alanna. "The doctor told you not to sing tonight."

"I couldn't disappoint all our fans," Alanna said.

"It's better than ruining your voice and never singing again." Ciara waved her beringed hand. "You're already picking up an American accent."

Liam faced the open door, and a frown darkened his face. Alanna glanced around and saw their new manager, Barry Kavanagh, standing in the doorway. The blokes seemed determined to square off like two bulls. Their first manager had let Liam run things as he pleased, but Barry was more hands-on. His background as an attorney was probably to blame.

The man's easy smile came as he stepped into the room. "I noticed your throat is troubling you, Alanna. I took the liberty of calling my doctor to come examine you. We can't be too careful with our star." The Southern accent in his words was almost a caress.

Alanna glimpsed a man in a black suit behind Barry. She nodded. "I'd be glad to have him look at it."

The doctor unzipped a compartment in his rolling bag and extracted a light and a tongue depressor. "Say ah," he ordered. Alanna complied and the doctor frowned. He stepped closer and pulled out a mirrored instrument. He peered deeper into her throat, then flipped off his light. "A bit of a sore throat. I'll give you some medicine, and you should be fine for the weekend's performance."

Alanna's hope surged. "You see no nodules?" Maybe the other doctor had been overly cautious.

"It's just a little sore throat," the doctor said, snapping shut his bag.

"That's not what the specialist said." Liam's suspicious stare went from Barry to the doctor, then back. "She needs to rest her throat for a few months. She might even need surgery. I'm going to cancel the bookings."

She clutched his arm. "Liam, you can't! The venues are sold out. Sold out, love! Everything we've worked for, prayed for, is happening now. We might never regain our momentum."

"Alanna is right," Barry said. "Ceol could be the next Celtic Woman. They could be as big as Enya. We must capitalize on the group's rising popularity."

Liam crossed his arms, muscular from his workouts at the drums. "Not at the risk to Alanna's throat."

"We'll be having three more concerts scheduled in the next week," Ciara said. "Can she finish the tour and then take some time off?"

Liam shook his head. "Not if she wants a chance to avoid surgery. The specialist said she has to rest."

Barry nodded and put his arm around Alanna. "My doctor says she'll be fine."

His proprietorial touch made her lean away just a bit. Alanna couldn't think, couldn't decide what to do. How could she stop now when the group was a shooting star? "You think the specialist was wrong?"

"You'd be believing a bloke like this?" Liam stabbed a finger in the doctor's direction. "And get your hands off my wife."

Barry's smile dropped away and he removed his arm. Alanna glanced at Ciara and found her glaring at Barry as well. No one liked the way Barry seemed focused on her. She didn't like it either, but the man was a marketing genius, and the group had soared to a new level under his management. They couldn't afford to offend him.

Alanna touched her husband's hand. "Liam, let's talk about it privately."

Liam's jaw worked, then he glared at Barry. "This is our decision, not yours."

Barry shrugged, then ushered the doctor toward the door. "I'll leave you to discuss it."

The moment he was gone, Ciara flipped her cornrows away from her face and scowled. "What an *eejit*. We'll wait for you in the hall. You two can be hashing it out."

Alanna didn't ask if she meant Barry or the doctor. The band trooped out the door.

Liam shut the door behind them, then went to the keyboard

and pulled out the chair. He settled in front of the keys and began to play.

"What's that?" The haunting tune filled the room, evaporating her anger, lifting her spirits as she finally placed the melody. "It's from my sister's music box." She stepped closer to him and laid her hand on his shoulder.

"It is." He continued to play.

The melody with its pure passion sent chills down her spine. One of her clearest memories was of a music box her sister, Neila, had been given by their great-grandfather. Alanna never heard the melody anywhere else, though she'd never forgotten it and had picked it out on her fiddle the moment she learned to play.

Liam began to sing and Alanna gasped. "You wrote words for it."

His intense gaze fastened on her, and love shimmered in his eyes. "Two souls bound and none can sever. This nightsong is for you. Our love will last through darkness, fire, and trouble. This nightsong is for you. Though death may try to break our hearts, I'll find you where'ere you go. This nightsong is for you."

The words bound themselves to the music and filled Alanna's heart. "I've never heard anything so beautiful," she whispered as the music stopped and faded.

He took her hand. "We're beautiful together, love. We can't let anything come between us. Not Barry, not Ceol, not our families." He rose from the chair and took her in his arms. "Promise me."

"I promise." She burrowed her face against his chest and inhaled the scent of him deep into her lungs, into her very being.

His lingering kiss ignited her senses, and she snuggled closer, then sighed and rested her head on his shoulder. "In just five months, we'll be parents, Liam. We must tell everyone soon. Your parents, our mates."

"It's lucky we are that you aren't showing much, but yes, we will need to let the world in on it soon."

She put her hand on her belly, and his cell phone rang. She sighed and pulled away. "It's Jesse wanting you."

"I know." He pressed his lips to her hair, then opened the door for her.

They found the rest of the group, along with Jesse, waiting by the exit. Jesse opened the heavy metal door into the dark alley where their van and Jesse's car were parked.

Some fans lined the back alley and screamed out Fiona's name. The beautiful blonde played Irish spoons and sang backup vocals. Fans bought the Celtic jewelry she designed, and Alanna spotted more than one of the beautifully crafted necklaces and earrings.

Fiona, Ciara, and Alanna stopped to sign a few photographs, but Ena kept her pink-dyed head down and ran for the van with her pennywhistle without looking at any of the fans calling her name.

Liam tugged Alanna to the van, then dropped a kiss onto her lips. "I'll be back in a few hours."

"Have fun. You think Jesse will let you drive?"

He grinned. "I doubt it. He's smitten with that car."

She watched him disappear around the corner to join Jesse, then climbed into the back of the van with her friends.

"Deadly concert tonight," Fiona said. "We'll be having them

all the time now." When no one answered her, she glanced at the set faces and shut up.

Alanna wanted to say something to break the tension, but she ended up leaning her head against the back of the seat and closing her eyes. The music industry was filled with examples of people who left the operating room with their singing voices changed forever, husky and rough, and she refused to think about a fate like that. But the high notes she used to hit with ease had become harder and harder to reach, and Barry's blather hadn't dislodged her fear.

An explosion shook the van, and she turned to see smoke pouring from the corner where she'd last seen Liam.

"Liam!" She screamed. She pushed open the van door and rushed to the corner.

She rounded the end of the concert hall and gasped when she saw flames billowing from a yellow sports car. "Liam!" She started for the car, but Ciara grabbed her.

"The fire department is coming. You can do nothing."

A siren's wail grew louder and mingled with her own sobs as Ciara held her close. Alanna couldn't tear her gaze from the burning car and could make out no figures inside. Deep inside, she knew no one could survive the intensity of those flames.

Two

lanna rubbed her eyes, gritty from crying. She padded on bare feet to the window of her hotel room and turned up the air conditioning. Peering through sheets of rain, she stared down onto the wet street.

Liam was dead. She still couldn't process the reality. The fire department had taken two men away, and the driver was clearly dead. She'd clung to hope that Jesse hadn't allowed Liam to drive, but when a paramedic asked the survivor his name as he was loaded into the ambulance, the badly burned man had whispered, "Jesse."

Generations of Irish women before her had faced widowhood with their chins held high. She must show similar strength. A cry of *Why Liam, God?* hung on her tongue, but she kept it locked inside. There was no answer to such a question. Liam had possessed a strong faith. Her own was weak in comparison, especially now when faced with such suffering.

When she had called the hospital fifteen minutes before,

Jesse was still clinging to life. His parents had the top plastic surgeon in the country standing by for 3-D facial reconstruction, and that would be done as soon as he stabilized. She should be glad he lived, but why couldn't it have been Liam? Why was her husband in the morgue while an *eejit* like Jesse would recover?

Alanna closed her eyes. Would she want Liam to go through what Jesse was enduring right now? Liam would have been grieved to see his old friend in such bad shape. The doctors had put him into a medically induced coma as they worked to save his life, and she'd been told he would require many surgeries. Maybe Liam was the luckier man.

Her eyes filled again. Liam would never flip his longish hair out of his eyes so he could wink at her. He'd never come in from planting flowers with mud under his fingernails. He'd never step into the yard with his bubble-blowing tools.

How could such a bright light just . . . cease to exist? He'd been her real family. She hadn't seen her mum or her sister in years, and the Lord alone knew if they were even still on this earth. She touched her belly. At least she had his child.

A knock came on her door, and she turned. The police had called an hour ago, and she'd expected them before now. She opened the door to find Barry standing there with two policemen.

Her manager stood in the hall with his hands in the pockets of his impeccable suit. A lock of blond hair fell across his forehead. His grave eyes looked her over, and both policemen were somber.

Alanna focused her blurry gaze on the nearest policeman. She wiped her eyes, then drew in another trembling breath.

"Come in." She stepped aside to allow them to enter, but her pulse throbbed in her throat. "Do you know what happened yet?"

Detective Adams was a small man with red hair. His pale skin was covered by a mass of freckles on his face and arms. The delicate skin under his eyes sagged. He wore khaki slacks and a light-blue shirt. He glanced at his notebook. "A bomb exploded under the car. We're still investigating."

"A bomb." She swayed and reached out to steady herself on an armchair. Someone had done this on purpose. It wasn't some accident with the petrol tank. Her knees threatened to buckle again, but she managed to stay upright as Ciara, dressed in jeans and a Ceol T-shirt, came rushing through the still open door. She said nothing but came to stand close to Alanna. The presence of her friend gave her strength.

She stared out the window at the rainy Charleston streets. It was a soft old day. The sky was crying for Liam. She tried to focus on what the detective was saying, something about investigating the bomb-making materials, but her vision wavered and her ears seemed to have gone deaf.

"I must sit down," she murmured.

Ciara guided her into the armchair and pushed her head between her knees. "Breathe."

Alanna obeyed, and her vision began to clear. When she raised her head, Barry was just ending a call, and the policemen had gone.

Barry knelt in front of her. "I can get Liam's body transported back to Ireland as soon as his body is released. Adams said he'd push the coroner on the autopsy, and we should be able to leave in three days. Does that suit? I'll reserve the flights."

"That's perfect, Barry." She fumbled for her purse. "Let me give you my card number."

"I've already taken care of it," he said. "Don't worry about anything. I need to go to Dublin on business anyway, so I got myself a ticket as well. If there's anything else I can do, please tell me, Alanna. I feel badly there's nothing I can do to help."

"You've already helped so much, Barry." Her lips felt numb.

"I'll pick you up at ten on Friday morning to go to the airport. You have my number. Call me if you need anything." He rose and stepped back.

"I'll need tickets for the rest of the band. I-I need them with me." She reached out and sought Ciara's hand.

"I'm sorry, but no. All that was available were two first-class seats. We can get them the evening flight though." He turned toward the door. "I'll leave you alone now to grieve. I'm so sorry, Alanna." The door clicked behind him.

She would have liked to have had Ciara with her especially, but it was more important to get Liam back to the Emerald Isle, on his own soil.

Alanna sat in the blessed quiet and listened to the traffic outside along the street. They'd had such plans to see everything in Charleston this trip—the old plantation houses, the swamps, the City Market. Now all those dreams had to be packed up in a trunk that could never be opened and carted back across the sea.

"I'm going to go downstairs and get you something to eat," Ciara said.

Alanna knew she'd never eat a bite, but she needed to be alone for a bit, so she nodded.

Once her friend was gone, she stared at the phone. Liam's parents needed to know, but oh how she hated to call them. If she were a coward, she'd call their vicar and ask him to go by and drop the news, but Alanna didn't want to put that burden on him. He had enough problems of his own with a sick wife and two kids. She got out her cell phone and rang her father-in-law. It was around noon in Ireland. Her call would likely interrupt their dinner, and she nearly disconnected, but it clicked through before she made up her mind.

The maid answered, and Alanna asked to speak to Thomas.

"He's at his meal, miss," the maid said. Her tone of voice always made Alanna shrivel.

"There's an emergency," Alanna said. "This is his daughter-in-law." Only she wasn't anymore. The Connolly family would be only too happy to scrape her off their shoes.

Thomas came on the line a few seconds later. "Alanna? What's wrong?"

She caught her breath. How could she tell a father that his only son was dead? Her vision blurred and she blinked rapidly. "Thomas, it's very bad news I bring you."

"What's happened to Liam? Someone mugged him, took all his money. I knew it would happen. How much do you need?"

He sounded weary, as though he was used to them dunning him for money, and anger swept away Alanna's grief. Never had they asked Liam's father for a dime. "It's nothing like that." He started to interrupt her, and she went on quickly before she lost courage. "Thomas, please. It's much worse than you understand. Liam, he—he was in an accident." Though she could hardly call the deliberate planting of a bomb an accident.

15

"An accident, you say? He was injured. Sheila, Liam's been injured," he said to his wife, who must be standing near.

"No, Thomas. He was . . . killed." Her voice broke on the word. The stricken pause on the other end of the line brought more tears rushing to her eyes. Even though they disliked her, she knew the pain they were going through. "He was riding with his friend Jesse Hawthorne."

"No," Thomas whispered. "It's a cruel joke you'll be playing, Alanna. Tell the truth now."

"I wish it weren't true," she said, a sob breaking through her resolve to be strong, "but I saw his body myself. I'm bringing him home on Friday."

A moan came through the phone, then a click. Thomas had hung up on her, and she was thankful she didn't have to hear his grief. Her own was quite enough to bear.

Three

The green hills of Ireland greeted Alanna with an uncharacteristically fine day. She was the first out of the terminal, and her mates crowded behind her. They had managed to get onto her flight at the last minute.

Barry motioned to the driver of the van he'd rented, and the man opened the back to lift their bags inside. "The casket is being transported for you, so we won't have to worry about that. The driver will take you to your apartments. I have some business to attend to, but call me if you need me."

"Thank you, Barry. You've been grand. My mates will take care of me from here."

"Of course." He helped her into the van after her friends, and his hand lingered on her arm for a long moment before he stepped back. The van pulled away.

Fiona turned to look out the window. "The first thing I'll be having is a big plate of black pudding and a spot of real tea. Americans don't know how to make it."

"I want mash and bangers," Ena said. "And to smell the city." She sniffed the air.

Alanna listened with half an ear. The first thing she had to do was go see Thomas and Sheila, but she dreaded it. They would blame her for Liam's death. At least she would be able to tell them about the baby.

Ciara took her hand and seemed to read her mind. "C'mere. Do you want me to go with you? To see his folks?"

Alanna squeezed her friend's fingers. "Would you mind?"

Her chin jutted out. "Thomas won't be bullying you with a witness alongside."

"You don't know him." Alanna let her gaze wander over the bustle of traffic outside her window.

"I'll be finding out," Ciara said, scowling.

Alanna drank in the beauty of the city she loved. When they passed Leinster House, where the parliament of Ireland convened, her smile faded. Thomas was an Oireachtas senator, a member of the upper house of the Irish legislature. He was much loved by the Irish media and his blokes in the Seanad Éireann, the equivalent of the United States Senate. He was probably there right now, imposing his will on his mates, just as he'd always done to her and Liam. Escaping to her music had saved them both.

The van stopped in front of Alanna's flat. Barry had offered to get her a hotel so she didn't have to face the empty rooms, but she had to do it sooner or later.

All the members of Ceol had flats in this building. The van driver helped pile their suitcases on the sidewalk. Alanna paid him and stood looking up at the old brick building.

"Shall I be coming up with you?" Ciara asked.

"I need to do this alone," Alanna said. "I'll call you when I'm ready to go to Thomas's house."

Ciara squeezed her fingers, then grabbed her two bags and hauled them toward the entrance. Alanna inhaled and did the same. Entering the building, she realized she'd forgotten how old the place smelled. It *was* old, built back in 1829. She took the lift to the third floor and carried her suitcases down the hall.

She set her bags down in front of the door and fumbled for the key in her purse. The lock took a bit of persuasion, as usual, but too soon the door swung open, and Alanna looked at her life the way it used to be.

The tiny living room still held the old green sofa they'd bought when they were first married. Liam's collection of fishing flies sat on the coffee table. Alanna stepped across the stack of old mail and flyers the postman had left on the floor. The flat smelled stale and shut up.

Empty of Liam's presence.

She blinked back the moisture in her eyes. Maybe it was just as well she didn't sense Liam here. Her gaze went to the pile of old mail. Anyone who mattered knew how to contact them on the road, and all their bills went to a box at her accountant's.

She carried the pile to the kitchen and began to toss each piece of junk mail into the garbage. The return address on one envelope caught her attention. It was from the private investigator she'd hired. The last she'd heard, he'd failed to find any trace of her sister, and that was over a year ago. She hadn't expected to hear from him again.

She slit open the envelope and pulled out a single sheet of paper. The investigator had turned up one small bit of information during inquiries into another matter. From what he could gather, her mother was last seen at a Traveller's village outside Dublin in February. One month ago. Alanna didn't particularly care about her mother's whereabouts, but she hoped that finding her mum might lead to her sister, Neila.

Someone knocked on the door. Still stunned, Alanna went to answer it and found Ciara there. "Is it quite late?" Alanna asked, glancing at her watch.

"No, I just thought I'd help you. You might think you want to be alone, but I'm not having it. It's not good for you." Ciara brushed past her.

Alanna closed the door. "I'm glad you're here. Look." She handed the letter to her mate.

Ciara carried it to the sofa with her. She dropped onto the sofa and scanned the letter. "Your mum's right here?"

Alanna sank into the chair opposite the sofa. "She was last month. I want to find Neila. I don't care about my mum."

"So you say. You have to be having some feelings for her."

"Why should I have any love left for a woman who would just walk off and leave her three-year-old behind in a trailer, alone? She had so little care for me. But Neila had no say. She was only eight when Mum took her away with her."

Ciara looked up from the letter. "We should check this place out."

"I was hoping you'd say that."

"Mate, you know I wouldn't let you do this alone."

Alanna studied her friend's face. There hadn't been an

opportunity to tell Ciara about the baby. "I have news to tell them—and you. I'm pregnant."

Ciara's eyes widened, and her mouth dropped open. "Oh, Alanna. So a part of Liam is still with us."

"Yes, it's quite the comfort. I'm just over four months along. It's a boy."

"So far along! And you're not showing."

"I've been clever with my clothing choices." She stood and smoothed her loose top over her tiny belly. "See?"

"Just barely." Ciara folded her in a fierce hug. "Me and the rest of your mates will be here for you and that baby, Alanna."

"I'm counting on that." Alanna glanced at her watch. "It's time we go to see Thomas and Sheila. I want to catch them before supper. My Citroen was serviced and left in the parking stall. We can take that. It will be grand to drive on the proper side of the road again. Let me change clothes. Thomas will be quite scandalized if I show up in jeans. Even the news of the baby won't pacify."

She left Ciara in the living room, then dragged her bag to the bedroom, where she changed into a navy skirt and jacket over a crisp white blouse. The despised navy pumps pinched her toes, but she wore them anyway.

Outside, she soaked up the sights and sounds of Dublin as she led Ciara to the car: the honks, good-natured calls between mates, the smell of mead spilling out of the pubs, and even the car exhaust. If only Liam were here with her.

The black Citroen started on the first try. She drove through the streets and out to the countryside. Rolling down her window, she inhaled. "Nothing smells like Irish rain."

"I'm feeling a bit peckish. We should have grabbed some fish and chips," Ciara said. "Shall your in-laws have mercy and invite us to eat?"

"I'm hoping not. I'd rather not stay." Alanna applied the brakes as she neared the laneway to the Connolly manor. The large house sat back from the lane a fair distance so that only a glimpse could be seen by the common folk Thomas represented in parliament. She paused at the entrance, then stuck her arm out the window and punched in the code to open the gate.

Her heart was beating fast and erratically. She parked in the circle laneway, right in front of the house. Seeing Sheila's joy in the coming baby would make putting up with Thomas much easier.

"It's pale you are," Ciara said. "Are you sure you're up to this?"

Alanna wet her lips and nodded, though acid churned in her stomach. "We'll just stay a short time. We can tell them we have plans."

"I have a date with mash and bangers," Ciara said, opening her door. "The sooner we're done here, the sooner I'll be eating them."

It seemed a lifetime since she'd last walked this flagstone path to the front door. She rang the bell and tried to compose herself, without success.

The butler opened the door. His expressionless face changed as he looked her over. "It's sorry I am for you, missus. Come in. I'll let them know you've arrived."

They followed him into the drawing room, where he left them. Sheila had redecorated since Alanna had been here. The blue wing chairs were quite lovely, as was the camelback sofa and new rug. She heard footsteps on the wood floor and whirled to see

Thomas in the doorway. Sheila was right behind him. She usually wore makeup, but today her face was tearstained and strained.

Thomas was slim and tanned, handsome. His gray hair and impeccable navy suit exuded power and prestige. Liam would have looked like him someday. The thought made Alanna's heart squeeze. Sheila's blonde hair was perfectly coiffed, and she wore a pale blue suit and pumps. About three years younger than Thomas, she was the perfect wife.

Thomas looked Alanna over. "You should have called us from the airport. I would have sent a driver for you. The funeral director called to let me know he has received our Liam." He swallowed hard. "We should discuss arrangements."

He came forward and she raised her cheek for him to kiss. His dry lips brushed across her skin and lifted away as if any prolonged contact would sully him. Sheila waited until Alanna stepped back, then opened her arms. Tears lay tracks down her cheeks, and her face was white.

Alanna went into Sheila's embrace and touched her lips to her mother-in-law's cheek, scented with some kind of powder. Liam had gotten his sweet nature from his mother.

"When did you arrive?" Sheila asked as they separated and moved to sit.

"Just this afternoon. I came straightaway. The furniture is lovely, Sheila. I like it very much."

Alanna knew the precise moment that Sheila realized she was pregnant. The sun piercing through the window highlighted the swell of her belly when she was two feet in front of the sofa. Her mates had seen her every day, so the change was harder to notice. Sheila hadn't seen her in over a year.

Sheila gasped and rose. "Alanna, you're expecting?"

Alanna smiled into Sheila's joy-filled face. "I am. Just four months along. It's a piece of Liam, Sheila. A boy." Her eyes welled with tears when she said the words.

Thomas was standing by the drink table pouring a glass of Scotch. He whirled and the liquid splashed onto his hand. His gaze went from her face to her belly. "A child? Liam's child?" His voice rose, and there was no mistaking the joy in it.

"Yes, Thomas. The little one will be making his appearance in August."

"This is jolly news, Alanna. Jolly indeed." He put down his drink and came to embrace her. "I'm so pleased."

Sheila rose. "Can I get you something? Sit down, dear."

Thomas set his drink on the sideboard. "Yes, yes, sit down and rest."

She allowed Sheila to push her onto the sofa. Her helpless gaze found Ciara's. Her mate had found a seat on an armchair out of the way. She rolled her eyes when their gazes locked.

"I'm fine, really," Alanna said.

"Any sickness?" Sheila asked anxiously. "I remember when I was carrying Liam how I couldn't look a blood pudding in the face." She gave a delicate shudder.

"I had a few mornings of nausea, but it's not been too bad," she said.

Thomas frowned. "How long have you known you were pregnant?"

She'd known this moment was coming. "Just a few weeks. I didn't pay attention to . . . to my monthlies." Her face heated to be discussing such a thing with Thomas there. He was so proper. "It was only when I discovered my jeans not fitting that I began to wonder and counted back. Liam didn't want to call and tell you that kind of good news over the phone. We'd planned to come to see you next month."

"That's good, that's good," Thomas said. "We have many plans to make. I'll call the architect and have him start straightaway on redoing the west wing for you and the baby."

"And I know just the pediatrician for you," Sheila put in. "He's the best in Dublin." She was practically clapping her hands. "A baby," she marveled. "I can't take it all in."

Alanna should have expected this. She must have been mad to have been gobsmacked by their plans. For just a moment she allowed herself to think of how wonderful it would be to let someone else worry about her life, but she gave a slow shake of her head. "I have a concert schedule to keep. I must go back to America after Liam's funeral. Most of the upcoming concerts are sold out, and if we cancel now, this chance might never come again. I will come back when the tour is done."

The lines on Thomas's brow deepened. "But of course you'll stop that music madness. It's no life for a child. Being hauled from pillar to post on a bus. A child needs stability, a normal home. A chance to go to church."

Alanna hadn't thought beyond getting through her grief while fulfilling her contracts and having the baby. "We're on the cusp of making a name for ourselves." She shook her head. "Our manager thinks we will be bigger than Celtic Woman someday. I have a responsibility to my mates to see it through. And not only that, it's my dream and Liam's too. I can't throw it all away when it's nearly in my hands."

"I forbid it!" Thomas thundered. "You cannot subject my grandchild to such lowlifes."

"I'm sorry if I sound disrespectful, Thomas. I don't mean it in that manner. But I'm nearly thirty years old. I'll make the decisions for my own child. I *am* his mother."

The burn of tears was in her eyes. She hadn't wanted it to go this way. In her imagination, she'd dreamed Thomas would promise to throw his influence behind bookings here in Ireland. He would offer her the little gardener's cottage at the back of the estate for when they were off the road. Such a foolish daydream.

Sheila gasped and Thomas said nothing for a long moment. Alanna prayed he saw the futility of his orders. They might yet have a decent relationship. When she saw his brows gather again, she knew he wasn't giving up so easily.

"Then you leave me no choice," he said heavily. "I wouldn't want to take the child from you, but I will if I have to. As the mother, you should be the first to recognize that."

Alanna rose and grabbed her purse. "You can't take my baby from me." The Irish law was very clear about who should be raising a child.

"I can do most anything I want," Thomas said. "All I have to do is make a phone call and report you as unfit. I can have your visa revoked, and you'll have no choice but to come back to Ireland."

Alanna's knees threatened to give way when she realized he meant what he said. And he had the power to carry it through. She had to figure out a way to thwart him before the baby was born.

Four

"The *eejit*!" Ciara fumed as she jerked the car into gear and tromped on the accelerator. "You okay?"

Alanna still felt shaken, too upset to drive. She'd rushed from the house with a strangled promise to think things over. There was nothing to think over, of course, except how to get out of Ireland as quickly as possible to protect her child. But Thomas wouldn't let an ocean get in his way. She knew him too well. All he had to do was pull the strings to get her visa cancelled, and she'd be back here under his thumb.

"He'll do what he says," she said in a trembling voice. "You don't know him, Ciara. He always gets what he wants. He knows I was raised by the Travellers. The courts will take one look at his lovely mansion and compare it with my circumstances and upbringing. It will be all over. I won't have the weapons to fight him if he forces me back here."

She couldn't let her child have the same upbringing that Liam did. He'd often talked of how differently he would treat his children—with warmth and unconditional love, not chilly perfectionism. If it hadn't been for Sheila, Alanna would have felt justified in keeping her pregnancy from them.

She saw Ciara bite her lip and knew her mate wanted to offer encouragement, but the reality was Alanna was right. Thomas held all the advantages. "I'm going to go back to America right away. Barry is connected. Maybe he will have a suggestion."

"I hope you're right." For once Ciara's tone didn't indicate disdain. "Barry's an attorney. He might be knowing some tricks to foil Thomas."

Alanna stared out the window. Around the curve, the field opened up and revealed a ragtag assortment of trailers and ramshackle cottages. Dozens of dogs ran through the dirt between the trailers. It was the Travellers' community the private investigator had mentioned in his letter.

The camp was much like the one she remembered from her childhood. Constant commotion: yelling people, barking dogs, shouting children. Hearing those same sounds through the open car window brought back the desolation she experienced when she realized she'd been abandoned by her mother. Other women had cared for her, but always with impatience. She remembered being lonely, so very lonely, while surrounded by people. The day she met Liam had changed everything, and the moment she left the community had been the happiest day of her life.

"Ready?" Ciara asked after putting the car in park.

"Right." She shoved open her door and stepped out into a light breeze that brought the smell of cooking stew over an open fire to her nose.

"Where shall you be starting?" Ciara asked.

"With that group of women around the fire." Alanna realized she had left her shoes in the car. With her feet in good Irish dirt, she was a child again, but it wasn't a good feeling.

She walked toward the group of six women. Dressed in brightly colored clothing and jewelry, they stood around the campfire chatting in a language she hadn't heard in over ten years.

She greeted them in Cant, amazed it came so easily to her lips. "I'm Alanna Costello, daughter of Maire. I heard she passed this way recently."

The oldest woman, her hair wrapped with a red kerchief, looked Alanna over, glaring from under heavy brows. "You have the look of Maire," she said grudgingly. "She was here."

Alanna couldn't hide her disappointment. "She's not now?"

"She left two weeks ago. Went back to America."

"America? Has she been living there all these years then?"

The woman nodded. "Twenty-five years now, she said."

She'd deserted Ireland totally. Not even concerned about the three-year-old daughter she left behind. What could cause a woman to leave her child? Alanna couldn't imagine leaving the baby she carried under any circumstances. She wanted to ask if her mother had asked after her, but she knew the answer.

She reminded herself that her mother cared only about Neila. "Did she have her daughter with her?"

"You were saying that you are her daughter."

Alanna's fingers curled into her palms. "I am, but I have a sister. Neila. Did you see her?" Though Neila would be in her midthirties, Travellers often lived together all their lives.

The woman shook her head. "She was alone."

Of course she was. She'd probably abandoned Neila along

the way somewhere too. Alanna would never find her. "Do you have any idea where Maire lives?"

The woman bent over to stir the stew and her ornate necklace dangled perilously close to the pot. "Somewhere in the South."

Alanna felt her last grasp at hope slipping away. "The South is a large area. You wouldn't know what state? She said nothing that might indicate where her home is?"

"From something she said, I think she was near water, maybe the Atlantic."

The woman's tone held an air of dismissal. She took a bowl from the woman on her right and began to ladle up the stew. "We eat. You go now," she said. "I cannot help you more."

Alanna nodded. "Thank you for the information." Near the Atlantic and in the South. She could research Travellers' communities there and see how many she could find. Surely there weren't more than a dozen, if that many.

She slipped into the car. "Well?" Ciara demanded.

"She's not here," she said. "She went back to America."

Ciara dropped the car into drive and pulled away from the side of the road. "America?"

"According to the woman I spoke to, she's lived there twenty-five years. She must have gone there straightaway."

Ciara glanced at her. "Shall you be dealing with it okay?"

"I knew long ago she didn't care anything about me." Alanna managed a shrug though she wanted to cry. To sit in the dust and howl. She didn't have any blood relatives left, and with Liam gone, there was no one who really loved her. Oh she had no doubt Ciara and her other band members cared. But someday they might go their separate ways.

Her hand smoothed her tummy. She would soon have her child. The minute she laid her eyes on her baby, she would know him. His imprint was already part of her. But first, she had to get out of Thomas's long-armed reach.

"We must get home to pack," she said. "We'll leave as soon as the funeral is over. Thomas won't be expecting me to return to America so quickly, and I shall be able to escape."

"Can you be getting a plane ticket out so soon?" Ciara asked. "Our flight back isn't scheduled for another week."

"I hope so." What would she do if she couldn't? "I think I'll call Barry. He might be able to change flights for us."

Ciara didn't object. Alanna pulled out her cell phone and dialed their manager's number.

Barry answered on the first ring. "Alanna?"

"I need your help, Barry."

His brusque voice changed to a softer one. "Alanna, are you all right? You sound upset."

How did so few words tell him that? Barry often seemed connected to her in a strange way. "I need to get back to America as soon as possible, Barry, right after Liam's funeral. And could you find out what I have to do to become an American citizen?"

"Of course, but what is this all about, sugar?"

When had he started calling her by the endearment? The first time it had startled her. Now she liked it. It gave her a sense of belonging. "Liam's father is going to try to get custody of my baby."

"You're pregnant." Something changed in his voice, a new alertness.

She told him what had happened in the confrontation with the Connollys.

"I'll get you a flight home right after the funeral. Leave it to me."

"You're so good to me, Barry. Thank you."

"I'd do anything to help you, Alanna. You should know that by now."

"I knew I could count on you." She put her phone away after Barry promised to check into the immigration protocol and call her back.

Ciara drove downtown, where the women ate dinner in a local pub. Alanna was only able to pick at her bangers and mash with a side of chips. The grease on the chips turned her stomach, and the spice in the bangers, usually something she loved, made her tummy burn. Ciara didn't have much to say either, and the women spent an hour in the pub staring morosely at their plates.

Darkness descended while they were eating.

"How's your throat?" Ciara asked as they walked back to the car. "You're sounding a little hoarse. Too much talking today." A yeasty smell of mead rolled out of the bars along the way.

"I'll rest it tomorrow."

She needed to follow up with the throat specialist when they got back to the States. What if her voice was already ruined? She had a baby to support. Would the audience respond as well to Ceol if all she could do was play the fiddle?

So many things to worry about.

Most pressing was Thomas's threat. Much more than a threat. What would she do if he succeeded? She'd have to throw herself on his mercy and move in with them. She shriveled inside at the thought, but she couldn't allow the Connollys to raise her baby without her influence.

She shuddered at a new thought. "Maybe I should do what Thomas wants," she said. "If he wins his suit, he's vindictive enough to deny me any contact with the baby. If I give in now, at least they would prepare an apartment for us. I'd raise my baby myself, even if it's with their interference."

Ciara pulled the car into the parking bay and shut it off before she spoke. "I'm not smart enough to be telling you what is the right thing, but think hard about it, Alanna. You'd be giving up any life of your own. Thomas would own you. You'd be making no money of your own, have nothing that belonged just to you. Your career would be over. And Ceol's."

Alanna knew she had a responsibility to her mates. She was Ceol's driving force. The audience roared when she played the fiddle and danced barefoot across the stage. The papers were filled with her image in the towns where they played. Critics compared her voice to Loreena McKennitt's pure, crystal tones. Now she sounded more like a frog.

"Maybe my career is over anyway," she said softly.

"Even if your voice is gone, you can play the fiddle like no one ever has," Ciara said. "The Irish reels that pour from your instrument make the audience want to get up and dance in the aisles. Sometimes they do."

Liam used to say that God had given her a gift. She didn't have the right to turn her back on it. But maybe she wouldn't be doing that if she moved in with Thomas and Sheila. She could train up her child to follow after the music.

Ciara reached over and grabbed her hand. "Don't be making any decisions until you hear from Barry. He may have a way out of this. And don't be thinking I'm saying this because of Ceol. I care about *you* more than the band."

Alanna knew her mate spoke the truth. She returned the pressure of Ciara's fingers. "Good advice." She nodded toward the building. "We should go in. I still have packing and sorting to do."

"Want me to help?"

"No, you get some rest. I'll see you in the morning." Alanna told Ciara good-bye. When she got to her flat, her cell phone rang. She glanced at it. It was Barry. She put the phone to her ear.

"Cheers," she said.

His Southern accent held an edge. "Sugar, I just got off the phone with my buddy who works for immigration. The news isn't good. In most circumstances, there is a three- to five-year permanent residency requirement."

Alanna exhaled and sank onto the old green sofa. "So that idea's out. He'll get my visa revoked, Barry. I know he will." Tears burned her eyes, and she blinked furiously. She would *not* cry. Whatever she had to do, she'd do it.

"There's one way out. I know it will seem a little drastic, but I'm sure it will work."

Her sinking hope rose. "I'll do anything to keep my baby. What can I do?"

"Marry me."

She gaped, then gulped. "I don't understand."

"Come here. When the child is born, it will automatically be a citizen. I'll adopt him and Thomas will have no power over us."

She clutched the phone. "But why would you do this for me? Tie yourself down like that."

"Why not? You're special to me, Alanna. You always have been. It could be a marriage in name only, at least for now. Later—maybe later we'll find there is more for us as a couple than we can imagine now."

Her spirit rebelled at the idea of being married to anyone but Liam. "For how long?"

"However long you want it to last," he said. "I'd like it to be forever, but if you want to be free after Thomas is off your back, I'll do whatever you want. What do you say?"

"I'll do it." She soothed herself with the knowledge the arrangement needn't last long. Just until her son was safe and Thomas realized he couldn't control them.

Five

*L*ass, don't do this," Ciara whispered fiercely in Alanna's ear.

Alanna tugged on the antique wedding gown and tried to summon a smile to reassure her mate. Luckily, the dress had an empire waistline that left plenty of room for her belly. If it fit today, it would still fit tomorrow when the actual ceremony took place. Ena snapped off a series of pictures in quick succession. Her pink hair was all that Alanna could see behind the huge camera and lens.

The last eight weeks since Liam's funeral had flown by with the speed of a Mark 4 train. She stared at herself in the mirror. Her turquoise eyes were wide with trepidation under the mass of red curls that were tousled yet controlled. The perfect bride for a man from an old Charleston family. All just part of the charade. She was six months along now, and she couldn't hide her belly under the dress.

"Call it off," Ciara said. "It's not too late."

Alanna turned away from the mirror. Her image depressed

her. Through the window, she saw the bay out past the Battery. Through some transformation she didn't understand, this place had become like home to her. Her hand went to the swell of her belly. "I have no choice if I want to keep my baby."

"I don't trust *Barry*." Ciara spat the word as though it were the breath mint she hated.

Her mate had hit the roof the minute she heard of Barry's proposal. Alanna turned her back on Ena's camera, though no doubt she had already captured their scowls. Tomorrow would be better. She'd pin her smile in place, and no one would guess her heart was breaking.

Ciara gestured from the top of Alanna's head to her feet. "Look at you. He even picked out the dress. It's never a thought of your own that you'll be having now."

Alanna smoothed the ivory silk. "It's not a sin to be caring about history and tradition. His grandmother, the Lord rest her soul, wore this. His mother too."

Ciara sighed, then shrugged her slim shoulders. "I'm wasting my breath."

Alanna turned away from her friend's accusing gaze. She heard a knock at the door.

It opened, and Fiona stuck her head into the room. Her blonde hair hung in a shining curtain to her shoulders. "I made something for you." She stepped into the room and held out an intricate gold necklace.

The pendant—a Celtic cross—caught the light. The center held a garnet, Alanna's birthstone. "Gorgeous." Alanna touched it. "I love it."

"Turn around, and I'll put it on you," Fiona said.

Her cool fingers touched the back of Alanna's neck. Alanna touched the chain and held it while her friend fastened the necklace. The cross hung in exactly the right place for the dress's neckline. She hugged her friend. "Thank you, Fiona. It's lovely."

Fiona smiled. "It's a beautiful bride you'll be making." She tapped on her lip. "The police detective is outside wanting to speak to you."

Alanna frowned. "What about?"

"He didn't say," Fiona said.

Alanna glanced at her watch. Barry would be here to take her to dinner soon, and she needed time to change. "I've got five minutes. Let him come in."

Fiona stepped to the door and opened it. She thrust her head out. "You can be coming in, but only for five minutes." She stepped back and allowed the detective through the doorway.

Detective Adams ran his hand through his red hair. "So sorry to disturb you when you're busy with final wedding preparations." Fatigue draped his freckled face. "I'll be brief."

"What is it?" Alanna asked.

"Do you know for sure which man was driving the vehicle?"

Alanna shook her head. "Liam had wanted to drive it, but Jesse told him he couldn't. Why do you ask?"

The detective pursed his lips. "Were you aware of Jesse's state of mind the night of the bombing?"

"These are odd questions, Detective."

"Jesse was recently fired from his job over a sexual harassment accusation. Were you aware of that?"

Alanna wasn't, but neither was she surprised. She frowned. "As far as I could see Jesse was himself."

38

"His usual envious self," Fiona muttered under her breath.

Detective Adams turned to her. "Explain."

Fiona blinked as if she hadn't expected to be heard. "Oh, you know. He held Alanna special mainly because he couldn't have her. Otherwise he never turned a pretty girl away." Her cheeks flushed.

The detective nodded thoughtfully.

Alanna gripped the back of the chair. "Are you saying Jesse was jealous of Liam?" she asked Fiona.

"Was he?" Adams asked.

All four women just stared at him.

"You're not saying . . . ?" Ciara didn't finish her thought.

"Saying what?" Alanna wanted to know.

Detective Adams kept a patient eye on Ciara until she was flustered into speaking.

"You think Jesse did this?"

Ena gasped. "Like what? A murder-suicide?"

Alanna felt faint. She shook her head. It wasn't possible.

"Do you think Jesse Hawthorne would have been capable of doing something like that?" Adams asked.

This time, no one spoke.

He glanced at his watch. "I don't want to keep you too long. I know you have a lot to do before your wedding."

Ciara scowled. "Unless we can talk her out of it."

Snap, snap. Ena continued to take pictures. Alanna turned her back, not wanting her shock and horror to be caught on camera.

The detective blinked. "You don't want her to get married?"

"It's too soon," Ciara said. "She's running on fear and not thinking it through."

"Barry Kavanagh is very much respected," Adams said. "He's done a lot for Charleston, donated money to help disadvantaged kids, restoration work around the buildings, all kinds of things. Every mama with an eligible daughter has been trying to catch him for years."

Ciara's face softened. "Don't be minding me. I'm just jealous." She walked the detective to the door and closed it.

Alanna hugged her when she returned. "Let's not be talking of jealousy. There's no reason."

"I am afraid you'll be drifting away from us," Ciara said in her ear during the embrace. "Barry wants you all to himself."

"No, he only wants to help."

"He pushed you after Liam died until you couldn't sing anymore."

Alanna hid her pain with a smile. Her surgery last month had successfully dealt with the nodules, but she was seeing no signs of improvement in the way her voice had changed. "Am I hearing you say my fiddle playing is lacking?" Her smile widened to a genuine one.

"I'll not be saying such a thing!" Ciara linked arms with her. "I fancy some American pizza. Change your clothes, and I'll treat you."

"The baby wouldn't say no." At least Ciara had left off with the attack on Barry and tomorrow's wedding.

Pain pulsed at his eyes again. Jesse Hawthorne pressed his fingers to his eyes and willed it to go away. He put down the bodhran.

The sound he got from it wasn't nearly as good as Liam's expert touch.

"Need a pill?" his mother asked, jumping up and hurrying toward the hall before he answered.

"I'm fine, Mom," he said. "It's not bad."

"You don't have to pretend to be so strong." She frowned.

He laid his head back against the gray velour sofa scented with cinnamon from the spray his mother used. For just a moment, in his mind's eye he saw a different living room. One with rain slashing the windows that looked out on the sea. A place he'd never been, he was sure.

This place was alien to him. He slept in a room he didn't remember next to a bookcase of young adult novels he was sure he'd never read. An array of football awards covered the dresser, and he had no idea what position he'd played. The doctor said his memory would likely return, but Jesse had begun to lose hope. Maybe this twilight would be his destiny. When he'd checked out his condo, he found nothing familiar there either.

"I'm going to move back to my condo today," he said.

His mother clasped her hands together. "It's too soon, Jesse! You're not ready. Who will be there if your vision blacks out or you fall? You need to stay here for now. The doctor thinks you shouldn't be alone yet."

"I'm never going to get back to normal if you keep coddling me." He didn't want to hurt her, but he was tired of being treated like an invalid. Restlessness plagued him, and he needed to find a purpose for his life. This endless drifting made every day drag.

"You don't have a car," she pointed out, her eyes hardening. "And I won't let you use mine for this foolishness."

"Then I'll go buy one. I still have money in my account." In his previous life, he'd worked for the FBI for a time, or so he'd been told. A bean counter. He'd looked at his resume and discovered he never worked anywhere longer than three years. Perpetually climbing the ladder or easily bored?

"You're being very foolish, Jesse," she said. "I'm going to call your father."

"Mom, I'm thirty-two, not fourteen! Your hovering is about to kill me, okay? I've got to get on with my life. Get a job, pick up the pieces."

"How can you get a job when all you do is sit in your room and practice that stupid drum? And all because of a dare from a dead man. You don't even remember how to balance accounting books anymore, do you?"

He glanced away from her challenging gaze. "I know how to do it. It's just not keeping my attention. Maybe I should start a new career." Noodling over numbers had become a habit in recent weeks, but it brought him no joy. Wasn't his job supposed to be something he actually liked?

"You have a master's, Jesse. It took you six years to get it. You're going to throw it all over to do something else? You need to stop jumping from job to job and settle into your career."

He rubbed his forehead as the pain intensified. "I don't know what I'm going to do."

Her face softened. "You're just antsy, son. Be patient. It will all come back."

"If I'm back on my own, maybe I'll *have* to remember."

His mother stepped closer and took his hand. "I know it's

hard, Jesse. You've held up so well under the strain. It will get better soon. It has to."

He didn't know where she was getting her information. It didn't have to get better. This half-life of his could go on and on. He went to the window. The sunshine shone on the live oak trees lining the yard, and roses raised their heads to the light. The cheerful view did little to lift his spirits.

He wished he'd died instead of Liam. He was going to have to get dressed if he wanted to attend that wedding, much as he hated the thought.

———

Ciara went to the mirror and fussed with the bright blue beads she'd put into her black cornrows. "I'll be chasing off the people at the wedding when they see this hair," she moaned. "You sure I can't be talking you out of this?"

"When have you ever talked Alanna out of anything?" Ena asked from behind the lens.

"Like, *never*," Ciara said, giving up on her hair.

Alanna linked her arm with Ciara's. "Be happy for me, Ciara. You know I have no choice, not if I want to keep the baby out of Thomas's clutches." Even talking about the trouble he'd caused made her ache down deep.

"They should be shot," Ciara declared. "Especially Liam's dad. It's all his fault you're doing this."

"Is Jesse coming?" Fiona asked.

Alanna released Ciara and gave the veil a final tug. "I invited him before I heard the explosion might have been his doing. Maybe he won't come."

She followed Fiona and Ciara down the magnificent staircase to the library downstairs to await the first strains of the bridal march. She found Barry standing by the window. "You should be waiting in the great room," she scolded. "It's bad luck to see the bride before the wedding."

He turned with her shoes dangling from his left hand. "I thought these might belong to you." His smile broadened when his gaze went to her bare feet. His eyes lifted to her neck. "What's that?"

Alanna's fingers caressed the fine necklace. "Fiona made it. Isn't it lovely?"

He swiped at the lock of blond hair falling across his forehead. "She's very talented. You should be wearing pearls though." He produced a velvet case from his inside jacket pocket and opened it. "These pearls belonged to my great-grandmother."

Though the pearls held the fine patina of age and quality, the cross seemed a talisman to her, and she touched it protectively. "This is special to me. Fiona made it for good luck."

His sternness evaporated with a slight smile. "And you should wear it. Do you mind wearing the pearls too?"

She shook her head. "I'd love that." Her fingers tightened around the cross, then she turned her back to him. "Would you fasten the pearls?"

His warm fingers touched her neck. The next thing she knew, the lengths of the gold necklace dangled in her hands.

"Oh, I'm so sorry," he said, his voice full of regret. "The clasp on your cross necklace broke."

"I had some trouble with the clasp," Fiona said. "I'll try to get it fixed, but I don't think there's time before the wedding."

The cool brush of pearls lay against Alanna's neck as Barry fastened the string. "Perfect," he said, stepping back. "You look beautiful." He indicated the Celtic cross in her hand. "Maybe you could tuck it somewhere since it's so special?" He laid the shoes at her feet, then began to back out of the room.

Alanna slipped her bare feet into the dainty heels. She hated wearing shoes, especially heels, but it was necessary. "Sweet of him to know how special the cross is." She tucked the cross into her bra. "He's a good man."

"But you don't love him," Ciara said.

"No. But I could easily fall for him once I'm able to love again."

"What if there's another great passion out there, someone like Liam?" Ena put in, snapping another picture. "Maybe you should be waiting for that and not settling."

There would never be a love like she'd had for Liam. Alanna turned to stare at her. "I thought you liked Barry."

Ena lowered the camera. "We just want you happy."

"I am! Deadly happy," she said through clenched teeth. She wobbled on the heels as she marched to the door. "Let's get this day over with."

The music started, and her mates walked the white runner to the front on the arms of the best men, Barry's friends she'd never met. Her gut clenched. She started down the aisle and saw Jesse turn to look at her. His face was still a bit swollen from his surgeries, but he looked better than she'd imagined. What could make a man desperate enough to take his best friend's life in addition to his own?

She averted her gaze and stepped on the rose petals strewn along her fateful path.

Six

The Mercedes rolled past giant live oak trees with Spanish moss dripping from their branches. Alanna caught sight of the glimmer of water from the swamps. A glorious sunset was the backdrop to a scene worthy of a picture postcard. Though they were only twenty miles from Charleston, it was another world.

Sluggish water moved in the river running beside the laneway. "It looks black," she told Barry.

He pointed to trees half submerged in the murky water. "Cypress. The tannin in the trees stains the water, and it moves so slowly that it's never fully purged." He turned his head and smiled at her. "Happy?"

She smiled back. "Deadly happy."

In reality, she'd never been so tired. Her face hurt from the smile she'd forced on it as she accepted the snarky congratulations from society women who'd had their eyes on Barry. His friends had likely only shown up to gossip about the grieving young widow. Everyone in Charleston knew of Ceol's tragedy. And she'd remarried so quickly.

She stretched and kicked off her shoes. "I'll be glad when the rest of the band joins us. And I can't wait to see the studio you had done up for us. The tour starts in six weeks. That's not a lot of time for practice. And we still have to find a-a new drummer." Her throat closed at the thought of replacing Liam. The percussionist they'd used right after Liam's death had gone back to Ireland for another gig and couldn't be coaxed to return. They'd interviewed dozens to replace him, and most didn't know the difference between a bodhran and tambourine.

He cleared his throat. "About the studio. The contractor was delayed by rain on another project."

"Oh, Barry, we have so little time! When will it be finished?"

"A couple of weeks." His smile broadened. "It will be okay. You all can practically read each other's minds. It won't take much practice to get you ready."

Alanna started to object, then closed her mouth. She studied her nails, blunt cut and unpolished. She often thought Barry saw her this way, as someone to be molded and honed. He'd find out she was more stubborn than he thought.

"I see." She made no attempt to hide how cross she was.

His smile faded. "The studio will be finished soon, and Ceol will be here. Don't worry about it. Let's enjoy getting to know one another better."

She turned her thoughts away from the sticky situation of a marriage that wasn't real. "We can't wait two weeks to start practice. Will you have a car for me to travel to the city? Though

I'll need time to remember how to drive on the wrong side of the road."

"We'll work it out," he said.

There were other problems to iron out as well. "What about my citizenship application? How long will it take to get it through?"

"Not long. I brought home papers for you to sign, and I'll take them to my friend tomorrow. He's promised to run them right through. He got your permanent residency done the minute you returned to the States, so he knows what he's doing."

Alanna allowed herself to relax. The car rolled through the line of trees shielding the estate, and she caught her breath at the first sight of Blackwater Hall when they were still one and a half kilometers away. Her awe caused her Irish brogue to return in full force.

"It's huge, it is," she said.

The stone plantation house's foundation appeared to have been laid when the area was first settled, though Barry had told her the home was built in 1890. Such a grand place for someone like her to occupy. Her toes crept across the car's soft carpet and found her shoes. She slipped her feet into them.

"It's beautiful." The manicured lawn went on forever. The grass was a soft green, the perfect foreground to the magnificent mansion waiting to greet them. She craned her neck and peered through the windshield as the Mercedes rolled closer to the home.

Four stories high counting the attic, the stone edifice towered over the lawn, and the mullioned windows reflected a blank stare that made her think the mansion kept centuries-old secrets. Two wings sprawled out from the main house. She had no idea how many rooms the house had, but she suspected it was at least thirty.

It was only as they reached the mansion that she noticed the way vegetation had chipped away some of the foundation. After she stepped from the car, she saw the peeling paint on the windowsills and the rotted frame around the massive double doors.

This banjaxed place formed a sharp contrast to Barry's pristine home at the Battery. It intrigued her. She approached the porch and heard mewing. "I'm hearing kittens?"

He grimaced. "I hate cats. I'm allergic."

She ignored his comment and got onto her hands and knees to peer under the porch. Three pairs of eyes looked back. "There are three of them. Here, kitty, kitty." She waggled coaxing fingers in their direction.

He grabbed her arm and pulled her upright. "There might be snakes under there. Poisonous ones."

Alanna brushed the dirt from her hands and shuddered. "You have poisonous snakes?"

"Copperheads and coral snakes. You won't see any coral snakes, but you might see a copperhead or two."

"I want to see the kittens," she said. "Can you pull them out for me?"

He shook his head. "I told you, I'm allergic."

"But they're so cute! I love kittens. And dogs. I want a houseful of pets," she said.

"I don't like an animal to touch me. You'll have to keep that houseful outside." His smile was indulgent, and he nodded toward the house. "I know it's a bit unkempt right now, but we'll soon set it right." Barry slipped his hand under her elbow and led her up the chipped steps, nearly three meters wide, to the porch. Avoiding warped floorboards, he guided her to the front door and twisted the knob.

She tried to peer through the sidelights. "It's not locked?"

"The lock is broken. No one bothers things out here anyway. They think it's haunted."

She stopped on the threshold. "Haunted?"

He shrugged. "You know how people can be superstitious. They see lights or hear a creak from a broken shutter and think it's a ghost."

"You've not been seeing anything?"

"Not since I was an impressionable kid."

She tipped her head to one side. "Is that the ocean I hear?"

"Sure is, sugar." He pointed to the right of the house. "The ocean is just past the sea grass. You can see a hint of blue."

She stared out past the waving sea grass, marveling at the lovely view. No wonder he was quite taken with this place. She could love it too. "What about hurricanes?"

"We're pretty sheltered here, but when we get heavy rains, we can be flooded in." He shoved the door open the rest of the way. His smile widened as he scooped her up in his arms. "I think we'd better follow the protocol."

Carried in her new husband's strong arms, Alanna entered her new home. No one but Liam had held her in so long, and the situation was just—wonky. She didn't dare struggle to be put down. After all Barry had done for her, he deserved better.

A cool dankness greeted them, a dark smell that made her think of dead things and vampire bats. She barely suppressed a shudder. Barry set her on her feet, and she glanced around.

The wallpaper, a faded rose pattern surely dating from when the house was first built, bulged in places where the glue had let loose from the wall.

The floors caught her attention. "Mahogany, are they?" she asked.

He shook his head. "Brazilian cherry," he said proudly. "They're in perfect condition."

They were the only thing she saw in perfect condition, but Alanna could make out the strong bones of the grand lady. She could envision the house in its old glory. She walked past a curving staircase to an entryway and passed into a large drawing room. The ornate fireplace had some plaster missing, but it must have been beautiful in its time. In this room the paper had been stripped and rose-colored walls gave the room a cheery glow. The rug in the center of the floor appeared new, as did the rolled-arm sofa and chairs.

"It's lovely." The décor was not her cup of tea, but what did she know about such things? She'd add her own touches and make it a home. She was lucky to be living in such a mansion.

Barry beamed. "I had it done last week, just for you. The fireplace will be repaired next week. Your bedroom is finished too. Would you like to see it?"

She nodded and followed him back to the entry hall and up the stairs. The curving stairway was ten feet wide with a polished wood banister that matched the floors. "This place must have been something in its day."

Barry frowned. "It's lovely now, full of history. I thought you'd love it."

"I do," she said hastily. "I meant I can see the grandeur of it.

The wallpaper must have been quite beautiful when it was new." When his frown didn't lessen, she knew she was digging herself deeper into the hole. "How lucky you are to have grown up here. I'd love to hear about your family." He'd said little about his heritage.

"Our family," he corrected. "My parents will be back from Europe soon, and you'll meet them."

She stopped on the stairs and gulped. "I thought your parents were dead."

He smiled. "Why, no, Alanna, why would you think that?"

Not dead? But he'd brought that antique wedding dress to her and asked her to wear it. He said it was his grandmother's, and his mother had worn it too. It would make him so happy to see her in it, he'd pleaded. But he'd never actually *said* she was dead. Maybe it was her fault. Her grief had blurred so many things.

"Then why didn't we wait for their return before the wedding?" she asked, still confused.

He sighed. "Let's not get into this now, sugar. It's not important."

She stopped at the landing halfway up the stairs. "How can you say that? It's very important." The more she thought about it, the more upset she became.

He ran his hand over his blond hair and sighed. "My mother . . . is difficult." His pointed gaze went to her protruding belly. "She would object to my raising another man's baby, and I didn't trust her not to make a scene. Besides, she can be rather overpowering, and I wanted to spare you her meddling."

Alanna cupped her hands around her belly, which clearly showed her condition. She would have to defend what she cared about most to Barry's mother. She'd thought the next few months would be easier with Barry to lean on, but the thought of a confrontation with his mother dried her mouth.

She finally choked out a response past her disappointment. "I would have been glad to have had her input." In truth, she'd been overwhelmed by the trappings of a society wedding. Today she'd wished a family of her own were present, though her mates were as close as sisters.

"This way," Barry said, obviously not willing to discuss his parents any longer. He took two more steps.

Alanna started to follow him, then her gaze went to a large portrait on the landing. The brilliant hues of the picture hanging on the wall at eye level mesmerized her. The woman in the painting stared back with eyes as turquoise as Alanna's own. The full lips parted as though she were about to speak. A circle of red curls lay piled atop her head.

"She looks like me," she whispered.

His eyes wide and unblinking, Barry stared up at the painting. He took a step closer to it and placed his hand over the woman's hand on the canvas. "Yes, she does." His voice was hoarse. "I noticed the first time we met."

Alanna stepped closer, staring in fascination. Even the heart-shaped face could have been her reflection. "Who is she?"

"An Irish woman my grandfather loved and wanted to marry. She refused him though, and he never got over her."

Alanna couldn't tear her gaze from the woman's secretive expression. "What was her name?"

"I don't remember." His tone ended the conversation, and he took her elbow and guided her up the last flight of stairs.

She eyed his set face. Strange he didn't know. She let him lead her down the wide hall, papered with a green acanthus leaf pattern, to the first door on the right. The rest of the hall rambled on out of sight. How large was this place?

He pushed open the heavy wooden door. "Here we are. I had it redone especially for you. What do you think?"

She gasped at the opulence of the room, such a sharp contrast to what she'd seen so far. "I'm gobsmacked!"

Luxurious silk bedding in a pale moss color drew her gaze first. She walked across polished wood floors until she stepped onto the plush area rug where the high bed rested. She reached past the mosquito netting that draped the white poster bed so she could touch the bedspread. "It's real silk."

Barry stepped to the bed and draped his arm around her. "Of course. Nothing but the best for my bride. If there's anything you need—anything at all—just tell me and I'll get it. I want you to be comfortable."

Alanna's instinctive reaction to the weight of his arm around her was to step away. She wasn't ready to confront any expectations from Barry yet. "It was jolly good of you." She avoided his gaze and kept her attention on the bedding.

Pillows lay heaped on the plush bed. It was so high she'd need to jump into it, and it would be as fun as leaping into warm Atlantic waves. The furniture gleamed with newness, and she could smell the fresh paint. The walls glowed with a pale lavender paint. The gentle colors drained the tension from her shoulders, and she sank into the welcoming embrace of an overstuffed rocker by the window.

She touched the soft fabric of the chair arms. "I quite adore it—all of it!" She gazed at the touches a woman could appreciate: candles, a mirrored dresser with pots of face cream, even a silver-plated hairbrush and comb. A light, fresh scent hung in the air, and she realized the bouquet of primroses on the dresser was real.

"Primroses!" She crossed the floor to touch a delicate blossom. "Mixed with shamrocks." She whirled to face him, surprised to find him right behind her. "Oh, Barry, it's too good of you."

Barry put his hands on her shoulders. "I know these are your favorites." His voice was husky. "I had the flowers and the shamrocks flown in from Ireland so you'd feel at home. I'm glad you like them." He sounded almost shy. His fingers moved to her neck, and he rubbed his thumb along her collarbone.

She closed her eyes and felt like purring. "That's nice." Tipping her head, she brushed her lips across the back of his hand. "Thank you, Barry." Attraction to her new husband flared in a way she hadn't experienced before. She raised heavy lids and stared into his face.

She could see in his eyes the desire to kiss her, and it brought her to her senses. It was too soon to feel this way, with Liam just gone. "I'm tired and I'm sure you are too."

He stilled, then stepped away. "I'll leave you to unpack. I'll be just across the hall in my room."

Relief drained the tension from her shoulders. She hadn't been quite sure what would happen once the wedding vows were taken. Barry loved her, and she knew it. At least he was giving her time to get over Liam and learn to love again.

If it was even possible.

Seven

Jesse's mother touched his arm. "The detective will be here soon. Maybe you should take a pill."

"I don't want a pill!" His mom winced, and he quickly added, "Sorry," to apologize for his sharp tone. He rubbed his head as he stood staring out the window, and the pain began to ease. A van drew to the curb outside. "I think he's here."

It wasn't a man who stepped from the van, but three women. He recognized them as members of Ceol. The beautiful black woman was Ciara. She sang alto. The pink-haired one, Ena, played the pennywhistle and the guitar. Fiona, the blonde, sang lead now that Alanna was recovering from throat surgery. How was Alanna doing now? She was married as of eleven this morning.

Her marriage was something he'd done his best not to think about. It was his fault she'd lost Liam. But he couldn't ignore the gnawing jealousy in his gut at the thought of her with another man. He felt as though she belonged to him, even though he had no conscious memory of them ever dating.

He met the band members at the door. "Hi." Opening the door wide, he stepped aside so they could step in.

Ciara's white teeth flashed in a smile. Her high heels clicked on the tile floor as she stepped inside. "It's good you're looking, Jesse." Her dark eyes assessed his face. "The scars are healing."

He touched his chin where the most prominent scar lingered. "I'm hoping this was the last surgery."

"Your voice doesn't sound quite so gruff either," Fiona said. "Your vocal cords must be healing too."

"So the doctors say. Come on in and sit down. I'm sick of my own company." He led them into the living room.

His mother came through the doorway from the living room with a pot of tea and cups. "Just in time to join us," she said, smiling.

"We can't stay long," Ciara said, always the spokesperson. But she still moved to the sofa and sank onto the overstuffed cushion. The others imitated her action. She tossed her black cornrows behind her shoulders and laced her fingers together over one kneecap. "We need your help."

"Oh my dear, Jesse is in no shape to help anyone," his mother said. "He's still recovering."

Jesse straightened. When was the last time he'd done anything other than wander the house aimlessly and lie on the sofa? It was driving him crazy, and the thought of escaping this place held appeal. "What do you need?"

Her lips lifted in a coaxing smile. "We need a percussionist. I heard you play the last time we were here. You're good, very good, especially on the bodhran. Our tour is coming up, and we haven't been able to find a new drummer."

"I'm a novice," he said. "I'm not sure I can keep up with what you need."

"It's desperate, we are. Say you'll at least practice with us in the morning? For Liam's sake?"

He needed a purpose. Maybe this was it. "I'm not nearly as good as Liam, and what about Alanna? I doubt she wants me around."

"Alanna will do what's best for the band."

The thought of seeing her again was a major enticement. "I'll give it a shot if you're sure."

"Son, you'd better ask the doctor first," his mother said.

He set his jaw at her protest. "I think it's for me to decide," he said. "I've got to find something to occupy my time."

"A tour schedule is grueling," Ena said. "Maybe your mum is right about checking."

"It's the inactivity that's bugging me," he said. "I want to try." He'd been practicing since he was well enough to pick up a drum, and his teacher said he'd never seen a faster learner. He felt more together when he played the bodhran, too, more himself. It might be good for him to be around Liam's friends.

His mother pressed her lips together but said nothing more.

"Shall we pick you up in the morning and drive out to see Alanna?" Ciara asked. "We'll be having Liam's drums loaded in the van."

He nodded. "About nine?"

Ciara smiled and went toward the door with the other two women trailing her. "See you then!"

The triumph in her voice made him smile. She might not be so happy after she listened to him practice with them. He waved as they got in the van and drove off, but his elation didn't last long when a police car turned the corner and stopped in front of the house.

"Here we go again," he muttered.

His mother twisted her hands together. "Why can't they let you be, Jesse?"

"They're just doing their job." He stepped out onto the stoop to meet Detective Adams, who scampered up the drive with a toothpick in his mouth. The man's small stature and sharp features reminded him of a rat.

Jesse nodded at him. "Detective Adams. What's this all about?" He wasn't sure he wanted to know.

Adams took the toothpick from his mouth. "Got any of your memory back yet?"

"No."

"Talked to the court-appointed psychologist you saw the other day. He thinks you're starting to recall things."

Nothing that matters. Just stuff like the smell of an Irish bog and the green of an Irish summer. It was worrisome but nothing he could explain, especially not to this detective with the cynical eyes. "I don't remember what happened."

"Don't or can't? How about just before you met Liam Connolly that night?" He leaned closer, and his minty breath washed over Jesse. "Like the fact you'd been talking about suicide."

His pulse skipped in his chest, and he tugged at his shirt collar. "Who told you that?" Had he been depressed? No one had mentioned it to him.

"Sometimes people in distress think death is the only way out. And they take out a loved one with them. Everything I've heard says you and Liam were as close as brothers." He jabbed a finger in Jesse's chest. "I think you planned for both of you to die that night, but you couldn't quite bring yourself to put the bomb under your seat. So you put it under his."

Don't show any agitation. "I wouldn't have done anything to hurt Liam."

Adams looked smug. "I thought you didn't remember anything."

"I-I don't. But I wouldn't do something like that." Lame, very lame. He had no idea what he wouldn't or wouldn't do, but the thought he might be that kind of man scared him.

"There's more to this than meets the eye, and I'm going to find out what it is." He tossed his toothpick to the ground, then turned on his heel and walked back to his car.

Jesse's knees threatened to give out as he went back to the house. His thoughts rambled through all the detective had said. Just last night on the news there had been a report of a man who shot his wife and kids, then himself. He'd wondered what drove a man to carry out such a heinous act. Surely if he'd tried to do something that horrific, he wouldn't have had such a strong reaction against the idea of it.

His mother was waiting by the door. "What did he say?" She followed him into the living room when he didn't answer. "If he's harassing you, I'm calling our attorney."

"Mom, was I depressed before the explosion? Did I talk about suicide?"

She pressed her lips together. "The doctor said you were going to be fine, just fine. Don't try to force the memories to come."

"Did I seem unstable?" he asked, knowing he was going to have to pin her down somehow.

"You were just going through a bad spell. You'd lost your job. What man wouldn't be upset after a false accusation?"

This was the first he'd heard of it. "What false accusation?"

She waved her hand in a dismissive gesture. "That secretary. She accused you of sexual harassment."

"And my boss believed her?"

She shrugged. "She's his sister. Women have always pursued you, Jesse. It's not your fault. I've seen it play out before. When you didn't show the interest she wanted, she set her mind on revenge." She touched his arm. "You were getting on top of things and had two job interviews lined up. Things were looking up for you."

Maybe he *had* been the sort of man to do these things. Maybe he had harassed this woman, even planted that bomb under Liam's seat. "What was the woman's name?"

Her nostrils flared. "Rena Mae Anderson." She spat the words like they had a bad taste.

He was going to have to go see this woman, find out the truth. "How well did I know Liam and Alanna?"

She sighed. "Why are you going over all this, Jesse?"

"I have to know."

She sat on the sofa and drew her legs up under her. "You went to college with Liam in Ireland. The two of you roomed together for four years. He was your best friend, and even after college, you talked to him at least once a week."

So he *had* been to Ireland. The memories he had of seeing the sea were real. "What about Alanna?"

Her nostrils flared. "You met her first and dated a few weeks before she threw you over and took up with Liam. You saw Liam maybe twice a year, but she usually wasn't along."

Then why did he feel this connection to her? Why was her name the first one on his lips in his initial coherent moment after the explosion? "I think I should see Dr. Phillips."

"I'm sure he'd be glad to see you. He's called several times."

The psychiatrist's messages were the only reason Jesse knew the name. "You have his number?"

She nodded. "By the phone in the kitchen."

He went into the kitchen, found the number, and called the doctor's office. There'd been a cancellation that afternoon, so he took it. Two hours later, he was in Dr. Phillips's office sitting in a chair by a window that looked out on the Atlantic.

"I need you to tell me what my mental state was like before my injury."

Dr. Phillips was in his sixties, and his expression of easy competence probably calmed his patients most of the time. His light brown eyes under sandy hair were shrewd as he looked Jesse over carefully. "Why?"

"Do you think I could have tried to kill myself? Put that bomb under my own car?"

The doctor pursed his lips. "We'd talked about doing a voluntary commitment the week before the bomb incident. Your depression was profound, and I feared you might try to harm yourself."

Jesse slumped back in his chair. "And *my best friend*?"

"That question's more difficult to answer."

"So I really am going crazy," he muttered.

Eight

The croak of bullfrogs from the swamp made the hair on the back of Alanna's neck rise. The noise made her think of alligators and snakes, reptiles she knew inhabited the murky waters as well. She sat cross-legged on the bed with both windows open to the cooling night air. Though it was hard to call that moisture-laden breeze a cooling one.

Barry hadn't appeared since he left her two hours ago. She tried to sleep, but the strange sounds in and around the house kept her eyes from drifting shut. A loud roar from outside sent her bolting from the bed. Running to the window, she stared into the dark yard. The moon glimmered on the water, but she didn't see whatever had made that horrifying sound.

Reaching for her cell phone, she dialed Ciara's number. Her friend answered almost immediately. Hearing Ciara's voice calmed Alanna's nervousness. "How are you, it's me?"

"What's wrong?"

"Nothing, not really. I miss my mates."

Ciara's voice softened. "We miss you too. How's the new studio look?"

"It's not done yet."

"What? He said it was going to be ready for us to come next week."

"A problem with the work crew. Now it will be a couple of weeks, so he says. But I'll come to the city, and we'll figure out where to practice," she added before Ciara could explode into new objections.

"Barry did this on purpose," Ciara said. "The *eejit* swooped in and took you over."

"Ciara, stop. He's done everything possible for us. The concerts he's arranged for us this summer are deadly."

"At the sacrifice of your voice!"

"I don't miss it," Alanna lied. If she told Ciara how she really felt about the loss of her singing voice, the argument would be full on. She rubbed her forehead. It wasn't Barry's fault, but her own. "You're determined to dislike him, aren't you, Ciara? What's he ever done to you but try to help us? I know you're jealous, but be giving me a little more credit than that. I'll never walk away from any of you. Just knock off, okay?"

While it was true they had spent less time together in the month leading up the wedding than when she was married to Liam, it was only because Barry's position demanded she attend a lot of dinners and events with him. "He likes you, all of you. He's told me many times how lucky I am to have friends like the three of you. And he's even building that studio for us to practice in. What more can he do to prove himself to you?"

Ciara sighed. "I'm feeling like he wants to separate us from you."

"If that were true, he wouldn't be inviting you out here to the studio, now would he? Or inviting you all out to stay at the summerhouse when it's fixed up."

There was a long pause before Ciara answered. "I don't like all the changes. And everything has changed since Liam died."

"Believe me, it's something I'm aware of every day," Alanna said softly.

"I need you to be telling me this one thing," Ciara said. "Can you learn to love him?"

Alanna thought of Barry's kind blue eyes. "I don't know. But Barry makes me feel safe and protected. He's giving up his freedom to help protect the baby from Thomas. That's enough for now."

"There is that," Ciara said. "I'm worried about you. That's all. You know the bloke loves you."

Alanna hadn't wanted to face what her heart knew, but she couldn't evade Ciara's bald statement. "I know. And he knows I still love Liam."

"He's hopeful you'll forget him."

Alanna couldn't bring herself to answer. The pain of Liam's loss was still too raw to imagine loving anyone else.

Ciara cleared her throat. "What about practice? I have a percussionist for you to hear."

"Oh? When can I meet him?"

"Can you come to town tomorrow to practice? See what you think of him?"

"Barry said we'd work it out, but right now I'm not sure how to get there."

"We'll come there then. We can practice on the garden, if nowhere else."

"Righto. See you then. Cheers." Alanna clicked off her cell phone.

She had to get out of this room. Exploring her new home might get her mind off of the discomfort she felt. Slipping a silky robe over her nightgown, she opened the door and stepped into the hall in her bare feet. A faint glow from a nightlight by the baseboard guided her. She found the hall switch and flipped it on.

Blinking at the brightness, she glanced at Barry's door and found it still closed. Good. He probably slept. He'd looked tired, and she'd been little help in planning the wedding in a strange country. He'd arranged the catering and all the details. Let him sleep. She didn't need a keeper.

The hall formed a T. Too many doorways to count left her dizzy. She wasn't sure whether to go downstairs now or explore her surroundings up here. She turned right from her doorway and walked past a myriad of rooms. The only stairway this direction led to the next floor up. She retraced her steps to her room.

Warm milk might help her sleep. The dank scent of mold made her sneeze. She stepped into the brighter glow of the bulb overhead. The main staircase lay in front of her. The light illuminated the first few steps, then faded into the dark first floor.

Descending the inky steps was like walking into a black hole. She should have searched for a switch to illuminate the steps. Clinging to the banister, she reached the bottom without mishap. Groping for a light switch, she touched something sticky. A spider web? A trickle of legs ran up her arm, and she snatched her hand away.

Barely suppressing a shriek, she shook the spider, or whatever it was, from her skin. Still shuddering, she found the switch and flooded the room with light. A black spider raced away on the floor by her feet. It had been on her. She rubbed the goose bumps on her arms.

Something clanked in the next room over. "Barry?" Maybe he was up after all. She followed the noise. Pushing open the door, she found herself in the kitchen. A light shone brightly. "Barry?" She stepped deeper into the room.

The cabinets were a dark wood. The finish was cracked and old. A stained white sink held sudsy water and pots. Was Barry doing dishes? She couldn't quite see her new husband washing up. She found a plastic cup in an upper cupboard.

A door opened, and a young man stepped into the room. At the sight of his broad shoulders and orange-dyed mohawk hairstyle, Alanna shrieked and dropped her cup. Backing away with her hands in front of her, she screamed Barry's name again, then whirled to flee from the intruder.

The man grabbed her arm. "Hey, calm down." The rich tones in his voice held no threat. "You must be Alanna."

He knew her name? The panic beating against Alanna's chest eased until she could draw in a lungful of oxygen. She clutched her robe around herself more tightly. "Who are you? What are you doing in my kitchen?"

"Taking charge right away, are we?" The young man grinned

and leaned down to pick up her cup. "Good thing this wasn't glass."

She snatched the cup back, narrowing her eyes at him. "Who are you?" He knew her name, so he must belong here. Her gaze went to the black tattoos on his bulging biceps. His style statements didn't surprise her as much as his presence. She'd thought she and Barry were the only ones in residence. "You haven't answered my question."

"I'm your new brother." He unfurled his arms and held out his hand. "Grady Kavanagh."

She touched her fingers to his, then withdrew. *More* family she was unaware of? Grady appeared around twenty-six or -seven. Smudges of dirt marred his big arms and face as though he'd been playing in the mud. "You're Barry's brother? You weren't at the wedding."

He shrugged. "I hate getting dressed up, and Barry said I didn't have to go if I didn't want to. He knew we'd meet sooner or later. I thought I wouldn't see you till morning. Sorry if my banging around woke you up." He glanced back toward the stove. "Hungry? There's still some she-crab soup left."

She was suddenly ravenous. "I wouldn't say no to a spot of soup."

He stepped to the stove and ladled up some soup. The bowl was warm when she accepted it from him. "Smells good. You made it yourself?"

"I'm a fair hand at cooking. I do most of it here. The great Barry Kavanagh can't be bothered with such things." He pulled a chair out from the painted table that had seen better days. "Have a seat." His smirk came back when he glanced at her cup. "Want some soda in that?"

"Milk will do." She set her soup on the tabletop and scooted closer in the chair. The way he stared at her gave her the jitters. He stood there like some kind of judge with his arms crossed over his chest and his blue eyes trying to see inside her.

She swallowed a spoonful of soup as he turned to pour milk into her cup. "Very good."

"Glad you like it." He put the milk away and returned to staring at her.

She put down her spoon. "Why are you staring?"

"Just curious about the woman who managed to snap up Barry Kavanagh. The society moms in the area are going to hate your guts. I can see how you caught him though. You look just like Miss Deirdre."

"Is that the woman in the painting on the landing?"

"That's her. She's been quiet this month. I haven't heard a peep out of her."

"What do you mean?" Alanna didn't mask her confusion. "She's living here?" Hadn't the woman been young in the 1940s?

He grinned and tugged at his lip ring. "In a sense. If you hear a banshee howling around the house, it's Miss Deirdre. Or so my dad says."

A banshee. Alanna barely held back a shudder. He was just trying to scare her. "Leave off! I'll not be believing such a story." But in this house, she could almost accept a myth like that. She scooped up a spoonful of soup and swallowed down her uneasiness.

His grin widened. "A banshee is the least of your worries.

Wait until Barry's mom gets back and finds out he's married. Whooee, the fireworks will go off then."

She swallowed the suddenly tasteless soup. "She doesn't know about it at all?"

"Nope." His eyes danced, and his smile widened. "She had other plans for Barry."

Alanna realized he'd called Mrs. Kavanagh Barry's mother, not his. "She's not your mum?"

Grady shrugged. "She barely tolerates me here. Her perfect husband had to admit his infidelity when I was fifteen and my mother died. Pop was left with a son he had tried to hide for all those years. It was quite something to watch him dance around the three of us."

She'd had enough of his stares. "Is that what you'll be doing with your life . . . watching?"

"Bugs you, does it?"

She tipped up her chin. "No."

He laughed. "Liar." His eyes studied her again. "You're going to shake things up in this house, and I've got a front-row seat. But I like you, Red. You've got spunk."

She'd didn't want to hear any more. Pushing back from the table, she rose. "Thanks for the soup."

"You barely touched it." He grinned.

She backed out of the kitchen and fled down the hall. Nothing was as it seemed in this house. Not the manor, not Barry's family. When she reached the bottom of the stairs, she heard a rumble like a lion's roar. The sound vibrated through her bones, up her spine and into her hair, which felt like it was standing up on end.

Her throat closed in a spasm, and she turned toward the door, though she wanted to rush up the stairs to her room and hide under the covers. The roar came again when she reached the front door. She peered out through the sidelight windows, but it was too dark to see the source of the horrifying noise.

Before it could come again, she raced for the steps and the safety of her room. Alanna flung herself against Barry's door. "Barry, what is that noise?" The rumble came again, and panic battered against her chest. She pounded on the door, and when he didn't answer, she pushed into the bedroom. It was empty.

She took a deep, calming breath. Whatever was making that sound was likely something indigenous to the area. No need to fear. It was just the strangeness of everything.

Before backing out of Barry's room, she glanced around. A plain gray sheet covered the bed, every edge tucked in. She could bounce a coin on the taut surface. No pictures on the somber gray walls. The room was a sterile cell, almost monk-like. Even the painted floorboards were gray. She picked up two medication bottles and stared at them. The medicine names on them were meaningless to her, but perhaps he had trouble sleeping.

The rumble jolted her bones again, and she left, pulling the door behind her. Were there big cats in this area? If so, one could be after the kittens under the porch. Maybe she could coax them inside from the porch. Gathering her courage up with both hands, she went back down the stairs to the front door.

The blackness outside the windows was complete other than a glimmer of moonlight on the water. Her glance took in a switch by the door, and she flipped it up. Pale golden light flooded the porch and the first few feet of the dark yard. The door creaked when she opened it and stepped out onto the warped floorboards.

A splash sounded to her left, and she glanced that way. The moonlight caught a thick black tail disappearing into the murky water. An alligator? She shuddered. Did it make that kind of sound? "Here kitty, kitty." Only the frogs answered her.

Hugging herself, she backed toward the door. And bumped into someone. A scream erupted from her throat until familiar hands gripped her shoulders.

"It's okay, sugar. It's only me," Barry said. "What are you doing out here?"

"There you are." She burrowed against his chest, taking strength from the steady beat of his heart. She felt safe and protected in the circle of his arms. "That sound, it scared me."

He lifted his chin from the top of her head. "What sound?"

"Some kind of rumble."

"The alligators. They're beginning to mate."

"It sounded like a lion." She shuddered. "I was afraid a big cat was after those kittens. Where were you? I called for you."

"I was feeding Pete. He's the alligator you just saw. He loves marshmallows."

"That thing is a *pet*?"

A ghost of a smile lifted his lips. "Well, not really a pet. He'd take my arm if I let him."

Alanna fell back a step. "Then why do you mess with him?"

Barry shrugged. "The thrill of it, I guess. It's exciting to know I have to be on my toes. Gators are interesting too. You'll see."

She shook her head. "I'll not be messing with an alligator." She seized the doorknob and yanked open the door. "I met your brother. I'm beginning to think I don't know you at all, Barry. First, you have parents I didn't know you had, and now I've just met your brother." She stepped into the cool dankness of the house. "It's a good thing our marriage is a business arrangement." She marched up the steps, eager to escape the questions raging in her head. Like why she had thought this rushed marriage was anything but insane.

He followed her, reaching for her arm as she reached her bedroom door. "Is that all it is, Alanna?"

She turned to face him, and her hand crept to her belly. "You know I'm grateful for all you've done. Liam's dad is powerful. He scares me."

"He can't touch you now." His fingers tightened on her arm. "You know how I feel about you. I'll protect you from him."

She searched his inscrutable gaze. "It makes for a romantic story. Tragic widow saved by handsome manager. A fairy-tale news article that makes the fans rush to the next concert. Was it all about protecting the money you've poured into promoting Ceol?"

His intense gaze scorched her. "You know it's more than that. I love you, Alanna."

She'd hoped he wouldn't say the words for a while. If nothing else, she found Barry physically attractive with his broad shoulders and the way his blond hair fell over his forehead. He was like a young lion, proud and aristocratic, with a gleam in his blue eyes that told the world he intended to own all he surveyed. And right now that gaze was fixed on her.

"I've always wanted you." He reached out to cup her cheek. "You're so beautiful. You make me feel alive."

His eyes burned with an intensity that made her want to turn and run, but the passion was compelling in some way too. What woman didn't want to be desired? But love was more than that, and she couldn't forget Liam's warm brown eyes so quickly. She turned away so his hand fell from her face, then stepped into her bedroom and shut the door.

Nine

Though she'd been convinced she'd never sleep a wink after the turmoil of the night, Alanna awoke to bright sunshine flooding her room. She rolled over and looked at the clock. Nearly eight. She sat up and pushed her heavy red hair out of her face. Her fingers itched to practice her fiddle. There'd been little time for it in the days leading up to the wedding.

Everything would seem different this morning in the daylight.

Her cell phone rang and she scrambled to grab it from her purse. Glancing at the screen, her gut twisted. She wanted to fling it away, but he'd just keep calling until she answered, so she forced herself to flip it open. "Alanna here."

Thomas's voice boomed out. "What's this nonsense about remarrying? If this is a ploy to keep my grandchild away from me, it won't work, lass." He said something else, but the words cut out.

Her pulse rebounded in her chest. She moved to the window

and got an extra bar on her phone. "It's not nonsense, Thomas. In fact, I'm already married. The wedding was yesterday." When he didn't answer right away, she lifted the phone from her ear and stared at it. Had he hung up on her? She put it back to her ear. "Thomas? Did you hear what I said?"

"What daft thing have you done, Alanna?" His voice was hard, but shaken. "I saw it in the newspaper, but I thought it had to be wrong."

"I'm married to an American now. All your political power can't touch me."

"That baby is all we have left of Liam."

"And I would have shared him with you if you hadn't threatened to take my son from me."

The sound of teeth grinding came over the phone before he spoke again. "I've never liked you, Alanna. You're showing your tinker roots with this little move. Does your new husband know about your past?"

She didn't answer. He would sense the lie if she gave it. "This is useless, Thomas. I'll be ringing off now."

"Wait, you can't do this! We want to see our grandson."

"You can come here and see him anytime." The thought of not seeing the green hills and valleys of her homeland brought a lump to her throat, but she had to protect her baby. Liam would expect her to protect their child. Though Thomas's political power was lessened by her marriage, she didn't trust him.

"Cheers, Thomas." She closed her phone. It rang again a few moments later, and she turned it off.

Thwarting Thomas should have felt good, but his dismay left her with a hollow sensation. She didn't like hurting people, but what else could she be doing? Thomas's power reached across every facet of Irish life.

But she'd disarmed him in one blow and in a way he hadn't expected. All thanks to Barry's generosity. Her heart warmed at the thought of all her new husband had done for her. What a great bloke.

After showering and dressing, she walked past Barry's empty bedroom and descended the stairs with her fiddle in her hand. The place was needing a woman's touch. The first thing on her agenda would be to wash the streaky windows and sweep the front porch, make it more welcoming.

She heard no movement in the kitchen or living room. Through the kitchen window, she saw Grady working in the yard. His dyed orange mohawk was garish in the sunlight. She'd meant to ask Barry why he hadn't mentioned his brother to her. Where was Barry? The mansion felt empty.

She carried her fiddle case to the front porch. The early May morning already shimmered with humidity laced with the promise of heat. She saw no sign of Barry, and the Mercedes no longer sat in the driveway. She laid down her case and decided to go for a walk in the cool of the morning.

Dew still hung in pristine droplets from the flowers blooming along the flagstone path that wound through the garden. With grass on one side and flowers on the other, she wandered through the expansive acreage. The birds sang out from the shelter of the live oaks and cypress she passed. Even in the bright daylight, the water was a sluggish black. Murky and unappealing. She made sure not to get too close.

The wind freshened, and she smelled the marsh. Its salty

scent drew her out to the waving sea grass, past the lagoon and camellia garden, until the house was in the distance. She should have put some shoes on. Her bare feet were wet with dew. The sound of the ocean grew louder, but she would need a flat-bottomed boat to get out to the waves past this marsh.

Disappointed, she stopped and let her gaze sweep the horizon. Was that a pier? She drew nearer and saw that a rickety structure ran out over the marsh to the waves. Watching where she put her bare feet, she walked to the pier.

Some of the boards were missing, and it didn't look safe, but she tested it with one foot.

"I wouldn't try it if I were you, not in your condition," a voice said to her right.

Alanna peered into the shadows of a large cypress tree and saw a black woman seated on a quilt. "Cheers," she said, moving closer to the woman, who looked to be weaving a basket.

The woman had one of those ageless faces, the dark skin smooth and unblemished. She wore her white braids wrapped around her head like a coronet. White shorts revealed long shapely legs, and the red tank top revealed muscular arms. Sandals lay discarded on the quilt.

She put down her basket and patted the space beside her on the quilt. "Rest, little one. I'm Hattie Bellamy." She held out a slim hand, sinewy with muscle.

"Alanna Co—, um, Kavanagh."

Hattie smiled. "Caught him, did you?"

"Not exactly." Alanna sank onto the soft quilt and studied the basket. "It's quite lovely."

Hattie picked it up. "I've done better. Your man lets me grow sweet grass out by the lagoon. I picked this a few days ago and dried it, but I think it needs to dry a bit more."

"I love this one," Alanna said. "Such a beautiful shape, like a boat. What will you be using it for?"

"I don't know yet. Its purpose will come to me." Hattie studied Alanna's face. "You're a little bit lost, aren't you?"

"Yes," Alanna admitted, not willing yet to say more though she'd warmed instantly to the woman.

"Irish, I hear." The woman picked up her basket and began to weave the grass into it again.

Alanna found watching her most soothing. "Guilty, I am. Irish through and through. Have you lived here long?"

"Born here." Hattie squinted through the trees. "You can just see my tiny place through the trees."

"You live on Kavanagh property?" Alanna was sure Barry's property went clear to state land.

"I was your man's nanny once upon a time. His mama deeded over the old place for as long as I live."

The woman must be older than Alanna thought. "There's so much about the family I don't know," she said. "I thought Barry's mother was dead. Now I'm finding she's very much alive and most likely will be outraged he married me."

"She's been wanting a grandchild. I suspect she'll be pleased once she gets over the shock."

Alanna shook her head. "It's not Barry's child." She found herself pouring out the story. Hattie listened with an impassive face. When Alanna was finished, she realized her cheeks were wet, and swiped at the tears. "Sorry."

"Lass, you got troubles. Miss Patricia won't take well to this situation." Hattie hesitated. "And there's darkness in that house. Scares me. You have anywhere else to go?"

Alanna shook her head. "Thomas's reach is long. Only Barry can protect me."

Hattie put down the basket and gripped Alanna's hand hard enough to make her wince. "You listen to me, lass. Watch yourself. Things aren't always what they seem. People aren't always what they appear. If you sense danger, you come to me. Just run right out of that house and head for my cottage."

Alanna smiled even though she could tell Hattie meant every word. "I don't think anyone would be harming me," she said. "Unless you're talking about the banshee."

The older woman snorted. "That banshee doesn't worry me. It's the flesh-and-blood folks who do the most damage."

A low sound in the background began to escalate in volume.

"What's that?" she asked, tipping her head to one side to listen. "A dog?" The whine intensified when she rose and approached a line of flowering shrubs. "Here, boy," she said.

"Prince won't come out," Hattie said. "He's scared of humans, ever since . . ."

"Ever since what?" Alanna asked, glancing back in time to see Hattie snap her mouth shut.

"Never you mind. It's not important." She nodded toward the bushes. "The dog's a stray and fears humans."

Alanna crouched in the soil and held out her hand. "Come here, boy," she said softly. She'd never met an animal she couldn't charm. When the dog didn't respond, she thrust her hand into her pockets, searching for something to offer him to eat. They were empty. She turned back to Hattie. "Do you have any food?"

The woman nodded and reached for a battered red cooler just off the quilt. She lifted out a sandwich and handed it to Alanna. "Won't do any good though."

Alanna unwrapped the turkey sandwich and broke off a small piece of meat. The bread wasn't good for dogs. She went back to the shrub and held it out. "Here, boy, come on now. I won't hurt you." She placed the bit of turkey on the ground so Prince could easily grab it if he came out from the bushes, then she settled down to wait.

The seconds stretched to minutes as she called gently for the dog. She was about to give up when she saw the leaves begin to rustle and a black nose poked out. "Good boy," she said in a soft voice. "Come out to me."

The branches parted and the dog's head came out, and she smiled. "You're an Irish Setter." One foster family she'd lived with bred setters. She had a favorite once and cried for days when he was sold. "Here you go. You can have it."

The emaciated dog crept close on his belly, then gently lifted the morsel from the ground. Alanna knew better than to try to touch him. She broke off another piece and laid it on the ground in front of him. He gobbled that up too. She continued until he'd devoured the entire piece of turkey except for one bite.

She left that on her palm and extended it. His dark, sad eyes broke her heart. When he edged slightly closer and nuzzled the bite from her palm, she gently laid her other hand on his head and stroked his ears. Those ears went back in alarm, but she spoke soothingly to him, and he crouched lower on his belly.

She ran her hands down his back and flank. "You're so skinny, Prince. I'm going to fatten you up. Good boy, such a good boy."

She smiled when she saw his tail begin to gently wag. It was barely a movement, but she saw it. "No one will be hurting you with me here, lad." She stroked and talked while he lay quivering.

Hattie rose behind her and approached with a bag of chips in her hand. "Poor dog. He can have these too."

At the sound of her voice, Prince yelped and ran for the bushes. Alanna called to him, but he stayed in the bushes. Still, it was a start. "I'll start bringing him scraps after meals until I can be getting him some dog food."

Hattie's dark eyes shifted toward the house, then back. "Just don't let anyone in that house know you're feeding him. He'll come up missing."

Alanna's fingers curled into her palms. "What do you mean? Who would hurt him?"

"I've said more than I should." Hattie bent down to fold up her quilt. "I must get back. Just keep it to yourself. And remember where I live if you ever need me." With her belongings under her arm, she picked up the cooler and set off in the direction of her house. Her long strides quickly took her out of sight.

"Alanna!" Barry's voice came from near the house.

She waved at her husband, then looked around and saw Prince running from the bushes as fast as his legs would carry him. Poor pup. Frowning, she walked to meet her husband.

He draped his arm around her. "I wondered where you'd gone, sugar. What are you doing out here?"

"I wanted to be seeing the water, but the pier doesn't look safe."

He turned her back toward the house. "It's not. You need to stay off it. I'm going to have it repaired."

"Why has this place fallen into such disrepair, Barry, when you love it so much?" When he frowned, she knew she'd gone a little too far. "I mean, your place in the Battery is in perfect condition."

He stopped and gazed down at her. "I was waiting to marry. Here is where I want to raise a family. I wanted my wife's input on how to restore it as well. Now that I'm married, it's time."

She gulped, realizing he was saying he wanted a real marriage with her eventually. When would she be ready for that? Right now it felt like never. All she could manage was a smile as she took his hand and started back to the house.

Ten

Barry left her at the porch. "I've got some work to do at the office," he said. "You'll be okay until I get back?"

She nodded. "My mates are coming out in a bit. We might practice on the porch or in the garden."

"Fine." He dropped a kiss on top of her head and went around the side of the house. A few minutes later, his Mercedes rolled past. He waved, then the live oaks swallowed up the sight of his car.

Alanna glanced at her watch. Ceol should be here in a few minutes. She had time to get warmed up. Opening the case, she lifted her fiddle out and grabbed the cube of rosin. After running the horsehair bow across the rosin, she settled her chin on the chinrest, closed her eyes, and laid her bow across the strings.

A reel flew from her bow, and her bare feet slapped against the floorboards. Her long hair flipped around her shoulders as she danced across the porch with the scent of roses blowing against her cheeks. It was Liam's favorite reel, and she imagined him sitting on the swing and smiling as he watched.

Her smile faded as the music did the same. She lowered her instrument. The fiddle by itself left her lonely, and she glanced at her watch again. She thought her mates would have been here by now.

The exertion had left her sticky and hot. It wouldn't be any better inside with no air conditioning, so she sat on one of the rockers and fanned herself as she gazed out over the lovely landscaping of live oak trees, roses, and camellias. She should have stayed out on the other side of the mansion where the sea grass waved. It was cooler there.

The place was as isolated as an island, and it was as if the city were hundreds of miles away. The sight of such beauty should have calmed her, but she felt strangely agitated.

A vehicle rolled up the driveway. Squinting, she watched it come. The vehicle wasn't Barry's silver Mercedes, but a familiar blue van with a Ford emblem. Alanna stood and waved at the vehicle. The van stopped by a row of azalea bushes. Ciara hopped out of the passenger side and waved at Alanna. A wild rush of joy filled her. It had only been yesterday that she'd seen her best friend, but it seemed an eternity.

"You're in the boonies." Ciara slammed the door behind her. "I nearly called for directions again. I passed by this laneway twice."

"Pretty though, isn't it?" Alanna called back. Putting down the fiddle, she started for the steps. A man stepped out of the car, and she caught her breath. For just a second, with the sun in her eyes, the breadth of the man's shoulders and the way he held his head made her think it was Liam come back to her. Then his bulk blocked the glare in her eyes and she saw his face.

Jesse Hawthorne. If he had never showed up to take Liam for a drive, her husband would still be with her.

In an instant, the horror of that night and the following days rushed over her. The flames, the heat, the agony of identifying his mangled body. She thought of it every time she saw Jesse. It was worse since the detective had told her he might have intended to kill Liam along with himself.

She paused at the top of the steps. "What are you doing here?"

Ciara stepped in front of Jesse. "Calm down, Alanna." She motioned for him to follow her. "I know what Adams said, but give the bloke a chance."

He hadn't given her husband a chance. Alanna bit her lip and said nothing as they approached. The sunshine threw the fading scars on his face into sharp relief, though the doctors had repaired much of the damage. He would still be a handsome man when the scars faded.

A slight smile lifted his lips. "You look beautiful as ever, Alanna." His voice still held a raw, husky edge from the damage done by heat and smoke inhalation.

What was she supposed to say to that? Flattery didn't erase the way he'd destroyed her life. In the end she said nothing, just continued to stare at him until he shuffled and dropped his gaze.

"What are you doing here?" she repeated, her gaze flitting from him to Ciara's pleading gaze.

"I need a favor," he said.

Her eyes snapped back to his face. "You're expecting me to do you a favor?" She didn't bother to hide the incredulity in her voice. His light brown eyes held her gaze. Maybe it was the color that so reminded her of Liam. In college, they'd often been mistaken for one another from a distance and thought it great fun.

"Takes cheek, you're thinking, right?"

"Did you kill Liam?" she asked, not caring when he winced. "You were talking about suicide. Did you try to kill yourself and take your best bloke with you?"

"Don't say such things," Ciara murmured.

Alanna turned a scowl on her friend. "Whose side are you on, Ciara?"

Ciara narrowed her eyes. "Yours, mate. You need to listen and not make judgments. Barry is rubbing off on you already, is he?"

Alanna swallowed back the harsh words forming. Ciara loved her and only wanted to help. She glared at Jesse. "For the last time, why are you here?"

"I wish it were me that died and not Liam," he said softly.

"You don't even remember him," she said. "So I'm thinking that's a nice platitude but hardly real." She studied his face. "You *haven't* regained your memory, have you?"

He shook his head. "I don't even recognize the face in the mirror every morning, but that doesn't keep the guilt away of knowing I killed a friend, even if I can't remember what happened that night."

She tried not to feel any pity, but she couldn't imagine living such a twilight existence. "What do you want from me?"

"A job."

Her eyes widened. "What kind of job?"

"Liam is gone, but I can fill in for him. I've been taking drum lessons, and I'm pretty good at it. Better than I expected. Ciara said you need a percussionist. You need a drummer, and I need a job."

She shot an accusing glare at her friend. "You *recruited* him?"

Ciara had the grace to look away at first, then lifted her chin and stared back at Alanna. "I did. We need a drummer, Alanna."

"Not just *any* drummer," she blurted out. "And it's more than drums. It's the bodhran, the bass, and the shakers. A new drummer wouldn't work."

"I've heard him, Alanna. He's deadly good," Ciara said. "Even on the bodhran. And you know how hard that is."

Alanna glanced back at Jesse. He stood with his feet planted apart and his hands in the pockets of his jeans. Liam used to stand just that way. The two men had shared many mannerisms after rooming together all those years, and it was even more disconcerting now than it had been when Liam was alive.

Jesse's gaze never wavered. "Give me a chance. I've been working hard on all of those things. I'm thinking I can do it."

Unbelievable, he was. "Why should I give you Liam's job?" The thought of anyone taking her husband's place on a permanent basis made her throat tighten.

Ciara stepped in front of him. "We're needing him, Alanna. Without a percussionist we're going nowhere. At least listen to him."

Alanna beckoned her to the porch. "I want to talk to you." Ciara sighed but went up the steps to Alanna. Alanna put her hands on her hips and glared at her friend. "I think he killed my husband. How can I see him every day knowing that?"

"Adams is still just guessing. I can't believe you'd think

of turning down our chance at having a decent percussionist. You're not usually being so judgmental."

"Judgmental?" Alanna took a step back.

Ciara gripped Alanna's forearm. "He's learned some of Liam's tricks, says he's been listening to CDs of our songs. We can pick up where we left off. Even his mother said all he does is practice."

Alanna barely heard Ciara's statement about Jesse's ability. Her gaze went back to Jesse, who stood waiting patiently. Liam had loved this man.

Still she didn't think she could take seeing him every day.

She opened her mouth to tell Ciara no, but the pleading expression in her friend's eyes gave her pause.

"Think," Ciara said. "Where are we going to get a good percussionist on such short notice? We need to start practice right away, even if the studio isn't done. Our first concert is right around the corner."

Ciara was right. Alanna needed to consider what was best for Ceol. She sighed and hunched her shoulders. "Let the bloke try."

"Shall we set up on the porch?" Ciara asked. "We'll be having shade that way."

Alanna nodded and went to help haul up the equipment, but Jesse shooed her away.

"Rest," he said, his gaze going to her belly. He opened the back of the van and pulled out his bass drums.

Alanna sat on the swing until they had the equipment set up. Fiona motioned for her to come join them. As she reached the area where the equipment was set up, Jesse began pounding away on the drums. Alanna stopped and listened to the staccato beat. Her lungs squeezed with pain as memories swept over her. The intensity on Liam's face when he'd play, the way he flipped his hair out of his eyes, the careful way he cared for his instruments.

She forced herself to listen as Ena snapped off pictures. Jesse wasn't Liam, but he was good, more than passable. He must have practiced a lot during his recovery.

Maybe she could deal with this.

He glanced up when she approached. In the shadows she couldn't see the scars from his plastic surgery at all. The surgeon had done a great job.

He stopped drumming and continued to watch her. "Well?"

"Not bad," she said. "How about the bodhran?"

Without another word, he left the drums and picked up the instrument on the porch, then sat down. He held the drum like Liam, resting it on his left thigh and forearm with his left hand acting as the "skin hand" so he could vary the pitch and timbre by where he touched the back of the skin. The tippers clicked against the skin at just the right times.

Alanna couldn't help herself. She grabbed her fiddle and lifted it to her chin. The dancing strains of a reel joined the fast thump of the bodhran. Closing her eyes, she danced in her bare feet across the worn floorboards of the porch. For just a minute she could imagine she was with Liam practicing before a performance. When she was done, he'd sweep her into his arms and dance around the room with her. She could almost feel his lips on her hair, the scent of his breath on her face.

She finally realized Jesse had stopped drumming a few seconds before. She opened her eyes and dropped the fiddle away from her face. Her face was wet with tears, so she turned her back and dried it while she made a show of putting her fiddle away. When she faced Jesse and Ciara again, she hoped she was looking composed and serene.

"I told you he was good," Ciara said, her voice smug.

"What do you say?" Jesse asked. "Will you give me a go at it?"

Alanna wanted to be saying no, but she couldn't come up with a reason that didn't seem selfish. The days were ticking away, and they couldn't go on tour without a drummer. Their futures hung on it. "All right. We'll try it for a week."

Ena put down her camera. "Let's run through our sets." She picked up her pennywhistle and began to play the tune to "The Last Rose of Summer."

Fiona began to sing the words in her crystal voice. Ciara harmonized with her. Alanna longed to sing with them, but she put her fiddle back to her chin and began to play. They ran through four songs. She had to admit Jesse was a passable percussionist. His competence with the bodhran surprised her.

They were about to run through another song when a plume of red dirt behind the tires of a car attracted her attention. She squinted and shaded her eyes with her hand. "I think Barry's back."

"Then I think I'm out of here," Ciara muttered.

Eleven

"ait and say hello," Alanna chided as her mate started off. Ciara stopped and turned back to join her, but her black eyes held rebellion. She twirled a cornrow in her fingers.

Ena picked up her camera and snapped off a few shots of Jesse. Fiona stood twisting her necklace in her hands. Alanna went to meet Barry at the top of the steps.

The Mercedes rolled to a stop, and Barry unwound from under the wheel. He pushed his blond hair off his forehead and smiled at them. "Hello. Good to see you, Ciara. You look as lovely as ever. Ena, Fiona." He glanced toward Jesse. "You look much better than the last time I saw you in the emergency room. The surgeons have done well by you."

"I'm doing okay." Jesse nodded toward the mansion. "Beautiful home you have here."

Barry beamed. "It's been in my family for generations. Would you like a little tour?"

Jesse glanced at his watch, then at Ciara, who quickly spoke. "We'd love a tour but not today, Barry. We have to be getting back. Thanks for the invitation though."

"Some coffee or tea at least?" he asked. "Since I had to go to town, I stopped for some benne wafers. Come on in. I'd like to talk to you about the plans for the studio, get your input."

Alanna noticed how Ciara's smile seemed genuine. Maybe she'd thaw toward Barry eventually. "Come on, Ciara, you can be staying a little longer."

"Are you having any chocolate benne wafers?" Ciara asked.

"Of course." Barry took her arm and led her up the steps.

Alanna suppressed a smile. Barry was pulling out all the stops to win over Ciara. He had to sense her hostility. The rest of the band followed them into the house with Jesse bringing up the rear.

Alanna stopped just inside the door, blinking at the dark interior. "I'll open these curtains," she muttered.

Jesse shut the door behind them. "Wow, this is really something." He glanced around at the faded wallpaper and inlaid floors. "I bet this was phenomenal in its heyday."

"So Barry says." She pointed to the hall. "I think they went to the kitchen." She didn't want to be alone with him, so she stepped quickly to join her husband and mates.

They weren't alone. Grady stood leaning his back against the counter. He had a benne wafer in his hand. "I finished the lawn and thought I'd start clearing out the rubbish in the summer-house you'll be using for living quarters for the band next." His gaze went to Ena and stayed there.

"Where is the building?" Alanna asked.

"In the trees." Grady gestured out the back window toward the ramshackle building just barely visible.

That was the place Barry intended for Ceol to live? "The place is practically falling down. Is it even possible to make it livable?" Alanna tried to keep the horror from her voice. It would take ages to make it ready.

"It appears worse than it is," Grady said. "A good cleaning will go a long way. And some minor fix-up." He couldn't seem to tear his gaze away from Ena, who was pretending not to notice.

Alanna exchanged a glance with Ciara. "We need to be practicing now. What about the ballroom I heard you mention? And the band could stay here in the house. It's huge and surely has plenty of space for them."

"The ballroom needs renovating," Barry said. "It's full of junk that I need to go through. And every bedroom that's been redone is in use. I'm sorry." His eyes were regretful. "The contractor promised he'd have it all done in two weeks. He has a large crew. It will be fine, you'll see."

"We can't really afford to keep staying at the hotel," Ciara said. "It's breaking the bank, it is. I think none of us would mind roughing it."

Alanna hid her surprise. Ciara's idea of roughing it was a Holiday Inn instead of a Hilton.

"I'll see what I can do," Barry said.

"I could work on the ballroom," Grady offered. "Get it cleared away."

"I'd rather go through it myself." Barry's smile faded. "You wouldn't know what was important family history."

Alanna glanced at the two men. Barry's shoulders were taut

while Grady appeared relaxed, though his expression held glee as though he'd been goading Barry. The question was, what was it all about?

Over tea and bennes, Barry discussed his plans for the band's space, then said his good-byes to take a conference call in his office upstairs. Alanna saw her group growing restless, and she saw Ciara keep stealing glances out the window. They all wanted to see that studio, and now was as good a time as any. She led her mates and Jesse around the side yard to the carriage house that looked out over waving sea grass and the distant blue of the Atlantic. The fresh tang of salt air sharpened her senses. When she reached the building, she stepped to the door and turned the doorknob, but it was locked. She peered through the dirty windows to a large open room that held stacks of lumber and other building material.

"It's not looking like he's even started it," Ciara said beside her.

"Likely more has been done than we can tell," Alanna said. "None of us knows two shillings about construction, and it's hard to see."

"This place hasn't been touched in years, maybe decades," Jesse said. "Look at the dust on the floors. Still thick as hay in a barn."

Hadn't Barry said they'd begun work? Maybe she had mis-understood. Jesse was right—no hammer had touched this place in many a day. Barry had said it would be ready in two weeks, but she saw no way of getting the place ready in time to prepare for the concert.

If her new husband wasn't going to make it a priority, she

was. "We must find a place to practice—and somewhere for you all to live," Alanna said.

Ena glanced back at the mansion. "Have you explored that place? Maybe there's room in the basement or the ballroom for the drums."

"Barry said the ballroom was a mess, but it still might suit. Shall we be checking it out?" Ciara asked.

"I haven't had time to explore yet. Some of the rooms might be livable too." Alanna's gaze rose to the top dormer windows. "The ballroom is on the third floor. We could go up there and look."

"Not sure I want to haul heavy drums up three floors," Jesse said. "The porch will do for now. Or just the yard."

Alanna hated to agree with him, but their options were few. She jerked her head back toward the house. "We'll be using the porch for now."

Jesse nodded and jogged back toward the van. Ena and Fiona followed him. Alanna turned her gaze from his broad back. The sooner he was gone, the happier she'd be.

"You're being a burk! You'll run him off," Ciara said.

"I should be so lucky," Alanna muttered, starting to the house. She despised herself for the way her eyes burned. She had to be strong. He'd already hurt her as much as anyone could. Alanna walked faster.

Ciara jogged to catch up. "What about the living quarters? Can we peek inside? Maybe just a cleaning will do, like Barry's brother said."

Alanna stopped and Ciara nearly bumped into her. "It looks dreadful from the outside." She glanced around the expansive garden, searching for the building she'd caught a glimpse of. She spotted the low-slung, ramshackle structure half hidden by tall trees and Spanish moss.

"That's it, is it?" Ciara walked through tall weeds toward it.

Alanna had a sinking feeling that this derelict place was just as bad inside as outside. From here, it appeared as if it were about to fall down. She followed her friend toward the gray, weathered boards of the residence. Cobwebs hung from the porch ceiling. The windows were filthy.

She wiped her hands on her jeans. "I don't think anyone has set foot here in years."

Ciara stepped onto the porch and rubbed a window with her fingers until it was clear enough to peer through. She stuck her nose to the glass. "This is it." She wiped her hands on her jeans. "Ick. It would take months to make this livable."

Alanna nodded. "The main house is huge. I'll find rooms for you there."

Ciara started back toward the mansion. "I'm thinking Barry won't want us that close to you, but you can let us know. We need to knock off for now and take Jesse home."

Alanna wanted to remind her friend the house now belonged to her as well, but she was too uncertain of her rights in this pseudo-marriage. Barry likely had a good explanation for why there was so little progress, and she'd make sure he was giving it to her when she saw him.

Twelve

The next morning Jesse threw back the covers and bounded out of bed. He had a job. Jesse grinned at the thought, even though he knew Alanna distrusted him.

A haunting tune ran through his head. At first he thought Ceol had played it yesterday, then he realized he didn't know what it was. He hummed the tune as he yanked on jeans and a T-shirt. Even as the notes echoed in his bedroom, he struggled to remember the words, but nothing came. This amnesia thing was getting old.

His parents were gone when he got downstairs. Just as well. His mother had already tried to talk him out of his plan for the day, and he didn't want to endure another argument. He downed a glass of milk, then grabbed the car keys.

Charleston had turned out for the beautiful spring day. Azaleas and dogwoods burst with color. Narcissus and pansies vied with camellias for attention. Jesse gazed at the spectacle as if he'd never seen it before. Every day was like that—this was the first spring in his memory. Somehow he knew the names of the flowers but didn't know how he knew.

He checked his GPS again, then drove along the streets toward Anderson Pipe Products. The building should be coming right up. There it was. The sight of the brick building didn't jog his memory. As far as he was concerned, he'd never been here before. But he was bound to find clues of some kind at his old job. Information about the kind of man he'd been. He had to figure out a way to prove that he was not the kind of person who would try to kill his best friend in a murder-suicide. He couldn't live with himself if he'd done anything to hurt Liam.

He parked and walked inside. The receptionist smiled and called him by name. She was an attractive brunette with a flirtatious manner.

He leaned his forearm on the counter above her. "You heard I was injured?"

She nodded. "I was sorry to hear it."

"How long did I work here? The amnesia hasn't lifted yet."

Her smile flickered. "About three years."

"Did you know me well?"

She looked down at her desk. "We, um, dated a few times."

Jesse glanced around the reception room. Pictures from the company's history lined the walls, but nothing was familiar to him. The furniture was brown leather, like so many other reception areas. Same magazines, same smells.

He turned his attention back to the pretty receptionist, wondering how to go about asking her what kind of man he was. She'd think he'd lost his mind. And if they'd dated, she might not be honest. He needed to talk to someone who disliked him enough to tell him the truth. "Could I see Rena Mae?"

The smile vanished from her face. "That's not a good idea."

"I think you're probably right, but I really have to," he said gently. "Maybe you could come with me if you think she might be uncomfortable."

She bit her lip. "Let me see if she'll see you." Her heels clicked on the industrial tile as she hurried out of his sight.

He exhaled and shoved his hands into his pockets. This wasn't going to be easy. How did he even start the conversation? He turned to look out on the bustling Charleston street. Taxis honked, and cars flickered by in a kaleidoscope of color. The clatter of the receptionist's heels caused him to turn back around.

"She's agreed to see you as long as you leave the door open." She bent over as if to offer her cleavage for his perusal. "Our favorite bar is having a special band in tonight. I'm free." Her long lashes swept over her blue eyes, then came up again.

"Maybe another time." He took his hands out of his pockets. "Where is her office?"

Her smile froze on her face. "Third door on the right."

His lungs squeezed as he went down the hall. He didn't know what he was going to say to her. How could he know she was even telling the truth? His steps slowed as he neared the door, which stood open. He paused in the opening and studied the woman behind the desk. In her late twenties, she was a beautiful brunette with chiseled features and large brown eyes. Her hair brushed the shoulders of her neat navy suit.

He cleared his throat. "Rena Mae?"

Her wary gaze flickered over him. "What's wrong with your voice?"

"Smoke inhalation from the bomb. Thank you for seeing me."

She folded her arms over her chest. "I don't trust you, so leave the door open."

"Of course." He stepped inside and stood opposite her desk. Not knowing what to do with his hands, he stuck them in the pockets of his jeans again. "I guess you heard I don't remember anything."

"So the rumors have it." Her tone implied she didn't believe it. "A convenient way to get out of your problems. What do you want anyway? If you want your old job back, forget it. You burned your bridges."

He winced. "I heard I lost my job because of sexual harassment. What did I do?"

Her lip curled. "You expect me to believe you've actually forgotten? You forget whom you're talking to here. I know quite well what you're capable of."

"But I don't," he said, keeping his voice even. "I'm trying to find out just who Jesse Hawthorne is. What I've found out so far shames me."

She narrowed her eyes. "Am I supposed to feel sorry for you?"

"No. But I'd appreciate it if you told me the truth."

She stood and walked to the window that looked out on a parking lot. Her gaze stayed on him, and she crossed her arms over her chest. Her movements were jerky, angry. "You were always making sexual innuendoes. At first I ignored them, but they got more blatant. Finally, one night when I was working late, you came through that door, shut it behind you, and grabbed me. If the janitor hadn't been here, I believe you would have raped me. He heard me scream and came running. I doubt anyone would have believed me without his having seen you on top of me."

Jesse felt like he might throw up. He swallowed down bile. He took his hands from his pockets, then put them back. "I'm sorry," he said. "I don't remember any of this. Maybe this whole memory thing is a way to start over, to become a better man. I don't want to be the kind of man who would attack a woman, that's for sure."

She turned from the window and studied his face. "The old Jesse never admitted what he'd done. He never said he was sorry."

"I *am* sorry. Very sorry. Are you okay?" The room felt hot, close. The walls closed in on him, and he knew he was going to have to get out of there soon or risk being completely broken.

She shrugged. "Your actions have made it hard for me to trust anyone, I can tell you that. And I don't work late anymore."

He saw tears shimmering in her eyes and realized how he'd damaged her. "I-I'm so sorry, but I've got to go. I hope you can forgive me someday." He bolted for the door and raced down the hall to the front door. Throwing it open, he stepped into the sunlight and inhaled gulps of fresh air. It didn't help, so he stepped into the grass and vomited the contents of his stomach.

He loathed Jesse Hawthorne. If he could rip off this face, this personality, and become someone else, he'd do it in a minute. He wished he'd died in that explosion, not Liam. No wonder Alanna hated him. She probably knew the real Jesse. The one who preyed on women.

He took a couple more deep breaths and his nausea subsided. Once he quit trembling, he walked toward his car. When he reached it he heard the pealing of bells. The beauty of the noise transfixed him. He cocked his head and drank in the musical tones. Where did they come from? His gaze swept the neighborhood and he saw a steeple peeking over the rooftops. The church bells pealed again, and he began to walk toward the beckoning sound.

He barely noticed the businesses and shops as he walked toward the entrancing bells. A few minutes later he stood outside an old church. The sign said it was St. Michael's Episcopal Church. He approached the open door and peered inside. A handful of people were gathered for midday prayers. He slipped into a back pew and listened. The minister's prayer touched something inside of him.

Jesse wanted to be different from the man he'd been hearing about. When the prayer ended, he slipped out, but he knew he'd return. Walking to his car, he thought back to everything he'd learned about himself. He'd attacked a woman. His depression might have caused him to kill his best friend in an attempt to kill himself. The job at Anderson Pipe Products had been his third one in eight years. Maybe because they found out what kind of man he was? Or maybe he moved on to find new women.

Though he hadn't thought himself depressed yesterday, a dark cloud hovered over him by the time he got to his car. Maybe he couldn't change. Maybe he'd slip back into the old habits as soon as his memory began to come back. He gritted his teeth and shook his head. No, he wouldn't allow it. This was his new start. He'd become a better man, a man of integrity. No matter what it took or what it cost him.

———————

The house where he'd been told he grew up loomed in front of him at the end of the cul-de-sac. He hadn't noticed until now how beautiful it really was. A two-story brick home on the historical register, it sat along a row of other equally beautiful homes. His mother's determined gardening showed in the rows of colorful flowers. How much did it cost to live here? He must have grown up with plenty of material comforts. Was that why he'd thought women were his personal playthings? His gut clenched again.

He entered the house and called out. His parents came from the kitchen. Mom must have called his father home from his investment firm.

"How did it go?" His father's tone was jovial.

Jesse stared at this man who had fathered him but was still a stranger. He said all the right things, did all the loving fatherly things, but Jesse still felt no real connection. Why was that? Was his dad gone a lot when he was growing up? He'd quickly warmed to his mother, but his dad was another story.

"Got any tea, Mom?" he asked.

"Made some fresh," she said. "Mint julep. Your favorite."

He followed her to the kitchen with his father trailing behind. His mother poured the tea over ice and handed it to him. "Thanks." He took a long swallow and bit back a grimace. "I saw Rena Mae. I was really a creep, wasn't I?"

His father's expression darkened. "Typical woman," he

scoffed. "Out for a ring on her finger. You're lucky she didn't claim you got her pregnant." He shot a glance at his wife, who colored and looked away.

Interesting. Maybe his mom had been pregnant with him when they married. He was an only child too. And obviously spoiled. "I don't think so. I think I really did what she said. She was clearly traumatized. And there was a witness."

His dad's gray brows drew together. "I hope you didn't admit to anything!"

"I apologized, but that doesn't make up for what I did." He glanced at them. "I stopped by St. Michael's today. It's a beautiful church." Both his parents stared at him as if he'd suddenly started speaking a foreign language. He'd been about to tell them of his desire to be a better person than the old Jesse Hawthorne, but their expressions of horror made him stumble over the words. "What?"

"You were in a *church*?" his father roared. "Have I taught you nothing? Religion is for the weak-willed. I've taught you to stand on your own two feet, not kowtow to some false sense of guilt. I've made sure you've never been in a church in your life, and now this?" He raised a clenched fist, and his wife caught his wrist before he could strike Jesse. He gave a final, furious glare, then stomped away. Moments later the front door slammed.

His mother sank onto a chair. "Don't infuriate your father like that."

Shaken, Jesse sat beside her. How was he supposed to know what infuriated the man when he didn't even know him? "Why is he so opposed to religion? I felt such peace in that place. Like maybe I could start over, be a better person."

She took his hand. "You're fine the way you are, son. A good boy. Don't go back to that church. I don't know what your father would do if he found out you ignored him."

The Jesse he'd been finding out about wasn't a good person. Besides, he was way past the age where his parents could make demands of him. He set his jaw. "But why? What's he got against church?"

"Your grandfather was a preacher. Strict and, well, abusive. He liked to use the strap on your dad's back. When your dad left there, he swore he'd never darken the door of another church."

"What do you think about God, Mom?"

She rose and carried her empty glass to the dishwasher. "There's no God, Jesse. What we make of ourselves in this life is all there is."

The words rang hollow in Jesse's heart. He hadn't done a very good job up to now, from what he'd heard. The old traps still lay ahead of him. When his friends began to come back around and he started visiting his familiar haunts, would the hedonistic Jesse return? The one who cared nothing about anything other than his own wants and desires?

He sure hoped not. This mission of self-discovery was turning into a horror show, and he was the star.

Murder-suicide. Could he really have been capable of killing Liam? Jesse feared the answer might be yes.

Thirteen

Her friends were gone, and the house felt too empty. Alanna paced the drawing room carpet and glanced outside from time to time. She was bored, that's all it was. Liam used to entertain her in the evenings with his giant bubbles. Or they'd go to the gym and work out. She wasn't used to such solitude.

The dog. She'd forgotten to take food to Prince. She went to the kitchen and rummaged in the fridge for leftovers. A container held the last of some roast chicken. Perfect. She carried it out the back door. A security light illuminated the garden and revealed the vast expanse of grass.

"Prince!" she called. She should have brought a torch. Did the dog even know his name? She heard a meow behind her. "Pussy," she coaxed. "Here, pussy." A tiny kitten approached her. She held out a morsel of food for it, and it nibbled from her fingers with sharp teeth. "You're wet."

The kitten was drenched as though it had been in the lagoon.

It complained plaintively and accepted another bit of food. Alanna saw a movement from the end of the garage. "Prince?" She held out a piece of chicken in that direction. "Come get your supper."

The skinny setter crept across the grass on his belly. His tail gave a tentative wag. Inch by inch, he approached her. Alanna barely breathed, afraid of causing him to bolt. He reached her and she laid the chicken on the grass, where he gobbled it up.

She touched the top of his head, and he flinched but didn't pull away from the food. His skin quivered as she petted him, and she saw the tension gradually ease from his body. "Poor love. No one will hurt you here."

Prince finished the chicken and lay quietly under her hands for several long minutes before he licked her fingers, then rose and slipped back into the night. She'd made progress. She stood and wiped her hands on her jeans.

The kitten still rubbed against her ankles. She scooped up the half-drowned scrap and cuddled it. It licked her chin and she carried it with her across the grass to the path around the lagoon. If she stayed on the path, she wouldn't have any run-ins with the alligator.

Her bare feet hit a pebble on the flagstone and she winced, then put down the kitten to brush the rock off her foot. The kitten hunched at her feet and cried. "What's wrong, little one?" She scooped it up.

She heard a splash in the lagoon and a loud meow from a different cat. Aiming her light through the gloom, she saw a white feline head above the water swimming furiously toward shore. A figure ran from the lagoon. Man or woman, she couldn't tell, but she suspected whoever it was had launched the cat into the water.

The cat yowled, and the note of despair in its cry galvanized her into action. She gasped and ran for the water. Was throwing the cat into the lagoon a deliberate attempt to feed it to the gator? She glanced around for the sinister reptile but saw nothing. The cat screeched again, and it turned a plaintive gaze toward her. Surely she could save the poor thing. She dropped the kitten to the ground and rushed to save the other cat.

Wading into the water, she felt along the muddy bottom with her toes. Ick. The gooey stuff clung to her feet. She listened for the horrific roaring she'd heard last night, but only the sound of tree frogs and crickets echoed around her. Her outreached hands touched the cat, and it practically climbed her wet shirt.

Alanna clutched it close and began to wade back to the shore. She heard a sound that made her mouth go dry. A rustle, then a loud splash. She glanced back to see eyes shining above the surface of the black water as the gator swam toward her.

The shore was still five feet away, and the muck on the bottom of her feet weighed her down like an anchor. Her pulse raced. What had she been thinking? She carried precious cargo—Liam's child.

She tried to move faster, hindered by the fact that she was clutching the cat. She spared another glance behind her. The gator was three feet away and gaining fast. She thought to hit it with the torch but knew that would do little good. All she could do was try to put one foot after the next in the muck and get to shore.

She saw Barry at the edge of the water. "Barry, help me!" Her shaking hands dropped the light. It sank into the dark waters.

"Hurry, Alanna!" He tossed something white toward the gator.

At first Alanna was confused, then she remembered that he fed the gator marshmallows. She moved as fast as she could. There was no time to look back. If she wasted a split second, the gator would take her in its jaws.

She heard those massive jaws snap and expected to feel searing pain, but the teeth hadn't clamped on her. On her knees at the edge of the water, she crawled the last few feet out of the murky lagoon.

Barry yanked her to her feet and propelled her away from the water. The moment her toes touched the flagstone path, she wanted to collapse, but she glanced back toward the lagoon and saw the gator again, only its eyes above the water. Looking for the prey she'd nearly become.

She dropped the cat and threw her arms around Barry. "Thank God you were here, Barry. He would have eaten me for sure."

He caught her in a fierce hug. "What were you doing out there, sugar? I could shake you."

"The cat," she babbled. "Someone threw the cat into the water to feed the gator, I'm thinking. I had to save it."

"You nearly were food to Pete yourself. I couldn't have endured it."

His mouth swooped down and claimed hers in a kiss. The fury and passion in his lips whirled her away from noticing she was wet and dirty and frightened. She clung to him and returned his kiss. How wonderful that someone cared so much if she lived or died. Barry was someone she could depend on. He'd been there for her since the day they first met.

His hand traveled down her back to her waist, and he pressed her more tightly against him. The movement brought Alanna to her senses. She wasn't ready for a real marriage yet. This was physical attraction, nothing more.

She tore her lips from his. "I need to draw a bath. I reek of the lagoon. Thank you for saving me, Barry."

"You're welcome," he said, his eyes intense. "Don't scare me like that again." He dropped his arms, then put his hands in his pockets. "The cat isn't worth your life."

"I had to help," she said. "I can't explain it."

The cat and the wet kitten still huddled at her feet, and Barry kicked at them. "Stupid cats, I'd kill them myself," he said fiercely. "Cats are good for nothing, and you nearly died to rescue one. What were you thinking?"

Alanna watched the cats streak away and dive under the front porch. "I wasn't thinking about the baby the way I should have been," she admitted. Her warmth toward him evaporated. "How did you happen to see me?"

"I was looking for you," he said.

She remembered the figure she'd seen by the water. Someone had thrown that cat in. "Had you been out here long? Did you see anyone?"

He shrugged. "A few minutes."

"How did you happen to see me?"

"When I couldn't find you, I decided to feed Pete. Good thing I did."

She couldn't be arguing with that. Still, the thought that he might have thrown the cat into the water haunted her. Who else could it have been? Grady was here. Hattie lived across the way, but Alanna couldn't see the older woman doing such a thing. So it had either been Grady or Barry, or possibly a transient. Though she doubted anyone would trespass to capture cats and feed them to the gator.

The kitten had been wet too, as though it had been put in the lagoon but managed to escape without being gator food.

"I need a bath," she said again. As she turned toward the house, she caught sight of a cardboard box by the water. "What's that?"

"Nothing important. Just stuff I was feeding Pete."

"What kind of stuff?"

He shrugged. "Garter snakes and lizards I've caught."

She shuddered. "Are they alive?"

He folded his arms over his chest. "Sugar, where is this questioning going?"

"They're alive, aren't they?"

He shrugged. "Pete likes to catch his food. It's fun to watch."

Alanna grimaced. "You watch him catch snakes and lizards? That's sick, Barry. You threw the cat in the water, too, didn't you?"

She watched him closely, wishing for a strong denial she could believe. When his shrug came, she took a step back. "You did it?" she whispered.

"I told you—I *hate* cats. The sneaky creatures slink around, and I fall over them when I least expect it. Don't make such a fuss about it, sugar."

Alanna felt ill. Did she know him at all? "I can't talk about it right now," she choked out. She ran for the house and paused only to scrape the gunk from the bottom of her feet on the grass by the porch. Inside the manor, she fought tears as she raced up the steps and to her bedroom. She grabbed pajamas and a dressing gown from her dresser before going into the bathroom.

Her cheeks were hot, and she sat on the toilet lid and turned on the shower. There was no bathtub in this room, and she was too dirty for a bath anyway. She shut the door, then stripped off her filthy clothes. Tears still rolled down her cheeks as she stepped under the hot spray. The water at her feet ran dark with South Carolina dirt.

Something creaked. The floor? The muscles in her throat tightened. "Is someone there?" she whispered.

"It's me, sugar," Barry said from the other side of the shower curtain. "I wanted to see how you are. I'm sorry if you didn't understand. I never imagined you would care so much about the cats."

She heard his steps come nearer and tried to cover herself with her hands. "Please leave, Barry. I'm not dressed."

"Say you forgive me first. I never meant to hurt you."

She was frantic to get him out of the bathroom. "I forgive you. Now please leave. I need to get out."

"Of course. I'll just take your wet clothes. And I'll leave your cats alone."

She heard the door creak again, then a click. Peeking out the shower curtain, she saw she was alone again. Shudders hit her then, an emotional reaction rather than a result of the cold. Her teeth chattered, and she turned up the heat until the water nearly scalded her skin.

Maybe she was overreacting. Not everyone loved animals the way she did. But her reassurances did nothing to stop her teeth from chattering.

Fourteen

The next day Alanna managed to avoid Barry until he left for the office. She didn't know how to face him now that she'd seen a side of him that dismayed her.

She took her tea and an omelet to the porch and sat, chewing on her lip. When Thomas Connolly accepted that she was actually beyond his reach, she might be able to gain more independence from Barry. She shied away from the word *divorce*. This issue with the cats was just a misunderstanding. His brutality might be accounted for by a cultural difference she didn't understand. For all she knew, Americans despised cats the way women she knew hated mice. She wouldn't have been so upset if he'd thrown mice to the gator.

Sunshine lit the garden. Her mates had promised to come out later to practice. She swallowed the last of her tea, then carried some scraps of omelet in a piece of plastic wrap with her in case she saw Prince. She could see Hattie now.

Not surprisingly, as she approached the shrubs at the far side of the garden, a black nose pushed out from under them.

"Here, Prince." The Irish Setter crawled toward her, his tail swishing ever so slightly more than it had. He was warming up to her. She petted and made over him, then left him licking his chops and made her way along the path to Hattie's cottage.

Such a fine spring day. With the birds singing and the sunshine warming her shoulders, she could almost forget the night's horror. A pregnant woman was supposed to be emotional. That might be a problem she hadn't expected. Her hands smoothed her belly, and she smiled when she felt the baby kick.

The cottage played peekaboo through the trees until she exited the grove and trod the stone path to the front of the small white house. The freshly painted green shutters matched the door. Planters of blooming flowers sat on the windowsills. More flowers lined the path as she neared the front. Hattie had a green thumb.

Alanna raised her hand to knock when she heard whistling behind her. She turned to see Hattie walking toward the house with a basket of grasses. Her hair was down today, a curly white waterfall that came to her waist. She wore capris and a matching top in a bold red Hawaiian pattern. Her feet were bare.

She hesitated when she saw Alanna, then smiled. "I hoped you'd come for a visit." She set the basket on top of a tree stump and came the last few feet. "Have you had tea?"

"I have." Alanna followed her inside. The scent of cinnamon greeted her, and she closed the door behind her. The drawing room was miniscule, just big enough for a small sofa and two wing chairs pulled into a cozy arrangement by the open hearth of a fireplace.

There were a couple of pictures on the walls, and she saw a photo of a young boy in a frame on a table by the sofa. She picked it up and studied it. The child was about five.

"That's your Barry," Hattie said. "He was quite a handful back then."

Alanna set the picture back. "When did you quit working for the Kavanaghs?"

Hattie settled on the sofa and drew her legs up under her like a young girl might. "Barry was fifteen. He didn't need me anymore."

"Did you care for Grady?"

"I was gone by the time he came. He's not been treated well, from what I can see. Poor boy. Patricia clearly hates him. You've not met her yet, you said?"

"Not yet."

"Be prepared. She hates all things Irish. It's a constant battle between her and Barry's father, Richard, who practically idolizes his heritage. Barry too. She'll hate your guts at first sight."

Lovely. Alanna sat in the wing chair. From this vantage point she could catch a glimpse of the manor house through the trees. She realized why she'd come this morning. She wanted to ask Hattie's opinion on the incident regarding the cats. It was a difficult subject to bring up.

She twisted a red curl around her finger and glanced around the room as she tried to decide how much to reveal. A sweet-grass basket held magazines by the door. Another one held pens and stationery on the table by the picture of Barry. She knew there would be more in the other rooms of the house.

"Do you sell your baskets?" she asked. "I'd love to buy one."

"I'll give you one," Hattie said. "What would you use it for?"

"I can't let you do that," Alanna protested.

"You can't stop me. I'll not take the money of a Kavanagh. I have three that are finished. Let me get them."

She rose and exited the room. Alanna wished she hadn't brought it up. She didn't want Hattie to think she'd been hinting for a gift.

Hattie returned carrying three baskets. One was about forty centimeters square, and Alanna's gaze was drawn to it. It would be large enough to store magazines and books by her bedside. The second was round and smallish. It might be good for pens and paper. The third was shaped like a boat.

"I can see you like this one." Hattie extended the large square one toward her. "Take it. I'm honored to give it to you."

Alanna's fingers closed over the basket. Even the texture and weight of it made her smile. "Hattie, I know this must cost you dearly. Please let me pay you for it." She'd heard what these baskets sold for. "I feel guilty to take it for free."

"You're family now, Alanna. Let this be the end of your protests." Hattie set the other two baskets on the sofa and curled back up into her previous position. "Now tell me why you really came. Something is troubling you."

Alanna clasped the basket to her chest and rested her chin on the top of it. "Is it usual for Americans to despise cats?"

Hattie frowned. "Cats? Why no. I have half a dozen kittens running around here most of the time, though usually different ones. No one cat seems to stay around for long. Most of us love our cats and spoil them rotten."

"Last night Barry admitted he'd thrown a cat to the gator. The gator nearly got me when I saved the animal."

Hattie blinked, then wet her lips and looked down at her hands.

"You're not surprised." Alanna tried not to show her shock.

"Barry has always been fascinated with the gators. From the time he was a child. Most often he fed them snakes and lizards. Sometimes rabbits when he could catch them."

Alanna fought her revulsion. "Why does he like the gators so much?"

"Once he told me he admired the gator's single-minded focus on its own needs."

"But Barry is so selfless! He's helped me through so many problems in the months I've known him, and he's never asked for anything in return."

When Hattie didn't answer, Alanna shifted restlessly. Yes, Barry was focused, but that was a good thing. He'd always put her needs ahead of his own, so his obsession with such a savage animal unsettled her. "Do you think he's thrown other cats to that gator?"

Hattie leaned forward and straightened an already perfect pile of magazines. "I really couldn't say."

Couldn't or wouldn't? "Did you see any evidence of cruelty when you were his nanny?"

"I shouldn't be discussing the family this way," Hattie said with an edge of firmness that warned she wouldn't endure any more pressure.

Alanna recognized that she'd get no more information out of Hattie. Likely the older woman already regretted saying anything. Would Grady be willing to tell her more? She couldn't say why it mattered so much to her. Maybe because such cruelty was so far outside her realm of thought. She'd thought she and Barry had the same values.

Now she wondered how well she really knew her new husband. "I'll be going now." She rose to her feet. "Thank you for the basket. You are too kind."

"It was my pleasure." Hattie followed Alanna to the door.

Alanna stepped outside. The heat and humidity nearly took her breath away. As she walked toward the house, she felt the weight of Hattie's gaze on her back. If she didn't know better, she would be thinking she'd seen pity in the woman's dark eyes.

The scent of flowers reminded her of a wake as she trod the path home, though she didn't know why the thought entered her head. Insects hummed at her ears, and she caught a whiff of decaying vegetation from the trees bordering the path. Something splashed in the lagoon, and she shuddered and averted her glance as she passed it. The alligator's eyes sent shivers up her spine.

When Alanna came around the end of the house, she spotted Barry getting out of his Mercedes. He hadn't been gone long—why? He waved to her. There was a folder in his left hand. Grimness strained his mouth, and she wondered if he knew how his actions with the cat had disconcerted her. Her steps dragged as she approached him.

"We've got trouble," he said before she could say anything.

He held up the folder. "Liam's father has wasted no time. He is suing for custody of your child."

She clutched her stomach. "Barry, what shall we do? Surely he knows he has no power over me here?"

"You're not a citizen yet," he reminded her. "I talked to my friend and he's going to try to hurry along the paperwork. You're to appear in Dublin in three weeks to answer the charges. I have another attorney working on delaying that order."

"What charges? I thought you said he wanted custody. Is there more?"

Barry nodded, his mouth tightening. "Liam's parents say you're unfit to raise their grandchild because you're a prostitute."

"*What?*" Alanna touched Barry's arm to steady herself.

Barry tapped the folder with his finger. "He says you worked in a strip club three years ago and includes a list of your clients, including current ones."

Did Barry believe it? "It's a lie." She dropped her hand from his arm and took a step back.

"Did you work at the Blue Dipper?" he asked, his gaze hooded.

She didn't want to admit it. "I was a barmaid, but all I ever did for customers was serve them drinks. I quit when the owner tried to pressure me into performing other services."

She wanted to shudder at the memory of that time, but she kept her gaze on Barry, willing him to believe her. Their gazes locked and the doubt in his eyes stung. "I'm not like that, Barry. You should know better."

He dropped his gaze. "You've never let me in, Alanna. How am I supposed to know all about your past?"

She nodded. "My past is not something I like to talk about." How would he react to knowing she was a tinker's daughter? So few people knew her background, and she preferred to keep it that way. Not even Thomas had ferreted it out yet. Barry's bloodline was as blue as the ocean across the sea grass. She should have disclosed her past to him before he agreed to give her child his name, but she hadn't deliberately attempted to keep him in the dark. Would he have married her if he knew about her past?

He raised his gaze to study her face. Was he thinking she'd duped him?

"Your word is enough," he said, breaking a silence that was beginning to grow uncomfortable. He thrust the folder into her hand. "We won't speak of it again. I'll take care of this."

There was something in his eyes she couldn't tear her gaze from. Was the darkness there a warning, or the passion she knew he felt for her?

Fifteen

Loneliness crept up on Alanna as she walked to the porch the next day. Barry had gone out to look at the summerhouse after announcing that his parents would arrive in the afternoon. She watched for Prince, but the dog stayed hidden. She couldn't sit around doing nothing but counting the minutes until she had to face Barry's parents.

Pressing her lips together, she marched up the curving staircase to the second floor. There were too many doors to decide which to peek into. She chose the one just beyond her own room.

The knob turned easily under her hand, and she stepped into a large bedroom. White dust covers draped the bed and other furniture. She walked toward the window and sneezed when dust flew from the floor. The rotted curtains felt greasy in her hand. She couldn't ask one of her friends to stay in this room.

But if she cleaned it up, got new linens and curtains, maybe it wouldn't be too bad. She went to the closet and opened it. Dresses from the twenties hung inside, and hatboxes were piled high on the shelf over the clothing. Old shoes lined the floor. This had been a woman's room. Alanna would have to pack all this stuff and take it to the attic.

Barry's voice came from behind her. "What are you doing?"

She turned with a smile. "Whose room was this, Barry? These things look like they're from the twenties."

He joined her at the closet and shut the door. "This was my great-grandmother's room. No one has occupied it in eighty years."

"It needs cleaning. I thought I'd look for new bedding and such. Ciara could stay here."

He put his arm around her shoulders and guided her to the door. "It's going to take more than you realize. The mattress is likely full of bugs and mildew and will have to be replaced. The drawers in the dresser are warped. The whole thing needs to be gutted and redone."

"Are any other rooms better?"

"Not really. By the time we could have rooms here ready, I'll have the summerhouse finished. A couple of weeks, tops."

"They can't be staying in the hotel that long. It's much too dear."

"Then they can move into my condo. I'm going to call Ciara and tell her I'll bring in the key."

It was good of him to take care of things. His dependability was one of the things she really liked about Barry. "Thank you. We'll need a place to practice. Any ideas?"

He frowned. "I've been thinking about that. The ballroom might not be a bad idea. I could get the boxes cleared away into the attic. Might take a couple of days."

"I could help."

"I wouldn't turn down the company."

His arm was still around her shoulders. She could smell the spicy tang of his cologne and the clean scent of his shirt. She turned her head to look up at him. His gaze held hers, and she saw the longing there. That hint of darkness she'd seen yesterday was gone.

He'd been so good to her. She leaned against him slightly, not fighting the warmth rushing through her limbs at his nearness.

He turned her to face him, then caught a red curl and twisted it around his finger. "No one has hair like yours." His voice was husky.

They were standing toe to toe. Alanna knew she should step away, but the warmth in Barry's eyes held her in place. She'd been so lonely without Liam. She missed being in his arms at night, missed the whispered confidences and the tender lovemaking. Barry wanted to fill that empty place in her life. Would it be so wrong to let him?

His fingers touched her chin, and he lifted it, then bent his head. His lips claimed hers in a kiss that told her the physical attraction between them was very real. She closed her eyes and kissed him back, laying her hand against his chest where she felt the pounding of his heart under her palm.

He muttered her name against her lips and drew her closer. For an instant, Alanna could imagine it was Liam who held her, who pressed his lips against hers so ardently. She forced herself to remember this was Barry, her new husband. A man who had every right to expect more from her than she was ready to give.

She put her hands on his chest and pushed off gently. He let her go and a crooked smile creased his face. "I-I'm not ready, Barry."

"I'll be here when you are," he said in a quiet voice. A car door banged outside, and he glanced toward the window. "My parents."

Her gut clenched, and she caught her breath. The moment she'd been dreading was here. They were going to hate her, she just knew it. He took her hand and led her down the stairs. More doors banged, and she heard footsteps across the porch. A woman's voice called out.

When they reached the entry, the door opened, and a woman stepped in. A man followed her. Alanna's gaze focused on Patricia Kavanagh. In her sixties, her blonde hair had even lighter highlights in the stylish layered bob. She wore a mint-green suit with heels that accented her slim legs.

Patricia's smile faltered when her blue eyes lit on Alanna. Her eyes went wide, and the color drained from her face. Alanna glanced at her husband uncertainly. Surely he'd told his parents about their marriage.

Patricia Kavanagh's gaze finally left Alanna. She glanced at her son with a question in her eyes, then stepped forward to brush her lips across Barry's cheek. "I missed you, son. Two months is too long to be gone. We're exhausted." She stepped back and stared at Alanna again.

Barry put his hand on Alanna's shoulder. "This is Alanna, Mother. My wife."

The words fell with all the power of a cannonball into the room. Patricia took a step back and went white. She shook her head, then stared from Alanna to her son and back again. "You look just like her," she muttered, her gaze focused on Alanna's face. "Just like Deirdre."

"I noticed that." Alanna sent an appealing gaze to her husband.

Patricia's lip curled. "You're *Irish*? How could you, Barry? You know how I detest that slovenly race."

"Alanna and I were married two days ago," he said. "I want you to welcome her into the family." His voice was hard.

Patricia blinked, then moved her gaze to her son. "You knew we'd be home today. How could you do this behind our backs after I asked you to postpone it?" Her stare at Alanna was fierce. "I suppose this was all your doing?" Her gaze went to Alanna's bare feet, and her lip curled. Her mouth fell open when her stare lit on the gentle swell of Alanna's tummy. "Are you *pregnant*?" she whispered.

Alanna's throat made an audible click when she swallowed. A simple yes would make it appear as though the child were Barry's. She didn't have enough moisture in her mouth to explain the circumstances. She and Barry hadn't discussed just what to tell his parents.

"Yes, she is." Barry's voice held a challenge.

"It's no more than I should expect."

Richard, Barry's father, cleared his throat. "Welcome to the family, Alanna," he said heartily. He brushed past his wife and took Alanna in his arms.

She returned his hug, which felt genuine.

"Don't mind my wife's reaction," he whispered in her ear. "She'll settle down." He raised his voice to a hearty bellow. "I'm sorry if we seemed less than happy. We're thrilled Barry has finally decided to settle down. Nothing could make us happier than to have a grandchild."

His warm words and embrace blew away a bit of the chill in Alanna's soul, but she hated that her new in-laws obviously thought the child was Barry's. She marshaled her thoughts to explain, but Barry cut her off.

"Alanna, would you want to put on some coffee for my parents? I believe there are still some bennes left. Let me take your bags, Father." He dropped his hand from Alanna's shoulder and leaned down to grab the suitcases.

"I'll help your wife," Patricia said, pressing her lips together.

Alanna had hoped to escape the inquisition Patricia was sure to spring on her. "I'm not sure where the coffee is," she said to Barry.

"I'll show you." Though the offer was warm, the words were cold. Patricia stalked into the kitchen and retrieved a bag of coffee beans from the cabinet. Instead of starting the coffee, she turned and stared at Alanna. "You're not fooling me," she hissed. "I know what you're after."

"Wha-what do you mean?" Alanna struggled to make sense of the other woman's hostility. Did she already know this baby wasn't Barry's?

"You're not the first, and you won't be the last, though I'll never know why Barry should feel such a misguided sense of responsibility that he had to marry you." She stepped closer.

"I don't understand."

Patricia's mouth twisted. "You're nothing special. Barry chases every redhead with even a superficial resemblance to Deirdre.

You're the first one he's married, though, so you might be smarter than you look."

"You don't understand." Alanna held up her hand. "Let me explain." It would be better for Patricia to realize there was nothing romantic in the relationship.

Patricia rolled her eyes. "What kind of fool do you take me for? I knew the truth the minute I saw the resemblance." She shook her finger in Alanna's face. "I'll have a talk with Barry and get to the bottom of this." She spun on her expensive heels and stalked out the kitchen door.

Alanna stared after her. Coffee. She turned back to the pot. Her hands shook as she measured out beans and put them in the grinder, then filled the carafe with water. The coffee prep wasn't enough to distract her from what had just happened.

Alanna shuddered at the venom she'd seen on her new mother-in-law's face. Maybe Barry could set her straight. She'd exchanged one set of in-law problems for another, though this one was Barry's fault.

The whole mess sickened her. All she wanted was to find someplace peaceful to grieve, a space to practice her music. She hadn't counted on such a hotbed of conflict.

While the coffee brewed, she put the cookies on a plate. Waiting on the coffee, she glanced out the back window and saw Grady approaching the back door. Maybe he could answer some questions.

He took his boots off on the back porch, then stepped into the kitchen. "Was that the great Richard and Patricia arriving?"

"Yes." She watched him walk to the sink and wash his hands. "They didn't want Barry to marry me."

COLLEEN COBLE

Drying his hands on a paper towel, he turned and leaned against the counter. "Doesn't surprise me." He tossed the towel onto the counter, then tugged at his earring. "His mother is a little controlling of everyone in her life." He twirled his finger around his ear. "Don't get on her bad side. She reminds me of Bette Davis in *Whatever Happened to Baby Jane?*"

Alanna wasn't familiar with the movie, but she didn't doubt his assessment of her mental health. "He'd not be telling his own parents about something so important?"

"The Kavanaghs aren't what you'd call close." He shrugged. "I'm a good example of how the Kavanagh men make their own rules. Patricia should have learned that a long time ago."

The coffee was done, and she'd have to rejoin the rest soon. "What about that picture in the stairs—the one that looks like me? Patricia seemed quite shaken when she saw me."

He shrugged. "Old Fergus would never let anyone take down that picture. She was some woman he was mad over. From Ireland, naturally. He loved all things from the Emerald Isle. Quite the opposite of Patricia. She despises the Irish. I bet she had a cow when she heard your accent."

Alanna ignored his comment. "Fergus was Barry's grandfather?"

"Great-grandfather. He died a couple of weeks after I came to live here. Never liked me. I think it was the tattoo." He leaned forward and lowered his voice. "I think Deirdre is the banshee we hear on rainy nights."

Alanna shuddered. "Patricia made her dislike of the Irish very clear." She told him what the woman had said.

He grinned. "I'd like to have seen her face when she saw

you. My mother looked a bit like the gal in that picture. The Kavanagh men seem to chase after the skirts who resemble her, and you're a dead ringer."

She poured the coffee into cups and put them on a silver tray. She wished she could put her shoes on. It was going to be a long afternoon.

Sixteen

The silence in the parlor was as suffocating as the inky darkness outside the window. Alanna sneaked a glance at her watch. It wasn't even nine. She stifled a yawn and wondered where Barry's parents were going to sleep. Maybe they were expecting to sleep in her room. If so, what would she do if Barry expected her to move into his room? She was worn out from the grilling Patricia had put her through and only wanted to fall into oblivion, not deal with what had happened between them earlier in the day.

She still needed to talk to Barry about his mother's misconceptions.

Patricia stood. "I think we'll head for bed." Without offering any acknowledgement to Alanna, she held out her hand to her husband. "Come along, Richard."

He rose obediently, but his gaze lingered on Alanna. She wished she could believe he saw her only as his new daughter-in-law, but after Grady's comments and Patricia's rage, she wondered if he saw her as a schemer as well.

"Where are they staying?" she asked Barry.

"They have a suite in the tower wing," he said. "You haven't been over there yet."

"Is there room for my band there?" Not that her in-laws would welcome her intrusion.

He shook his head. "It's just one bedroom, living room, bathroom, and small kitchenette. A self-contained suite."

There was so much of this huge place Alanna hadn't seen. She was going to have to go exploring at the first opportunity. The big old house whispered of secrets, and she suddenly couldn't go to bed without clearing the darkness from her brain. She needed her nightly walk. Mostly, she just wanted out of the oppressive atmosphere his parents had brought with them.

She stood. "I believe I'll take a stroll."

Barry was pulling out his laptop, but he paused to glance up. "I'd better go with you."

"You should be getting your work done. I'll be fine. I won't go by the lagoon."

He frowned. "Put on bug spray. The mosquitoes will carry you off." He put his nose back toward the computer screen.

Through the screen door she could hear the crickets and katydids and some other sound she couldn't identify. Barry had once said something about tree frogs. Perhaps that was the strange, almost musical tone she heard.

She spritzed herself with the bug spray she found on a shelf in the entry, then flipped on the porch light. Almost at once, moths and other flying insects raced for the dim glow. She stepped through the creaking screen door onto the porch. The moistness of the night breeze touched her skin with a refreshingly clean touch.

She paused on the top step while her eyes adjusted to the dark ahead of her in the yard. Maybe this wasn't the best idea, at least not without a flashlight. She wouldn't be able to see her hand in front of her face. She started to retreat for a flashlight when the moon came out from behind the clouds and touched the trees and shrubs with a faint glow.

Good. The thought of going back inside didn't appeal. She stepped down onto the brick walk and walked along the flowerbeds in front of the mansion. In the night, she couldn't see the peeling paint or crumbling brick. She could almost imagine she was a Southern belle strolling the yard in her hoop skirt.

She heard the sound of a motor, then headlamps swept the grass before the vehicle stopped in the laneway. She paused and strained to see in the dark. The lights went out, a door opened, and a man emerged from the shadows. She took a step back until he drew near enough that she recognized the police investigator, Detective Adams.

"Is there something new in the case, Detective?" she asked, brushing a mosquito from her arm.

He stopped two feet from her. "I hear Jesse Hawthorne is coming to work for you."

"Righto. As our percussionist."

Adams switched his toothpick to the other side of his mouth. "I want you to keep an eye on Hawthorne. See if he'll open up to you. Trust makes people want to confess sometimes."

"He doesn't remember," she reminded the detective.

His teeth flashed white in the dark. "So he says. I'm not sure I buy it. And why did he even take drumming lessons? Our psychologist says sometimes people deal with guilt by taking on the persona of the one they killed. He might be trying to become Liam Connolly."

Chills rippled down her back and gooseflesh rose on her arms. "That would make him flipping crazy."

"Like I said, keep an eye on him. If he's really trying to slip into your husband's shoes, he'll cozy up to you."

"Could someone else have planted that bomb?" she asked. "Just before my wedding, you mentioned Jesse might have enemies. Maybe someone was trying to kill him."

The detective shrugged. "I'm checking out every angle. He was fired for sexual harassment. The victim might have hated him enough to hire someone to snuff him out."

Acid burned her throat. A man like that lived while Liam had died. Life wasn't fair. "You have to find out who did this."

"I plan to." Adams said. "You'll let me know if you learn anything?"

"Yes." Her hand went to her belly. Her baby would grow up without a father because of Jesse Hawthorne. He'd either killed Liam himself, or his actions had caused someone to hate him enough to do away with him.

Adams's big hand came down on her shoulder. "Try not to worry. It's not good for the baby." He lowered his arm to his side. "I'll be in touch." He turned and melted into the darkness.

Even though the night was warm, Alanna shivered. She didn't want to think that Liam might be lying in his grave because of a suicide attempt, but the thought of an angry woman planting a bomb under him wasn't any better.

She wandered down closer to the waving sea grass until she stood at the edge of the lapping waves. Water calmed her and made her think she stood on the shores of the Atlantic in her homeland. Ireland was in her blood, her bones. Her fingers itched to hold her fiddle and play a mournful tune that would whisk her to Hibernia in her mind.

The wind sighed through the tall grass and brought the salt scent to her nose. Liam should be here with her with his arm across her shoulders and his thick brogue in her ears.

"Alanna?"

For a second she thought her daydreaming had conjured up Liam, then she recognized Barry's big shoulders and shock of golden hair. She put on a smile. "Barry, you startled me."

She heard a rustle, a slither, then he grabbed her arm and yanked her from the water. The next thing she knew, they were running up the slope. Water splashed behind her. "What was that?" she asked, panting. "The gator?"

Barry slowed their pace. "Pete about had you for dinner."

"In the seawater?" She'd thought she was safe.

"He sometimes moves around."

"In seawater?"

"It's brackish here, not fully salt water. Gators move through brackish water."

A shiver ran up her spine, and she studied his face. "Did you come out to throw him a kitten?"

His lips tightened. "No."

She didn't know if she believed him. Was it the air of danger under the surface that drew her? She didn't want to experience the warmth in her belly when she looked at him or the racing of her pulse when he touched her hand. Not a man like him.

She stopped at the top of the hill and turned back to watch the moon glimmering on the water. "It's such a beautiful place to hold such danger." When she tried to tug her hand out of Barry's, his fingers tightened. Her desire to pull away melted. He was her husband now. It was all right to enjoy the contact of skin on skin, to relish not being alone. She had no right to judge him.

Barry had feelings for her, and she longed to return them, to put the pain of Liam's death behind her. She stared up at him in the moonlight. "You've been so good to me, Barry."

His fingers brushed her cheek. "I love you, Alanna. I've always loved you."

"Me or the fact that I look like Deirdre?" She blurted the question that had been lingering in her heart every time she saw the portrait.

"Where'd that come from?"

"Grady says all the men in your family are obsessed with Irish women who look like her. Is that true?"

His lips tightened. "You have to be careful of anything Grady tells you. It's just a painting. I love you for much more than your beauty. I love your passion for life, the way you care about other people and animals, even the way you run around barefoot."

"And your desire to marry me hadn't anything to do with how I look like Deirdre?"

His gaze narrowed. "I'll not lie to you and say I didn't notice. I've got eyes in my head. You're a beautiful woman, and it is almost uncanny how much you look like her, but it wasn't what made me fall in love with you. Satisfied?"

"Why didn't you tell me how your parents would react to my appearance?"

He shrugged. "It wasn't important."

"She accused me of trying to entrap you. Have you told them the baby isn't yours?"

"My mother can be a little overwhelming, but they won't be here long before they're off on another trip. She was just shocked. Tomorrow she'll be fine."

She wouldn't get anything else out of him. And maybe it was enough. Maybe tomorrow would be better. "Did you get your work done?"

He brushed the hair back from her face with a tender hand. "No, but I worried that you might stumble into trouble. It appears I was right. Let's go in. You're shivering."

"You go ahead and I'll be along. I want to enjoy the night a bit longer. I'll stay away from the water."

He bent and brushed a kiss along her brow. "Don't be long."

She watched him turn and walk along the brick path to the house. Thanks to Barry she was in a lovely old house and her baby was secure. If not for him, she'd be wondering how she was going to make enough money to support her baby. She might have had to give up the band and live with the Connollys after all. Barry had saved her. Surely that was more important than his affection for an alligator.

He disappeared around the side of the house, and she wandered through the garden. A garden by moonlight held its own brand of magic. The scents floated from everywhere, and light gilded the blooms with gold. The summerhouse loomed at the end of the garden, but she knew better than to poke around there in the dark.

She retraced her steps to go inside. Passing the roses, she felt a hard shove between her shoulder blades. The blow knocked her forward. Her legs moved fast to avert a fall, but a slight drop-off unsteadied her even more. She put her hands out. She had to protect the baby.

She hit the ground on her right shoulder, then she was rolling down a steep slope that she hadn't even known was there. Thorns tore at her bare arms and tangled in her hair. She tried to protect her stomach, but her body slammed from one spot to another and gathered speed as she tumbled down the hill.

Her head rammed into a large tree at the base of the hill and she came to a stop. Crumpled into a ball, she lay stunned with the world spinning around her. Her hands roamed her belly, but she couldn't think, couldn't feel anything. Then her knee cried out, and her shoulder groaned. The pain of her abrasions began to penetrate her numb state.

Get up. She had to get up. Make sure the baby wasn't hurt. Groaning, she got onto her hands and knees and shook her head to clear it. Her blurry vision kept her from recognizing exactly where she was, though she saw trees marching off into total darkness to her right. The woods. She'd rolled down to the base of the woods.

She managed to claim her feet, though her legs trembled. Something trickled down her arm, most likely blood. Her hands cupped her belly. "Please, Lord, let the baby be all right," she mumbled. There were no cramps, at least not yet. Maybe the baby was unharmed, but she needed to see a doctor and make sure.

Who had shoved her? She shuddered and turned to stare up the hill, an impossible slope to climb in her state. A figure appeared at the top, then started down. Out of the darkness, a man called her name. In Liam's voice.

She strained to see. It *was* him. She recognized that walk, the way he held his head. Her knees crumpled, and darkness claimed her.

Seventeen

The baby. Alanna swam out of the darkness, her hand going to her belly. She struggled to sit up.

"Lie still until the doctor sees you," said a male voice to her side.

Liam's voice. Surely it was. She strained up, then opened one eye and stared into the face hovering over hers. Jesse, not Liam. Slumping back, she blinked against the moisture in her eyes. What had she expected—that Liam had come back from the dead?

"How do you feel?" Jesse crouched over her. He brushed mosquitoes from her arms. She still lay at the base of the tree.

Her hands roamed her stomach. "I-I don't know." Her arms and face throbbed from scratches, but she had no cramps or pain in her stomach. The baby was all that mattered to her. The other pain was a minor irritation.

Jesse brushed the hair back from her face. "The ambulance is on its way."

"Where is Barry?"

"In the house, I assume. I rang 9–1–1 on my cell."

"Help me sit up," she said. The detective's warnings rumbled around in her head. This man might have killed her husband. Was he trying to become Liam? The inflections in his voice suggested it, but she told herself to show no fear.

Had he shoved her down the hill?

"You need to lie still."

She pushed away his restraining hand. "I must get to the house." She managed to sit up, and her head swam. She waited until the spinning stopped, then struggled to her feet with his help. Before she could take a step, he swung her into his arms and started up the hill with her.

The scent of spearmint on his breath smelled like the same gum Liam used to chew. "It's too steep," she protested. "I can walk."

He ignored her protest and continued to lug her up the slope with his breath growing more labored. When he reached the top, he paused to draw in a few deep lungfuls of air before heading toward the house.

"I can walk," she said again, more convinced now that it was true.

Against her will, her fingers touched the curls at the base of his neck as she hung on for dear life. Liam's had felt just this soft and springy. She jerked her hand away.

"Almost there," he gasped.

"Put me down and go get Barry," she commanded. All she wanted was to get away from this man who reminded her too much of Liam.

They reached the porch steps and he carried her up them to the front door, which he banged with his foot. Insects dive-bombed them from the porch light. The breeze changed direction, and she smelled his cologne, Irish Tweed, just like Liam used to wear. The scent angered her. How dare he think he could ever hope to match Liam? There was no one like her husband.

His wearing the cologne convinced her of all the detective had said. "Put me down!" she said in her fiercest voice.

He stopped banging the door with his foot and glanced down at her before carefully allowing her to gain her feet. It was a mistake. Her head spun again, and she swayed before grabbing his arm for support. She hated that she had to depend on him for any help.

"I've got you," he said, slipping an arm around her waist. He opened the door with the other hand and half carried her over the threshold. "Kavanagh!" he shouted.

Barry appeared in the hallway, and his eyes narrowed. "What are you doing with my wife?" He rushed toward them. "Give her to me. Alanna, are you all right?" He swept her into his arms and carried her to the living room. "What did you do to her?"

"She fell down the hill," Jesse said, following them to the living room.

Shudders wracked her body, and she couldn't stop them. "What's wrong with me?" she stammered through chattering teeth.

"Shock, I think." Jesse shoved his hands in his pocket as he stood at the edge of the sofa where Barry laid her.

Alanna couldn't bear to look at him.

She clenched her teeth to keep them from jittering. "Can I have a blanket?" she asked Barry.

"Of course." He grabbed an afghan from across the back of a chair and laid it over her. He knelt beside her, and his warm breath caressed her face. He stroked her hair. "Are you hurting anywhere?"

The warmth enveloped her, but the shivers didn't stop. No pain in her belly though, and she laid still with her hands protectively over her child. She couldn't lose the only piece she had left of Liam. "I-I think I'm all right."

He frowned at her bare feet. "You were outside again with no shoes? You could get snake bit."

"You know I hate shoes."

From outside, the ambulance screamed up the drive, the siren growing louder until it stopped with a final shriek right outside. Footsteps pounded up the porch then the front door shuddered with a fist pounding it. "Paramedics!" a voice shouted.

"I'll let them in." Jesse disappeared into the hall.

"What's he doing here?" Barry asked, still stroking her hair.

"I don't know. When I came to, he was standing over me."

"Came to? What happened?"

She stared into his worried face. It was a bit dodgy that Jesse happened to be there right after she'd been pushed, but she couldn't afford to let Barry forbid Jesse to come on the property—not if she wanted to get to the bottom of what happened to Liam. Could he have pushed her, then played the hero? It made a twisted kind of sense.

"I fell down the hill," she said.

"I should have made you come in." He tucked the afghan

around her better. "I'm sorry I wasn't there for you." The paramedics came rushing in and he stepped back.

The paramedics checked her vitals and told her nothing serious appeared to be wrong. They bandaged the worst of her cuts and told her to rest. When a worried Barry asked if she should be transported to the hospital, the paramedics glanced to Alanna for input.

If her fall had damaged the baby, no doctor could fix it. "I think I'm all right," she said. "But I wouldn't turn down an ultrasound."

"Is it okay if I take her in?" Barry asked.

The men nodded. "She's in no danger."

When the EMTs left, she realized Jesse had gone as well. On the way to the ER, she reflected on her attack and tried to remember anything in that moment before she fell, but nothing was coming to her. No whiff of cologne, no sense of who her attacker had been.

Shudders racked her again, but this time they were from knowing a madman was out there.

Barry escorted her into the emergency room, and she was quickly taken back to a room. The ultrasound showed the baby moving around with a strong heartbeat. Once she knew the baby was all right, fatigue weighed down her limbs, and she nearly fell asleep on the way home.

"Want me to help you to bed?" Barry asked when they reached the entry hall.

She still ached all over, and her skin throbbed from the cuts and bruises. "If you're not minding, that would be lovely."

She took his hand and he supported her with one arm

around her waist. The warmth of his skin penetrated her clothing and strengthened her. His strength, his steadfastness, were what she needed right now.

He helped her up the stairs. The vertigo was disappearing, and she felt stronger by the time they reached the door to her room. Barry flipped on the light and led her to the bed, where he pulled back the covers and helped her climb in. The cool sheets that smelled of sunshine welcomed her.

"Could you get me a washcloth?"

He nodded, then stepped to the bathroom, and she heard water running before he returned with a warm washcloth. The bed sank as he sat on the edge by her feet and gently washed her face and arms. The hospital had tended to her cuts and scrapes, but traces of mud and grass still clung to her skin. The warmth of the water soothed her, and so did the steady grip of his hand on her ankle. Barry's touch was growing more and more welcome to her, but she couldn't help the feelings of guilt that welled up. Liam had been gone only a few months, and she had no business enjoying another man's attention.

She pulled the sheet up over her legs. "It's a good bloke you are, Barry," she said, her voice husky.

He tucked the edges of the sheet around her. "You want me to stay with you? I can sit right here in the chair."

"You need your rest. I'm fine now. Thanks for taking such good care of me." She caught his hand and pressed it to her cheek. He had broader hands than Liam. Square-cut nails that were well cared for. Liam's had been jagged where he chewed them sometimes.

Barry bent and brushed his lips across her forehead. His

breath whispered over her face. "I'll just be across the hall if you need me."

She smiled up at him, and he stared back with such an intense gaze that her smile faltered. The passion in his eyes made her wish she could respond the way he wanted. "See you in the morning," she said softly.

He retreated to the door and flipped off the light. "I'll leave the door cracked so I can hear you if you call."

His footsteps faded, and loneliness enveloped her. She nearly bit her tongue with the effort not to call out to him. The cacophony of katydids and other insects intensified in the dark, and she allowed the sound to drown out her longing for companionship. She'd been a twosome so long, and she hated sleeping alone.

Alanna moved her throbbing legs restlessly under the cool brush of the sheets. She'd never be able to sleep with that din outside. Lying in the dark with her eyes wide open, she went once more through the events leading up to the shove. Had she smelled anything, heard anything that might give a clue to the person who wanted to harm her?

And why push her down the hillside? The fall wasn't likely to kill her. Did someone want to frighten her away from the estate? The hatred in Patricia's expression came back to Alanna. Could it have been Barry's mother? His parents hadn't come to see what the sirens meant, which seemed strange now that she thought about it.

Maybe it hadn't been Jesse. Alanna had been quick to jump to conclusions, but she didn't think the shove down the hill had been a murder attempt. Once she found out why Jesse had come, she'd understand more.

Eighteen

The ambulance had pulled away without Alanna in it. Jesse stood in the shadows with the mosquitoes buzzing around his ears in the moist night air and watched the lights in the Blackwater mansion. He knew he should go home, but he wanted to be close to Alanna. So he hid his car in a grove of trees dripping with moss, then watched until Barry's Mercedes returned. Curling his hands into fists, he watched Barry help Alanna inside.

She belongs to me. That man had no right to put his hands on her.

The minute Jesse had touched Alanna, something happened to him. An overwhelming love welled inside of him, and he had no idea where it had come from. Visions of holding her, kissing her, had flashed through his mind. He wanted her for his own.

And in that moment, he realized he was being influenced in some way by Liam's spirit. Possessed maybe.

He shook his head. Maybe he was going crazy. He rubbed

his head and groaned. What a nutty idea. He didn't believe in demons or spirits, did he? But then again, how would he know? Maybe it was all part of his brain trauma.

The lights upstairs had gone on a little while ago, then gone out again. A figure passed in front of the big front windows downstairs. Barry's face peered out into the night, and Jesse shrank back into the shadows. He needed to get out of here before he was caught. If Barry ordered him off the property, he wouldn't get the opportunity he needed to talk to Alanna, figure out what was happening to him.

He thrashed through high weeds in a jagged trail to his car, parked halfway down the drive. Something slithered away in the undergrowth, but he only cared about not being seen by Barry.

He banged his shin against the car fender in the dark, then felt his way around to the driver's door. After half falling into the seat, he closed the door with as little noise as possible, then started the engine and backed out of the car's hiding place with no lights. Once he emerged from the trees, the moon lit the way.

There was no traffic on the road past the estate. He peered through the trees but couldn't see the house from here with the live oaks blocking the view. His hands trembled on the steering wheel, and he had no idea why he was so agitated. Was it leaving Alanna behind? Or maybe this crazy sense that she belonged to him.

He drove to the city and found himself passing by St. Michael's again. A man in a collar stood by one of the front pillars. Before he could talk himself out of it, Jesse parked his car and got out. Belching fumes, a truck rumbled by. Jesse waited for it to disappear around a corner before he walked across the street.

The priest was walking away from the church toward a small red car. "Excuse me," Jesse called. "Are you the rector?"

The man turned with a smile. "Why, no. I'm the priest for a parish in Louisiana. I'm visiting the area. Can I help you?"

Should he talk to this fellow? The man's blue eyes held a warm welcome in the wash of streetlight. What Jesse had to say would sound so crazy, but surely a priest could help him sort through the muddle he found himself in.

He put his hands in his pockets. "It sounds crazy. Maybe I *am* crazy."

In his midthirties, the priest was slightly built with a shock of sandy hair. He studied Jesse's face. "Have a seat." He indicated a park bench along the sidewalk, then sat down and glanced up at Jesse with an interested smile.

Why not? Jesse sat beside the priest and laced his fingers together around his knee. "What do you think happens to a man's spirit when he dies?"

"Is this a rhetorical question or do you have a reason for asking?"

Jesse didn't want to be drawn into a theological discussion. He wanted answers. "Do you believe a spirit can possess another person? Or at least bug the heck out of them?"

The priest smiled. "Who do you believe is possessed?"

"Me." Jesse watched for a reaction, but the priest's expression didn't change. This was a waste of time.

The man's gaze locked with his. "What makes you believe you're possessed?"

"There was this car bomb. My best friend was killed, and I think his spirit or some imprint of his memory moved to me. I know things about his life. Things I could only know if part of his spirit transferred to me."

"I see. We usually think of possession as by a demon. Maybe your friend told you some things and you're remembering them now. It sounds like you were close?" The man's voice was kind.

Jesse grabbed onto the idea, which would be much better than being possessed by Liam's spirit. "I'm sure my shrink would be saying the same thing."

"Why are you seeing a psychiatrist?"

Jesse told him about the amnesia. "And I had some depression before the explosion."

"Have you told your doctor about this idea that you're possessed?"

Jesse shook his head. "He'd lock me up."

"But you're still convinced it's the truth?"

Was he? His earlier certainty faded when he stared into the other man's calm eyes. "I suppose it's possible Liam told me some things and I'm starting to remember." He shook his head. "Some of the things I'm remembering are *feelings*. How can that be? Maybe I'm just possessed by the love he had for . . . someone. Maybe his love survived death. Is that possible?"

"Love is the greatest of all commandments. That shows the importance God puts on love. Love transcends eternity."

"Could Liam's love have imprinted itself on me in the moment of his death?"

The priest shrugged. "Some mysteries are beyond us."

The guy wasn't much help. Jesse rose. "Thanks for your help."

Or lack of it. He walked across the street to his car. The priest was right about one thing. This whole situation was a mystery.

In the darkness, pain radiated up Alanna's legs and arms. Muscles began to protest. She should have taken a Tylenol before coming up. The pills were still downstairs on the coffee table. Barry would be quick to run and get one for her, but she didn't want to disturb him when he'd likely nodded off already.

Stifling a groan, she slipped from under the sheet and went to the door. The door creaked when she eased it open, and she listened to make sure she hadn't disturbed Barry. The silent hallway assured her she was alone. Sliding her bare feet across the wood floor, she slinked down the steps, found her pills, and carried them back upstairs with a glass of water. When she reached the top of the steps, she heard something. The tinkling sound could almost be music. She put the water and pills on her dresser, then followed the music. The melody drew her down the long expanse of blackness, though she trailed her fingers along the wall in search of a switch.

The twisting corridors reminded her of a maze. In the darkness, she lost track of which way she went and how to get back, but the melody still drew her on. Maybe it was a music box? She couldn't determine what made the noise. No one should be in these rooms. She, Barry, and Grady occupied the bedrooms closest to the stairs. Her bare feet trod debris on the floor, and she wondered if she'd made a bad turn. At least Barry's parents were in a totally different wing on the opposite side of the house.

Her hand finally touched a light switch and she flipped it on. Weak light from a bare bulb in the ceiling illuminated a hallway that hadn't seen a paintbrush or a mop in years. Wallpaper hung in strips and revealed old milk paint on the plaster walls. Scratches scarred the wood floors. Maybe this had been the servants' quarters. The paper wasn't the expensive sort she'd seen downstairs.

She glanced back the way she'd come. Three hallways branched off this one. She would have difficulty in finding her way back. The melody had stopped. All the doors were shut tight but one, and it opened only a crack. She pushed on it and flipped on the light. A bare iron bedstead and a stand were the only pieces of furniture in the room. A music box sat on the stand.

She approached the handsome wooden box and raised the lid. Goose bumps rose on her arms when the melody she remembered from her childhood tinkled out. When she'd hummed the tune to Liam, he had set it to words in "Nightsong."

Transfixed, she listened to the music box tinkle. The only one she'd ever seen like it had belonged to Neila. This one was a twin to her sister's prized possession. Alanna had to have this box.

She closed the lid and lifted the heavy box reverently. Turning to carry it back to her room, she saw someone move by the window. She gasped and peered into the draperies' folds. "Is someone there?"

"Just me." Grady materialized from the shadows. "I was watching the moon on the lagoon. I thought you'd be in bed." His normally cynical smile held sadness. "Beautiful box, isn't it? I hope you weren't about to take it."

"Just to my room so I could enjoy it. Isn't that all right?"

"Barry will just carry it back here. The banshee doesn't like it to be moved. I heard her playing it tonight and came to see. Did you hear it too?"

"I heard something," she admitted. "That wasn't you playing it?"

He shook his head. "The box was open when I got here. I hoped to see her dancing around."

Alanna didn't know what to think though her goose bumps returned. "You've seen her?"

"Several times," he said, his tone grudging.

Back home in Ireland, she'd heard tales. Most who saw a banshee never lived to tell the story. A banshee was said to be a fairy, and to hear one shriek was an omen of death to one of Ireland's five major families. She'd heard tell that banshees emigrated with their families. Was Barry's family rooted to one of the five?

She suppressed a shiver. "What does she look like?"

"She wears a flowing white dress with her red hair down to her waist. She usually floats along the grass. Once I saw her sitting by the water combing her hair with a silver comb."

"And does she have wings?"

"Wings?"

"You know the legends, don't you? When a banshee leaves, you can hear the flutter of wings."

"I don't know about that. She's beautiful, just like you. In fact, she could be you." The cynicism was gone from his face again.

His description matched everything she'd always heard about banshees. Alanna put the music box back on the stand. "You're joking, righto? You've never really seen her."

"No joke. I'm sure Barry has seen her too. It's no wonder he was determined to marry you."

"He married me to help me," she said. "You mustn't think he had any agenda."

Grady's laugh held derision. "He's sure got the wool pulled over your eyes, Alanna. I knew the minute I saw you that he would have stopped at nothing to have you."

She hugged herself, ready to end this conversation. "You really don't like your brother much, do you?"

"What's not to like? A blue blood born to greatness who knows it. The great one bestowing favors on us peons." He gave a bitter laugh. "Barry always gets what he wants."

"Sure, but it's sad that you and your brother can't love one another," she said. "My sister . . ." She looked down at her bare feet peeking from the hem of her gown.

"What about your sister?"

"I don't even know where she is," Alanna said, wondering why she was telling him this. "I was taken from our mum when I was three and she was eight." Her fingers caressed the smooth wood of the music box. "She had a box just like this one."

"What happened when your mother left?" he asked, his voice gentle.

Wishing she'd never brought it up, she shrugged. "I don't remember very much, just crying for her. The woman she left me with slapped me and told me she'd come back someday. I never saw either of them again."

"Maybe it's better that way," he said, his tone turning cynical again. "Finding out the truth might be more painful than what you've already survived."

She didn't want to talk about it anymore, not to this young man with the orange mohawk and hooded eyes. "I'm lost. Can you be showing me the way to my room?"

"I'm headed that way myself." He glanced at the scrape on her arm. "What happened to you?"

If he hadn't been so hot and cold, she might have told him the truth. "I fell down the hill. You didn't hear the ambulance come?"

"I went to the bar for a few drinks and just got home. You're okay? And the baby?"

"We're both fine." She glanced at the music box again. It would be so comforting in her room. And wasn't she the mistress of the house now? "I'll be taking this to my room," she said. "Barry won't object."

Grady shrugged. "Suit yourself, but remember I told you so."

Carrying the heavy box, she followed him out the door. As she shut the door behind her, she thought she heard the flutter of wings, and a shudder went down her back.

Silly superstition. She followed Grady through the labyrinth of corridors. "I would never find this by myself. How do you know the way?"

"I've explored this old place many times." He stopped in front of a door and rattled the locked knob. "Except for this room. Barry has it locked up tight. He won't let anyone in it."

Alanna touched the cold knob. "What's in here, do you suppose?"

"No idea."

"Does he ever go inside?"

"Nearly every night before he goes to bed."

Her curiosity was truly piqued now. Barry was so indulgent with her. Maybe he would allow her access.

"Maybe he's an ax murderer and he keeps his toys inside," Grady said, grinning.

She rolled her eyes. "You really do hate him, don't you?" Still, she couldn't help giving the door one final glance before following Grady to her bedroom.

Nineteen

lanna thrust the curtains aside and allowed sunshine to stream into the room. She needed the brightness to wash away the nightmares of the night before. Every muscle in her body screamed with pain, and she hobbled as she went to the dresser. She wore a flowing skirt and loose top so nothing chafed her sore skin.

Her fingers caressed the wood of the music box, worn smooth by the touch of so many hands over the decades. She found the winding mechanism and twisted it. The lovely strains that tinkled out made her aches disappear. She had to find out about this melody and this box. Could it possibly be the same one her sister had? And if it was, how had it come to be here in this mansion? The tune haunted her, and she wasn't sure how to go about discovering the name of the song. Maybe Barry would know.

She ran her fingers over the smooth wood again. Practice was what she needed today. Playing her fiddle with her mates would get rid of this unsettled sensation she carried.

Her door opened, and Barry thrust his head in. "What are you doing with that, Alanna?"

She turned with a smile that ebbed when she saw his dark expression. "I heard it playing last night and found it in an abandoned room. I quite adore it, Barry. My sister had one like it. In fact, I was wondering if it might be the same one. How did it come to be here?"

"It's been here as long as I can remember. I've never asked where it came from."

"Do you recognize the tune?"

"No." He stepped in. "It needs to be returned to the room where you found it."

"Please let me keep it?" she coaxed. "Who can enjoy it otherwise?"

His attempt at a smile was more of a grimace. "I'm sorry to disappoint you, sugar, but I can't let you keep it here. Feel free to listen to it in that room anytime though."

"You don't really believe there's a banshee, do you?"

He didn't answer as he reached past her and closed the lid to the music box. The abrupt cessation of the delightful sound pained her. He lifted it in his hands and took it out. Alanna followed him, still disbelieving that her doting husband would deny her something that meant so much to her.

When he disappeared around the corner, she decided to see if he might take it to the padlocked room Grady had shown her. Her bare feet made no sound on the floor. When she reached the place where the corridor branched off, she saw Barry disappear around another bend. She followed him through the twists and turns of the halls until she was thoroughly lost.

She saw Barry pass the padlocked door and return the music box to its original location. She paused and leaned against the wall by the padlock until Barry exited the bedroom and shut the door. He stopped when he saw her standing there.

"I neglected to ask how you're feeling this morning," he said, his smile breaking out.

"I'm a little sore, but I will soon be to rights when I get a chance to practice with my mates," she said. She turned and yanked on the doorknob. "Why is this locked? None of the other rooms are."

He took her arm and pulled her away. "It's just got my business papers in it. I don't trust Grady not to meddle, so I lock it up."

His tone held tension under the casual words. She realized she didn't believe him. As far as she knew, he'd never lied to her before, but somehow she knew he wasn't telling her the truth. It made her more determined to see what was inside that room. But judging by the way he moved her along at a fast clip, she knew better than to ask for admittance. Maybe later.

Right now she needed her band, her music. And she needed to be finding out what Jesse was doing at the estate last night.

She tugged her arm out of Barry's grasp so he would slow. "I'll be meeting Ceol in Charleston today to practice. What car do you want me to take?"

He stopped walking and stared down at her. "I've got a conference call that will last several hours. I can perhaps take you after my business is concluded."

"I'm perfectly capable of driving myself. I've gotten quite used to cars on the opposite side of the road. I need to practice most of the day."

He frowned. "You shouldn't drive in your condition, Alanna." His gaze swept her bare feet. "And certainly not without shoes."

She smiled up at him. "But the nail polish is such a beautiful color."

His stone-faced expression didn't recognize her attempt at humor. "I really don't want you driving the cars. It's tricky driving on the opposite side of the road. If you listen to the radio or get distracted in any way, you'll veer to the wrong side."

"I'm not a lass, Barry," she said. "I've been driving fifteen years."

He took her elbow and led her down the corridor again. "Things are different here in the South, sugar. I'd rather drive you. I'll come find you when I've finished my conference call. You had a fall yesterday. Practicing all day would be too arduous anyway. Remember the baby. You don't know your own limits."

Maybe he was right. Liam had also said she pushed herself too much. Every muscle still ached, and she needed to guard the baby.

"Take a nap," he urged. "I can see you're limping. I doubt you slept very well."

"No. No, I didn't." She allowed him to lead her to her bedroom door. "Thanks for taking care of me."

He brushed his lips across her forehead. "I'll try not to be long," he whispered. He caught a strand of red hair in his fingers and kissed it before letting her go with obvious reluctance.

She closed the door behind him, then sat on the edge of the bed. Though her body ached, she wasn't sleepy. A nap didn't sound appealing. She'd rather find out what Jesse was doing wandering the estate last night. She rang Ciara and told her what had happened.

"I don't believe Jesse would hurt you," Ciara said after a long pause.

"Then what was he doing here? He'd left with you, then came back. And he appeared right after someone shoved me down the hill."

"I don't know, but I'm sure there's a good reason. The main thing is you're all right. The baby is okay?"

"The ultrasound showed him doing cartwheels," Alanna said.

"What about practice?"

"Barry will bring me in later today." She didn't know what to be making of his aversion to her driving. They needed to get that straightened out. She'd not be living as a prisoner in this place, her movements subject to Barry's discretion.

"Lass, we've got to get cracking on getting ready for the tour."

"I know," Alanna said.

"Where are we practicing today?"

She chewed on a hangnail. "I thought we might just work at the hotel."

"There's no room. It has to be at your house. The living room there is huge. Or we could even set up on that veranda again. I could get the girls together and grab Jesse."

Alanna had an idea of what her mother-in-law's expression would look like with the music ringing out on the lawn, but right now she didn't care. "Righto then, get them together. I'll tell Barry not to bother running me to town."

"We'll be there within the hour."

Alanna put her phone away and went to find her husband,

but the office door was shut and she heard the murmur of his voice behind the door. He'd already started his phone conference. She'd have to make sure they set up where the noise wouldn't disturb him.

The living room would be too close. So was the veranda. Maybe one of the upper floors would work, though they'd have to haul everything up there.

"Good morning."

She turned to see her mother-in-law standing in the living room entryway. "Good morning. I hope you slept well."

"Very well, thank you. I just made coffee. Would you care for some?"

"No thank you. I have to avoid too much caffeine."

"Oh, of course, the baby. I just made muffins though, and they're still warm. Come along to the kitchen." Patricia turned toward the kitchen without waiting for a response.

Alanna followed her. Patricia's attitude had done a major readjustment overnight, but she was wary of the sudden hospitality. "The muffins smell delicious."

"Chocolate chip." In the kitchen Patricia put one on a plate and carried it to the table. "Milk?"

"Yes, please." Alanna accepted the muffin, then slid into a chair. She took a bite of the warm bread. "Very good."

Patricia put a glass of milk in front of Alanna. "I want to apologize for my behavior last night. I was overtired and very rude. I do hope you'll forgive me."

"Of course," Alanna said. "I understand." In truth, Patricia's attitude still puzzled her. She thought it best not to bring up the baby again.

"What are you going to do today?" Patricia asked with a bright smile. She sat across from Alanna and took a bite of her muffin.

"My mates are coming out to practice. Our tour starts in a few weeks, and we're quite unprepared." She took a sip of the cold milk. "I'm trying to figure out where we might practice. Somewhere that the sound doesn't carry to the office. Barry is on a conference call."

"I know just the place! The ballroom on the third floor would be perfect."

"I'd thought of it, but we have quite a lot of equipment to haul up."

"There's a dumbwaiter for that type of thing. I'll show you when you finish your breakfast."

The idea of using the top floor grew on her, and Barry had even said it might work once he helped her clear out the rubbish. "What's the condition up there?"

"Boxes of things not in use and old furniture are stored up there, but you can have Grady move them to the attic. Or just shove them to the walls. There should be plenty of space."

Alanna gobbled the last few bites of her muffin, then stood. "I'd quite like to see the dumbwaiter now if you don't mind."

Carrying her cup of coffee, Patricia led Alanna to the pantry. There was a white door tucked away in a corner. She opened it and revealed a deep metal lift and a system of pulleys. "Plenty of room even for the drums."

"Fantastic," Alanna said. "Thank you so much. I'll run up the stairs and check out the ballroom now."

Patricia glanced at her watch. "I'd come with you, but I've

got a hair appointment in half an hour and just have time to get there. Follow the hall to the back. You'll find another flight of stairs to the third floor."

Alanna said good-bye, then did as her mother-in-law suggested. She found the stairway at the back of the hall. Dust coated the stairs. There were no prints to suggest anyone had been this way in quite some time. She reached the landing of the third floor and gasped. The ceiling towered at least sixteen feet over her head. Elaborate moldings detailed the ceiling painted in cherubs. The wood floor was smooth and tight. It would be a dream to dance here.

Lovely old furniture occupied part of the space as well as several trunks. Alanna went to the nearest one and lifted the lid. Colorful dresses lay inside, mostly silk and satin. They appeared to be from the turn of the twentieth century. She held up a cream one detailed in handmade lace. "Lovely," she murmured. She thought it might even fit her.

She'd have to have a try on sometime, if the fabric wasn't too delicate. Shoving a few of the lighter pieces of furniture aside, she thought they would have room to set things up. On the way back to the stairs, she saw the van arriving and hurried down to meet her mates.

Fiona hugged her when she met them at the entry. "You look blooming wonderful. Marriage must agree with you."

"Love your new necklace," Alanna said, eyeing the polished amber stones strung around her friend's neck. She hugged Ena, whose usual morose expression had lightened to a faint grin at the sight of her.

Ena fingered her pink hair. "Is Grady around?"

"Somewhere." There was definitely interest between them.

Ciara emerged last from the van with Jesse in tow. Alanna went still when she saw the man. There would be time to interrogate him later. She hugged Ciara, then beckoned them all to the house. "Grab your things and come along. I've got the perfect space."

By the time the creaky old lift had transported the instruments to the third floor, the band's voices had risen with the excitement of being together. The harp had to be carried up the main staircase by Jesse and two of the women. "We can be as loud as we want up here."

She watched Jesse set up the drums. He arranged them exactly as she'd seen Liam do a thousand times, and her irritation grew. He tested them in the same order as Liam too. Gritting her teeth, she set to making sure her fiddle was in tune.

"Let's get to practice," she said. She dragged her bow across the strings, then broke into a reel.

"Go, Alanna!" Ciara yelled. She pulled her chair closer to her harp.

Ena lifted her pennywhistle. "What first?" she asked.

"'Last Rose of Summer,'" Jesse said. He started the drum intro.

Alanna nodded and followed his lead. Before the drums faded to the softer part of the song, Barry stood red-faced at the top of the stairs.

"What's going on?" he shouted. "The sound is piped directly into my office."

Staring at her husband's angry face, Alanna realized Patricia had to have known how the sound carried. She'd been set up.

Twenty

et's get to the bottom of this." Barry took Alanna's arm and marched her down the steps. "Mother just came in from a hair appointment. She is cooking lunch."

"Did the noise interrupt you?" Alanna asked as she struggled to keep up with her husband.

"The house is designed so music wafts into the office. My great-grandfather designed it that way on purpose so he could monitor what was going on in the ballroom even if he had to be attending to business. So yes, I had to end my call prematurely."

They reached the first floor. The aroma of she-crab soup hung in the air. Barry led her across to the kitchen where they found a flushed Patricia stirring a pot at the stove.

Patricia glanced up with a smile that quickly faltered when her gaze lit on Barry. "What's wrong, son?"

"You tell me." He dropped his grip on Alanna, then folded his arms over his chest. "Why did you tell Alanna to practice in the ballroom when she told you I needed quiet for a conference call?"

Patricia pushed a lock of hair from her moist face. "Why, I never told her any such thing. I told her *not* to practice up there, whatever she did. That the noise would travel right to you."

The glib lie snatched away the protest in Alanna's gaping mouth. Patricia's expression was so disbelieving of her son's accusation that for a minute Alanna wondered if she'd misheard her mother-in-law. Then she remembered the dumbwaiter. "That's not true, Patricia. You even showed me where to find the dumbwaiter so I could get the instruments up to the third floor. I couldn't be knowing where it was otherwise."

"Of course you did," Patricia said. "I found you exploring it this morning. I warned you to be quiet up there."

Alanna's jaw sagged. She'd never met anyone who could lie so convincingly. And she had no way to prove Patricia had set her up.

Barry stared at his mother. "You're lying."

"Of course you'd believe that little tart," his mother spat.

"I'll not be listening to this." Alanna started for the stairs. She blinked at the moisture in her eyes. Why was everyone so hostile?

She marched up the steps to her bedroom. Nothing could convince her to remain in this house any longer. It would take only a minute to grab her few belongings and leave with her friends. She jerked her big suitcase out from under the bed, then went to the dresser and lifted an armful of clothing from the drawer. Her attempt to hold the tears at bay failed, and big drops slipped down her cheeks.

"What are you doing?"

She turned to see Barry in the doorway with his brows knit together. "I'm leaving right now," she said, turning back to her packing. She heard his footsteps start toward her but continued to the closet to grab her hanging clothes. When she turned, she plowed into him.

His arms closed around her, and he buried his face in her hair. "Don't leave," he whispered. "I need you."

Alanna struggled to maintain her anger. "You thought I'd lie to you."

"Of course I didn't. I wanted her to admit she lied. I never doubted you."

She pulled away from him so she could see his face. "Why would your mother be such a blackguard?"

His hand smoothed her curls. "There are always bumps in the road when you try to find your place in a new family."

His hand on her hair soothed her, and she kept her head on his chest. "She hates me, Barry. We'll never get along."

"Give it time," he whispered against her ear. "You're mistress of this house now. She'll just have to get used to it."

His warm lips brushed across her neck, and she shivered, then turned her head to meet his kiss. Physical attraction wasn't enough to base a marriage on, but it was enough to keep her head spinning. Still, what was physical attraction without the real intimacy she craved?

The kiss deepened, and she let go of the morning's pain. Snuggled against his broad chest, she could almost forget his mother's lies and the recent argument. She could push away the memory of the alligator and the kitten. The time was coming when he wouldn't be content to keep the bedroom door between them closed, and Alanna realized she was almost ready to let him past the guard she'd kept up.

Without bothering to hide her reluctance, she pulled away. "I'd better check on my mates," she whispered.

"How about I use my cell phone to finish my conference call?" he asked with a teasing light in his eyes. He still hadn't taken his hands from her waist. "I'll go sit out in the car."

"It's too hot," she protested. The temperature was close to thirty degrees Celsius.

"I can turn on the air occasionally. I'm used to this weather." He brushed his lips across hers in a final, lingering caress, then turned toward the door. "I should be done in another couple of hours. It's all for you, you know. I'm working on getting some new venues set up for the band."

Warmth spread up her neck. "Thanks, Barry." She watched him close the door behind him.

As she threw her things back into the chest, she noticed a small recorder. She grabbed it up, then went down the hall to find the room with the music box. She figured out the maze of halls and rooms and stepped inside the room. Maybe her mates would recognize the tune. It was a good place to start. She lifted the lid of the box and pressed the record button on the mini tape recorder. When the song had played long enough, she closed the lid and went to find the rest of the band.

Her mates sat on boxes by the open windows. Even with a cross breeze, the ballroom was stuffy. From this vantage point, she could see clear out into the Atlantic, past the waving sea grass and the cypress trees.

Ciara got up to meet Alanna when she stepped into the large room. "That man is insufferable! I don't know how you'll be putting up with him."

Alanna's smile faded. "It's his mum. She took one look at me last night and was prepared to hate me. We Irish disgust her. She told me to use this space when she *knew* the sound would disturb Barry's important call."

"He could have stood up for you. I wasn't liking his tone when he came up here." Ciara's black eyes snapped. She waved a crimson-tipped finger at Alanna. "He's too domineering."

Alanna remembered his refusal to let her use the car. That was just concern though. "He's trying to take care of me, make sure I'm not hurt."

Ciara sniffed and Fiona rose, stretching like a lioness. Her blond hair rippling to her shoulders added to the illusion. "Leave her be. You haven't given Barry a break since the first time you met him. I don't know what you've got against him. He's done a lot for Alanna. For all of us."

Only Ena and Jesse said nothing in the argument. Ena sat snapping pictures of the water with her camera, and Jesse had his back wedged into a corner while he listened to the exchange.

Alanna was tired of her life being picked apart. "Are we going to practice or not?"

"We are." Ena turned toward them. She picked up her pennywhistle. "I need to hear some music." Her gaze went to the recorder in Alanna's hand. "What's that?"

"Oh, I almost forgot. I found a music box in one of the bedrooms. The tune is one my mother used to hum to me, and the box is just like one my sister had. Have any of you heard it?" She rewound the tape and pressed the play button. The haunting melody spilled out, and she turned it up. She wouldn't mention the words Liam put to the tune. It was their secret, and she wanted to hoard it.

The band listened intently. Ena might be the one most apt to recognize it. Alanna watched the top of Ena's pink head as she sat with her gaze on the floor. Ena had been in so many foster homes and in so many cities, she was likely to have picked up more snippets of culture.

"I've heard it," Ena said when the music ended. "I can't think where though. Play it again."

Alanna rewound the tape and played the song again. The more she heard it, the more her dim memories of her mother sharpened. Mum had a mole at the corner of her mouth that Alanna had loved to touch when she was a little girl. She'd forgotten that until now. She could see the lips singing to this music, but the original words still eluded her. Alanna strained to recover more of the memory, but it slid away from her grasp.

Ena raised her pennywhistle. "My tired feet want to dance. This is getting us nowhere. Maybe it will come to us later. We need to practice now."

Ena was right, but Alanna hated to give up when the tune hovered just beyond reach. The rest of the band rose and went to their instruments, so she had no choice but to turn off the recorder and grab her fiddle. Once the smooth basswood was in her hand, making music was all she thought about.

Ceol ran through their entire repertoire in the next two hours, and Alanna's fingers throbbed when they finally put down their instruments.

Jesse wiped his perspiring forehead. "I'm ready for something to drink. Any chance you have some Club Orange?"

Liam's favorite soft drink. Alanna told herself not to overreact. Jesse had likely picked up a taste for it when he was in college with Liam.

She forced a smile. "It does sound good, doesn't it? Afraid all I have in the fridge is the typical American fare. I think I saw Coke and Sprite on the shelves."

"A Sprite will have to do then." He fell into step with her as the others trooped downstairs ahead of them. "How are you feeling today?"

She slowed her steps so the others would get far enough ahead not to hear their conversation. "Fair enough. A bit sore. One question though, Jesse. Why were you here last night? You never explained. It seems a bit dodgy."

He frowned and looked away. "I needed to talk to you, ask some questions. I feel drawn to you, Alanna. Like there is something between us." He stopped and rubbed his head. "I keep getting flashbacks of memory. Were we ever lovers?"

She hid her shock. "We dated briefly, but just as friends. I met Liam through you."

"Maybe that's it." His expression and voice held doubt. "I feel I know you so well." He rubbed his head.

"It was only through Liam. It's your imagination, Jesse."

"It's not just the memories of you," he said. "My friends and family tell me that I was agnostic and wouldn't set foot inside a church, but I find myself drawn to St. Michael's. The quiet, the sense of holiness there draws me. Was Liam religious?"

Liam had loved that church too. He'd made a visit there for

morning mass every day they stayed in Charleston. She backed away from him and wished the others were closer. The delusions this man held might make him capable of anything.

She began to walk toward the steps again at a faster clip. "I think you need to be talking to your therapist. I'm sure the explosion has caused these strange memories that aren't real."

"Maybe," he said. "But that's why I came last night. I wanted to ask you if we were closer than anyone else knew. I-I almost feel as if Liam is haunting me."

The blood drained from her head, and she felt faint. First banshees and now this strange blather from Jesse about a haunting. If Liam were going to haunt anyone, wouldn't he hover close to her? She wanted to strike Jesse with her fists and make him take back his crazy talk.

The dejection in his voice lessened her anger. He had suffered plenty these past months. He had to reconstruct his reality based on what other people told him. Between all the surgeries and the physical therapy, his life had become a roller coaster ride of pain and dark mists. She knew he'd stayed with his parents for a time while they tried to recover all the explosion had yanked away.

Had this man tried to kill himself and take Liam with him? The detective seemed so certain, and this crazy talk reinforced the possibility in Alanna's mind.

Sometimes she thought Liam wasn't really gone—that he was out there somewhere calling for her. She knew Liam was in heaven, but she wished she could believe some aspect of her husband lived on in Jesse. That she could gaze deep into his eyes and catch a glimpse of the man she loved. To know he was gone from her for the rest of her life was more than she could bear to think about.

She eyed Jesse again. "What are you saying? That you think Liam has possessed you?"

A muscle in his jaw jumped. "Something like that. Sounds crazy, doesn't it? Or maybe the love he had for you imprinted on me somehow. I don't know."

She had to keep a grip on reality. "Our only real connection was our mutual love for Liam. What do you remember about the explosion? Anything?"

He shook his head. "My past is just blank. I only know what I'm told. But I've been having these dreams . . ."

"That's all they are. Just dreams. Your regrets showing up from your subconscious."

"That's what my shrink says, but it feels like more. I want to get to the bottom of it."

"There's nothing to get to," she said, her voice sharp. "I'm sorry, but we've never even kissed, Jesse." They reached the bottom of the steps. "I've heard you had been thinking about suicide." She bit her lip, wishing she could pull back the words. He'd been opening up to her and she'd likely cut off that flow of confidence.

He caught her arm. "Who told you that?" His fingers bit into her flesh. "It was that detective, wasn't it? Adams. He thinks I'm too stupid to notice how he's been following me around. I know what he's told you—that I wanted to take Liam out with me in a murder-suicide thing. It's not true!"

"How do you know if you can't remember?" she asked, keeping her voice neutral.

"I'm not crazy!"

His raised voice frightened her, and she managed to get her arm out of his grip. "Of course not," she said soothingly. "I wasn't saying you were."

"That *is* what you were implying. That I'd try to take out my best friend, a guy I've loved like a brother since I was seventeen."

"Do you remember Liam?" she asked.

The anger drained from his face. "I'd like to be him," he whispered, passing his hand over his face. "He was a better man than the Jesse I'm learning about." He glanced down at her.

The glow in his eyes frightened her more than his anger. Obsession could be a dangerous thing. "Did you push me down the hill last night?" He cupped her face in his palm and she jerked her head back. "Did you want me to join Liam?"

He dropped his hand. "How can you think I'd want to hurt you? Besides, a little tumble down the hill wouldn't kill you. Whoever shoved you just wanted to scare you." His gaze went to her belly. "Or make you miscarry. You shouldn't stay here."

Miscarry. That thought hadn't crossed her mind. "I live here," she said past her racing thoughts. Maybe Patricia had pushed her. Alanna wouldn't put any scheme past her again.

Jesse must have noticed her softening expression. "I wouldn't hurt you, Lanna."

She recoiled at the use of Liam's pet name for her. "Don't be calling me that," she whispered. "Only Liam calls me that."

Even as her doubts surfaced again, she realized he had to have heard Liam refer to her as Lanna. It meant nothing.

Twenty-One

The band left after dinner, a strained, silent affair. Alanna couldn't look at either Jesse or Patricia, so she was glad to escape to her room once her mates pulled away in the van.

She stepped through the open French doors onto the balcony and let the moist air blow across her face. From her vantage point, she could see the last rays of the sun cast a rosy glow across the water in the distance. Her true home was on the other side of the Atlantic, and she missed the green hills of Ireland, the hubbub of Dublin, the sound of the Irish brogue rolling off tongues all around her. Most of all, she missed Liam.

Marrying Barry might have been expedient in the short run, but it was requiring a major lifestyle change for her. She glanced down at the shoes Barry had insisted she wear to dinner. She kicked them off and wished she had the nerve to toss them over the railing. Turning her into a Southern belle would be harder than he imagined, though she did want to please him.

As she leaned on the banister, a flutter in her tummy made

her pause. Was that the baby? She touched her skin where she'd felt the movement. Oh how she longed for her son to have Liam's golden-brown eyes. "Who are you, little one?" She stroked her belly.

Liam should be here sharing this with her. Sadness covered her like the mist hiding the sea grass. She was wise enough to know her attraction to Barry was an insufficient cover for her pain, a thin bandage all too easily yanked off.

The sun had set now, and the buzz of mosquitoes around her ears forced her inside. It was too dark now to make out much anyway. She picked up her shoes and carried them back inside. After shutting the doors behind her, she dropped the shoes on the floor and dug out her pajamas, green cotton ones with shamrocks. She slipped into their cool comfort, picked up her book, then crawled under the cool sheet.

Something stung her toe, and she yanked her foot away, then threw back the covers. A coiled snake lay on the sheet. She'd been bitten. Too shocked to do more than gasp, she scrambled from the bed trying to remember what she was supposed to do about a snake bite.

It depended on whether the snake was venomous. She stared at the small reptile. The bands of red, black, and yellow would have been pretty on anything else. Before they'd come to the South, Liam had made her learn a little rhyme about coral snakes. What was it?

"Red and yellow, kill a fellow," she murmured. "Red and black, friendly jack." Her horrified gaze landed on the yellow bands next to the black ones on the snakeskin. She backed away even more. "Barry!" she screamed. He might never hear her from downstairs. If she left, the snake might escape, too, and he probably needed to see it.

Keeping her gaze fixed on the coiled snake, she backed toward the door and threw it open. "Barry!" A faint sound of music came from downstairs. Could he hear her? She shouted his name again, then heard steps pound up the stairs.

"What's wrong, sugar?" he asked when he reached the top of the stairs.

She sagged into his arms as terror finally seized her. "A snake," she gasped. "In my bed. It bit me!"

He guided her to a chair just inside her bedroom door, then stepped toward the bed. She saw him recoil and knew the news wasn't good. "It's a coral snake, isn't it?" she whispered, her limbs growing icy.

"I'm afraid so. Show me the bite."

She extended her leg and pointed to her little toe. "Right there. Should we cut it and suck out the venom?" She shuddered at the thought.

His strong fingers supported her ankle, and he peered at her toe. "No, that's not recommended anymore. It drives more venom into the tissues." He frowned and looked at her foot again. "The bite isn't obvious. You're sure you were bitten?"

"I felt it."

"Sometimes you can't see puncture wounds. You need antivenom right away. I have some in the refrigerator." He stepped to the top of the stairs. "Grady! I need you right now!"

Alanna's teeth began to chatter and shudders racked her body. "Am I going to die?" Her hand crept to her belly. She had to live so her baby could live.

"No," he said through gritted teeth. "I won't let anything happen to you."

Grady bounded up the steps. "What's wrong?"

Barry pointed to the bed. "Get rid of that thing." He stepped to the door. "Don't move, Alanna. I'll get the injection." He exited the room and his feet pounded down the steps.

Grady stared at the motionless snake. "Coral snakes are the shyest ones of all. I don't think I've ever even seen one in the yard with all the work I do out there. How did it get clear up here? And into your bed?"

Alanna hadn't thought that through yet, but she remembered Barry saying they likely would never see a coral snake. How *had* it gotten up here? Patricia's face flashed into her mind. Would she go that far to get rid of her?

"I need a hoe or a shovel," Grady said. "Don't move."

She grabbed his hand. "Don't leave me." Her teeth chattered so hard she found it difficult to talk.

"It's just shock," he told her. "The venom takes hours to affect a person. We need to put compression on the foot. I've got an elastic bandage in my room from a sprained ankle last month."

"The baby," she whimpered. Her hand left his and cupped her belly.

"Stay calm," he said. He went across the hall, then returned a few moments later. Kneeling beside her, he wrapped the bandage around her ankle tightly. "It has to be really tight," he said.

Alanna had kept her eyes on the snake, which still hadn't moved. Why wasn't he killing the thing?

Grady stood and went near the bed again. "I need a shovel or a hoe," he said again. "And gloves."

"Can't you just kill it?"

He glanced back at her. "Don't you get it, Alanna? Someone put that snake in your bed. It couldn't have gotten up here by itself. It's not the snake's fault. I just want to take it back out to the woods."

She nodded. "You're a good man, Grady. Just get it away from here. I don't want to see it again." She turned at the tread of Barry's feet again.

"I've only got one vial," he said, coming into the room. "You'll likely need more."

"You'd better get her to the hospital before you administer it anyway," Grady said. "Allergic reactions are common. Life-threatening ones."

Alanna raised up on one elbow. "And what if it hurts the baby?"

"You'll be fine with some antivenom," Barry said. "I can probably get some extra from a neighbor."

"I want to go to the hospital," she said. "I want to talk to a doctor about this. Grady said symptoms wouldn't show up for a while. We have time."

"Don't you trust me, Alanna?" Barry asked.

This was no time to spare his feelings. "You're not a doctor. I need to find out the best treatment to protect the baby."

He touched her hair. "I'll bring the car around. Let's get you downstairs." He lifted her in his arms and carried her toward the steps. "Get rid of that snake," he barked over his shoulder at his brother.

Huffing with the exertion, he reached the bottom of the steps and set her on a chair in the entry. "Wait here." He rushed out the door.

Patricia emerged from the hall. "What is going on?"

Alanna studied the smooth skin, the carefully coiffed hair. Had this woman arranged for the snake in her bed? "A coral snake was in my bed. It bit me."

Patricia's mouth gaped. "I find that hard to believe. It was most likely a king snake."

A strange calm had descended on Alanna, and her teeth quit chattering. "No, it was a coral," she said. "Barry and Grady saw it too." If Patricia wanted a fight, she could have it. "Why do you hate me?" she asked softly. "I've done nothing to you."

Patricia's eyes narrowed, and her mouth grew pinched. "I'm not going to let you use my son." Her contemptuous glare swept over Alanna. "Barry finally told me the truth. Palming off another man's son onto him. It's incredibly wicked."

"It was Barry's idea," Alanna said. "I wouldn't trick him into anything."

Patricia opened her mouth, then closed it again when Barry came rushing back inside. "What can I do to help?" Her tone was disgustingly sweet.

"Call ahead to the hospital and tell them I'm bringing in a pregnant woman who has been bitten by a coral snake." He lifted Alanna in his arms and carried her out the door.

The car door stood open. He eased her inside, then shut the door and went around to the driver's side. His aftershave was strong in the confined space, but it was a scent Alanna was coming to like.

"How do you feel?" he asked.

"Calmer. The bite hurts, but I'm not lightheaded or nauseated." She cupped her stomach. "Just worried about the baby."

The car surged down the driveway. Alanna glanced in the outside mirror and saw Grady exiting the house with the snake dangling over a hoe. She averted her gaze and adjusted the vent so a wash of cool air hit her face. Her brain seemed wrapped in cotton. She struggled to think, to feel. Was she experiencing the effects of the venom already, in spite of Barry's assurances?

She tried to pray for the baby's safety, but she hadn't been on speaking terms with God since he'd taken Liam from her. Her heart was cold as a stone, and her prayers didn't rise above the roof of the car.

Moments later, or so it seemed in her numbed state, they reached the hospital's emergency entrance. For the second time in twenty-four hours, Barry ran through the doors and came out with a wheelchair. He helped her into it, then wheeled her inside where the sharp odor of antiseptic struck her. The pungent odor roused her from her stupor.

This was serious. Her baby might die.

She couldn't bear it if she lost the last bit of Liam she still possessed. She tried to pray again, but she knew God wasn't listening. Not with the anger she still harbored toward him. She barely listened as Barry related to the staff what had happened.

A nurse wheeled her back to an exam room. "I'm going to leave you in the chair to keep your ankle below your heart," she said. "The doctor will be right in." She put in an IV drip and adjusted it.

"I'm pregnant," Alanna said. "Is this going to hurt my baby?"

The nurse paused for a moment in the doorway. "I'm sure you'll both be fine." Her eyes flickered away, and she closed the door behind her.

Alanna grabbed Barry's hand. Her teeth began to chatter again. "I'm so scared. I can't lose my baby."

He knelt beside her and put her hand to his cheek. "It's going to be all right. We'll have more babies if something happens."

She jerked her hand away. "I want *this* baby," she shouted in his face. "It's all I have left of Liam." She had no energy to spare to soothe the hurt in his face. Such an insensitive comment. Did he have no compassion, no idea what this baby meant to her?

The doctor came in with the nurse trailing him. He wore jeans and hiking boots under his white coat, and he was young. About Alanna's age of thirty-two. "I'm Dr. Miller."

Alanna grasped his arm. "You've got to save my baby!"

He unhooked his stethoscope from around his neck. "I'll do my best." He motioned to the nurse, who wheeled up a fetal monitor. "We'll see how the baby is doing. Are you having any cramps?"

"No, nothing." Alanna leaned back in the chair and let the nurse attach the leads to her stomach. The reassuring *thump* of a rapid heartbeat filled the small room.

The doctor smiled. "That's a good sound." He bent over and listened to Alanna's chest. "No distress for you yet. I'm not sure what to do, quite honestly. Sometimes a coral snake bite is a dry bite with no venom—about twenty-five percent of the time. In that case, the antivenom can do more harm than good." He knelt, unwrapped the compression bandage, and examined her foot. "I don't see a puncture wound." He grabbed a light and a magnifying lens. "Ah, there it is. I see no signs yet of envenomation, but we can't really tell until you show neurological signs."

"What signs?" she asked.

"Paralysis, respiratory failure." He straightened. "We can't wait for that. Have you ever been told you're allergic to horse serums?"

"No."

"Good, then I'll administer the antivenom."

"What will it do to the baby?"

"There haven't been many studies on it, but the ones that have been done seem to indicate a higher rate of miscarriage. That may be a moot point because nearly thirty percent of all women bitten by a poisonous snake miscarry. The antivenom is your best chance at protecting you and the baby."

Alanna couldn't hold back the tears. Barry took her hand, and she squeezed it tightly. "What if it's a dry bite and the antivenom is harmful to the baby?"

"We have no way of knowing," the doctor said. "But I think we need to administer the antivenom."

Wait. The voice was a whisper in her heart. Was it God's direction? She'd been going through such a long, dry spell she wasn't sure. The assurance came again. *Wait.*

Is that you, God? Tears pricked the backs of her lids, and she waited, barely breathing.

Wait. The nudge came again, and she wanted to cry with relief. God hadn't forsaken her. He saw her pain, her need.

She lifted her head and looked at the doctor. "I'm not going to take it."

Barry's grip tightened on her hand. "Alanna! You have to take it."

"No, I don't. There's a chance I won't need it."

"But if you do and we wait until you show signs of envenomation, we might lose you both," the doctor said. "Once the neurological symptoms appear, they're very hard to reverse."

"I'm going to take the chance."

"No, she's not," Barry said. "Administer the shots."

The doctor glanced from Barry to Alanna. "I'm afraid she's the one who will have to give permission. You can't decide that for her, Mr. Kavanagh."

Barry took a step closer to the doctor and clenched his fists. "Do you know who I am? I donated the money for your pediatric wing."

"I realize that. But laws are laws. Only your wife can choose her care."

Barry's fists opened. He turned and knelt beside her. His eyes were moist. "Please, Alanna, you can't risk your life this way."

She took his hand. "I'm going to be all right. I sense it."

"Please, sugar, take the treatment." His voice broke. "I can't lose you."

She cupped his cheek in her palm. Her assurance deepened. "It's going to be fine. You'll see."

"I'm going to admit you to the hospital," Dr. Miller said. "We'll need to observe you for forty-eight hours."

"Righto." At least she'd be away from that house for a few days. Patricia couldn't get to her here.

"I want only the best for my wife," Barry said. "Give her a private room, the biggest you have."

Dr. Miller moved toward the door. "Of course, Mr. Kavanagh. I'll arrange it now." He directed his gaze at Alanna. "Call the nurse if you start feeling at all strange."

Calm descended on Alanna. Someone in that house had tried to harm her twice. This time was much more serious. Did Patricia know venom could cause miscarriage? Was she only trying to harm the baby, or was killing Alanna her real goal?

By the time the nurse got her settled in her room, it was close to ten. "You go on home," she told Barry. "Get some rest. I'll call you if anything happens."

His grip on her hand tightened. "I'm not leaving you. The effects could start any time. Please, take the antivenom."

"I am sure it was a dry bite, Barry. It was such a little sting. I feel fine. I'm just needing sleep." She squeezed his hand. "Thanks for taking such good care of me."

"That's all I want to do—take care of you."

She stared into his face in the dim light. "How do you think that snake got in my bed?" His mother had to have done it, but she wanted him to come to the conclusion by himself. An accusation from her could drive them apart.

He frowned. "I guess it dropped off the tree outside and crawled in through the open door. You leave that French door open sometimes."

She hadn't considered that. "Do coral snakes live in trees?" she asked.

"I'm not sure of their habitat. What are you getting at?"

"This is the second time in two days I've been hurt. First someone shoved me down the hill."

"You never said someone shoved you!"

"I didn't want to worry you. Grady didn't think the snake could get up into the bed by itself. He thinks someone put it there."

"Jesse was at the house both times."

She hadn't thought about that. "When would he have had time? He was with someone every minute."

"You followed him around? There was never a moment when he was alone? He could have brought in the snake in some kind of container and slipped it into your room very quickly. He went upstairs to the bathroom before the group left."

She remembered now. He'd been gone to the loo about five minutes. Plenty long enough to slip that snake under her sheets. But what was his goal? She didn't know what to believe about the man.

"I don't want him at the estate again," Barry said.

"He's part of my band. We need a drummer, and he's good. There's no time to replace him."

"I don't trust him."

Neither did Alanna, but she knew Liam would want her to give his best friend the benefit of the doubt. And she needed to know the truth.

"I'm tired," she told Barry. "You go on home, and I'll be seeing you in the morning."

He brushed his lips across hers. "I love you, Alanna. I couldn't bear for anything to happen to you. I'll sleep right there on the couch."

She wished she could repeat his words of love, but it was going to take time, so she smiled and kissed him back without saying anything. "Okay. Could you run home for a few things? It will be several hours before anything might happen."

He nodded and she wrote out a list. When he closed the door behind him, she sat up and reached for her cell phone. Detective Adams might be able to shed some light on this event.

Twenty-Two

"It's not unheard of for a coral snake to climb a live oak tree," Detective Adams said, chewing on a toothpick. Dark bags cupped his eyes. "And you say the French doors were open?"

Alanna nodded. The detective's assurances went a long way toward easing her fears. Believing the snake's appearance in her bed had been a fluke would make it easier to go back to that house of shadows.

"You see this?" Adams dropped the newspaper in his hand onto her bed. "You and your new hubby are on the front page of the arts section."

She opened the folded paper, dated the day before, and saw her face smiling back at her. She and Barry looked incredibly happy. Another picture was of her mates smiling at the camera— with the exception of Ciara, who scowled at Barry. The article told of her tragedy and her quick engagement to Barry, high prince of Charleston society.

Another picture showed her on stage with Liam pounding

away at the drums. She couldn't look away. Her chest squeezed at the way he was looking at her in the picture. His lips curved in a tender smile, and she well remembered the light in his eyes whenever he saw her. They'd had something so special. Even now, she couldn't believe he was gone.

"Mrs. Kavanagh? You okay?"

She tore her gaze from Liam's image. "Righto. Just reading."

He rose. "You can keep the paper. You talk to Hawthorne?"

She nodded. "You were right. He seems obsessed with Liam. And me."

The detective frowned. "He threaten you?"

"Oh no, nothing like that. He told me that he's been dreaming of me though." She wrinkled her nose. "It was a little wonky. He actually said he wondered if Liam has possessed him."

The detective grimaced. "You think he shoved you down the hill?"

Alanna didn't dare tell him her real suspicions—that her new mother-in-law might have had something to do with it. "I'm not getting that feeling." She glanced at her watch. "Barry will be back soon."

"I'll get out of here then. Thanks for bringing me up to speed." He went to the door, and it *whooshed* shut behind him.

Alanna turned up the light above her bed so she could look at Liam's picture again. The baby fluttered in her tummy, and the sensation brought a smile to her lips. She ran her fingers over the picture. "We're going to be having a baby, Liam. I wish you were here."

The door opened again, and she hurriedly put the paper under the sheet. She couldn't explain, even to herself, why she didn't want Barry to see it. But it wasn't her husband's face that peered around the edge of the door.

Her gaze met Jesse's. "What are you doing here?" Why had he come? Couldn't he sense his presence made her uncomfortable?

He stepped into the room. "Barry called Ciara. I asked to come along with her. She stopped off at the bathroom. How do you feel?"

"I'm going to be fine. My toe aches a little, but it's not numb or anything. I don't think the snake put any poison in." She was clinging to that hope for her baby's sake.

He stepped closer to the bed, then thrust his hands into his pockets. "You mind if I pray for you?"

Pray? That's what Liam would have done. "I don't mind."

She bowed her head, and Jesse launched into a prayer for her safety. With her eyes closed, she could imagine it was Liam praying for the safety of her and their baby. But when she peeked up at him, it was just Jesse, of course.

Jesse ended the prayer and stepped closer to the bed. "I looked up coral snakes. They usually burrow underground. How did that one get in your room?"

"They sometimes climb trees. It probably dropped onto my balcony and came in my open French doors," she said, parroting what others had told her.

He shook his head. "Think, Lanna. This is the second time you've been hurt. It's not safe for you to go back to that house. Go stay with your mates at the hotel. Something will happen to you if you go back there."

He'd called her by Liam's pet name again. "At the hotel? Didn't Barry get by to drop off a key to his flat?"

Ciara came through the doorway. Dressed in hot pink, she was a bright spot in the drab room.

"No, he did not. Was he supposed to be doing that?"

"He said he would."

"We need something to happen. We're all about out of money." Ciara sat on the edge of her bed. "You look pretty spry for someone who was just bitten by a coral snake."

"I think it was a dry bite."

Ciara approached the bed. "So Barry said. He also said there's an even better chance it *wasn't* a dry bite. That you really should be having the antivenom."

"So that's why he called you . . . to try to change my mind?"

"Someone is needing to. Do you realize how deadly that venom is once it starts depressing your breathing? It's a neurotoxin. Just take the bloody shots! We need you around."

Alanna folded her arms over her chest. "There's an even higher incidence of miscarriage with the antivenom. I'll not be risking it."

Ciara rolled her eyes. "I'm not knowing what to do with you."

"Keep the band practicing. I'll be stuck up here for forty-eight hours. It's time I can't really be affording."

"Where should we practice?"

"In the ballroom. All the instruments are still up there. I'll tell Barry you'll be coming." Alanna wanted Ciara to take Jesse and go. She couldn't take much more of the way he stared at her. It was as if he needed her to remember something for him. Working with him in the coming months would be harder than she thought if she didn't get past this wonky idea that she was seeing Liam in him.

Ciara seemed to grasp the plea in Alanna's gaze. She grabbed Jesse's hand. "We'll be getting out of here so you can rest. Talk to you tomorrow. Call if you get sick."

"I will." When the door shut behind them, she snuggled down in the pillow and closed her eyes. She never heard Barry come back and only woke once in the night when the nurse checked on her. Barry snored on the sofa.

When sunlight streamed through the windows, she stretched and wiggled her foot. It still felt perfectly fine. About twelve hours had passed since the bite. If she was going to get sick, she would have done it by now.

Maybe she could push the doctor to let her go home. Sitting up, she pushed her heavy red curls out of her face. Her hair was probably a frizzy mess. If they'd take out the IV and all these monitors, she could have a shower.

The doctor pushed through the door. "How are we this morning?"

She put on a bright smile. "Fine. Can I go home? It's been twelve hours."

He frowned. "Not just yet. Let's give it a few more hours. Symptoms usually develop within ten to fourteen hours though, so my gut says you probably did get a dry bite."

Barry jerked, then opened his eyes. "Alanna?" He sat up, rubbing his eyes.

She sent a smile his way. "No worries, Barry. I'm feeling pretty good. I'm trying to talk the doctor into letting me go home."

He swung his feet off the sofa. "She's going to be okay?"

The doctor looked up from her file. "Looks like it to me. It's rare for symptoms to start after this much time. If you're still feeling good after breakfast, maybe we'll let you go home. No excessive salivation, nausea, sweating?"

"Nothing like that. I actually feel very chipper."

Dr. Miller lifted the sheet at the end of the bed and examined her foot. "Any tingling or numbness in that toe?"

"No."

A smile spread across his face. "Excellent." He tweaked her big toe. "What would you like for breakfast?"

She was suddenly starving. "I wouldn't turn down a good fry," she said. At his blank stare, she went on, "That's rashers and eggs. *Em*, bacon and eggs. Or bangers—sausage. Mushrooms and tomatoes."

"I think we can arrange that. I'll check back midmorning."

When the doctor left, Barry approached the bed and pressed his warm lips to hers. He pushed the hair away from her face with a tender hand. "I'm so relieved you're feeling all right. I was so worried."

She recalled that inner voice. "God told me I'd be okay." Thankfulness welled in her soul, but she still couldn't let go of the last trace of her bitterness toward God for taking Liam.

Barry's smile faltered and he drew back. "That's good. I should call my parents and let them know. They were so worried. I'll have to leave the room to call. I can't get a good signal in here. I'll be right back."

Somehow she didn't believe Patricia would be anything but happy if Alanna suffered in the throes of snake venom. The thought of facing that woman again made her almost wish she could stay here another night. Almost.

When she was still feeling fine by ten, the doctor released

her. Barry brought the car around, and she stepped out into the sunshine. Everything felt different this morning after the panic of the night before.

Driving home, the car rolled past Hibernian Hall. The white, Greek-style building glowed in the sunshine, and she remembered the triumphant concert Ceol had enjoyed here just hours before Liam's death.

She peered through the window. Was that Jesse on the steps of the building? It was, she decided. He stood talking to a man by the front door. She wondered why he would be there.

"Cold?" Barry asked, leaning forward to flip the blower down.

"Thanks," she said, not wanting to explain that she wasn't cold. They were close to his mansion by the Battery. "Could we stay for a few days at your Bay Street house? It's gotten so hot and humid."

He frowned. "There's so much to do out at the estate. I intend for it to be the most gloriously restored mansion in the Low Country. The contractor is coming to look at the kitchen today."

"Can't we stay in comfort while it's being worked on?"

"I need you to oversee it, Alanna. I thought you liked it."

"I do," she said hastily. "But I'm pregnant, and the heat bothers me. The thought of taking on the project right now is more than I can handle. You'll need to do it. You know what you want anyway."

He pursed his lips and nodded.

"And I'm a little disconcerted by what's happened. What if another snake gets in?"

"Keep your French doors closed and you'll be fine."

"It's so hot though. I can't bear the heat and humidity. Ireland has cooler, rainier weather."

"You'll get used to it," he said. "I might sell the house by the Battery. Blackwater Hall will be much more awe-inspiring when it's finished."

She could push the issue and insist on moving to the city, but was it worth it the battle? Barry was doing so much to help her, and she couldn't seem to appreciate it.

She looked away from him, out across the Atlantic where storm clouds roiled. Her emotions were running high. She dreaded returning to the house in the shadow of the live oaks, though she kept telling herself it was just a house, nothing more or less. The churning in her gut had no basis in reality. She had nothing to fear.

Barry drove out of Charleston and turned onto a small country road. "A shortcut," he explained.

The line of trees ended and she saw a settlement of trailers and fifth wheelers interspersed with homes that looked new. In the center stood a Catholic church. It was a ragtag community that roused a homesick sensation.

"Stop a minute," she said. "What is this place?" But she knew. Oh yes, she recognized that assortment of dwellings, and she tasted something bitter on her tongue.

He pulled his car to the side of the road and stopped. "An Irish gypsy community."

"Irish Travellers, here?" she asked.

"They've been here for over a hundred years," he said. "Polluting the landscape. I tried to get them out, but their claim on the land was airtight."

She tried not to wince. His caustic words showed her how right she'd been to hide her background from him. "How are they affording such nice houses?" she asked, studying the children playing tag in one yard. One little girl in particular caught her eye. Dressed like she was ready to compete in a beauty pageant, complete with tiara, she wore a face-splitting smile.

"The men take to the road every summer doing home-improvement jobs. It's pretty lucrative. And there are some who say the scams they run fill the coffers too."

"Just because they're Travellers doesn't mean they're criminals."

He held up his hands. "What's got you riled? Just because they're Irish doesn't mean they reflect on you."

She'd caught the note of contempt in his voice. Alanna turned her gaze back on the settlement. What would he think if he knew he'd married the daughter of Travellers? Their backgrounds couldn't be more different.

"I'd like to buy a basket." She pointed to a roadside stand where baskets of Irish design hung.

He rolled his eyes. "I'll buy you some authentic sweet-grass baskets instead of these cheap things."

She didn't wait for his approval and threw open her door. "I want one of these."

The woman sitting in the stand watched her approach. "You like a basket, missus? I have good prices."

Though the woman's words were friendly enough, Alanna wasn't sure about the intense stare from the woman's brown eyes. "They're quite lovely," she said, though now that she was closer, she saw the cheap materials and workmanship.

Her mother used to make baskets. She dimly remembered sitting on the floor beside her mother in a booth much like this one. A trug basket to hold cut flowers would be a good choice. She picked it up. "How much?"

"For you, thirty dollars."

"Too much." Alanna haggled her down to twenty. Barry had gotten out of the car but stood back leaning against the hood. She fished a bill out of her purse and handed it over.

She could smell Irish stew bubbling in the pot over the open fire, an aroma she hadn't inhaled in years. Nostalgia swept over her. That life hadn't been so bad, even with her foster mother's harshness. At least she'd the freedom to play barefooted in the dirt.

"I will throw in a smaller basket," the woman said suddenly. "You wait here." She exited the back of the stand and went to a small trailer. The glance back toward Alanna before she entered the trailer held speculation. Almost recognition, though Alanna was sure she'd never seen the woman before.

"You done?" Barry called.

Alanna didn't really want a smaller basket. She'd only bought this one so she could see a tiny part of her past she'd all but forgotten. If the woman came back out, she might make it difficult for Alanna to get away. She grabbed her basket and joined Barry at the car.

His nose wrinkled at the sight of the basket. "There are much better ones around, sugar. We'll stop on the way home."

Alanna got into the car and fastened her seatbelt. As Barry pulled away from the ditch, she saw the woman come out of the trailer with a cell phone in her hand. She was talking animatedly into it and waved for the car to stop.

Barry accelerated. "I don't like the way she was staring at you. They probably recognized your accent and thought they had a gullible one on the hook."

Alanna said nothing though she bristled at his tone. She wanted to tell him the truth about her past, but the fake story their first manager had concocted sometimes seemed more real than the actual life she'd experienced. Why was she even thinking about all this? She'd never find her mother or her sister. She and Liam had tried many times. She had to accept the fact that she was alone in the world.

Except for God. She pushed away the whisper in her head. If God had answered any prayer, it had been Jesse's, not hers.

Barry reached across the seat and took her hand. "Are you okay, Alanna? I'm sorry if I was a little gruff."

"Just a little homesick."

He squeezed her fingers. "I know you'll never forget Liam, but I hope you can move on. We've got a future together if you'll open your hand and take it."

She stared into Barry's warm eyes. "Maybe you're right." It was about time she forgot the past altogether and just looked to the future. She knew he would do all he could to make their future together a good one. She squeezed his fingers. "You're a good man, Barry Kavanagh."

He smiled. "Too bad there's no demand for good men, huh?"

"Let's go out to dinner tonight, just the two of us?"

His eyebrows rose. "Really? How about we take in a concert too? I've got tickets to Hibernian Hall. A small symphony event."

She kept the bright smile on her face. Marriage was all about compromises, of each one growing and giving. She and Liam hadn't liked the same things either, but she'd learned to enjoy making him happy.

Twenty-Three

Barry stopped by the grocery to get milk then continued on to the house. The car rolled up the long driveway, and the shadows thickened as the trees blocked out the sun. An unfamiliar vehicle sat in front of the house.

"Who's here?" she asked.

Barry frowned. "No one I recognize."

The beat-up pickup had more rust than paint. One tire was almost flat. "Maybe it's the contractor," she said.

"He wouldn't be parking a vehicle like that in front of *my* house." Barry parked behind the truck and got out. He grabbed Alanna's bag from the backseat. She got out and approached the porch behind him.

A woman rose from the rocking chair at the end of the porch. Her hair was a gaudy dyed red, and she wore a skirt that was too tight across her stomach. The leather on the toes of her brown shoes had been scuffed away. The lipstick she wore was a slash of red that had bled around the edges of her mouth a bit.

Alanna took all this in with one glance. She didn't recognize the woman, and she saw from Barry's blank gaze that he had no idea who she was either. Pasting on the smile of a hostess, Alanna approached the woman with her hand outstretched. "How are you? Can I help you?"

The woman took her hand in a sweaty grip that felt too much like desperation. Her green eyes searched Alanna's. She gave a tentative smile. "Alanna, you've not been changing in all these years. I could have picked you out of a crowd."

Alanna tried to pull her hand away, but the woman kept hold. "Do I know you?"

"You'll not be knowing your own mum?"

"Pardon me?" She couldn't have heard the woman right.

"It's me, dearie. Your mum, come to see you." She released Alanna's fingers and fanned her face with her hand. "It's deadly hot here. Might you be having some iced tea to offer me?"

My mum? Alanna took a step back. Her gaze searched the woman's face, and she found a familiar landmark to guide her in the tiny mole by the corner of her mouth. Many people had moles, she told herself. Her mother's memory had long been buried in the mists of one foster mother after another. The only thing she remembered was the scent of heather.

And that aroma was wafting up her nose.

Thunder rumbled overhead as Alanna gaped at the woman. The weather forecast for the weekend promised heavy downpours and possible flooding. Alanna nearly let loose a flood of her own—of tears. Her mother's appearance here unsettled the future she was trying to build. How would she explain all this to Barry?

"Come in, let's talk this out." Barry held open the door for them. "Alanna, would you bring in some iced tea?"

My mother? Still in a daze, Alanna went past him into the house and to the kitchen. The pitcher of tea and glasses full of ice were on a tray before she realized she'd prepared them. She carried the refreshments into the parlor.

"It's sweet tea," she said. "That's all we have here."

"Sounds lovely," her mother said. She hiked her legs onto the ottoman Barry had brought her, revealing a run in her hose.

Alanna exchanged a glance with Barry. His manners were impeccable, but she knew he was as perplexed as she was by her mother's appearance. And was the woman even her mother? She poured the tea and handed one to the woman who called herself Maire Costello.

Maire took a sip of tea. "You'll probably be wondering how I found you." She put down her glass and rummaged in the gigantic cloth bag at her feet. She pulled out a newspaper with an air of triumph. "The minute I was seeing this, I knew. Knew it was my Alanna. I imagine you're surprised to see me." She opened the paper and revealed the article Alanna had seen at the hospital.

Surprised was an understatement for the gobsmacked sensation reeling in Alanna's brain, but she just nodded. Barry took her hand, and she curled her fingers around his. The comfort he offered was a lifeline in this sea of confusion.

She heard steps from the hall. Patricia stepped into the room followed by Richard. Patricia's eyes widened when she saw Maire. Her gaze swept the woman from her scuffed shoes to the spot on her scarf. "I'm sorry. I didn't know we had a guest."

"This is, ah, this is Alanna's mother." Barry's fingers twitched in Alanna's hand.

Alanna bit her tongue so hard she tasted blood. Her gaze went back to the woman. Her mum? Really and truly? The woman's skin was that pale coloring found on many redheads, including Alanna. Maire's eyes drew Alanna's attention—clear green with gold lights, just like her own.

A sudden rain lashed the screens in the windows and began to blow onto the wood floors. Barry sprang to close the panes, and his father hurried to help him. The three women stared at one another, and Alanna had no idea how to ease the tense atmosphere. She wasn't comfortable with either woman.

Maire twisted her hands in her lap and glanced at Patricia. The fear in her eyes made Alanna frown. She would have guessed that Maire *knew* Patricia. Her mother-in-law had a warning glare fixed on Maire, who kept her gaze down.

"How . . . how will I be knowing you're really my mum?" Alanna eased onto a chair.

"All you need to be doing is to look at the two of us. You're the spitting image of me when I was your age."

Alanna suppressed a shudder. She saw no hint of herself in this woman, other than the eye color and skin tone. The hideous dyed hair covered whatever the natural color might have been. "I think we'll need more proof."

Maire shrugged, then hefted her bag onto her lap and began to dig through it. "Here we be." She dragged out a large manilla envelope. "Your birth certificate is in here, and some pictures of the two of us."

Alanna's hand trembled as she took the envelope and opened

it. A birth certificate fell out. The name on the certificate was Alanna Maire Costello. Born to Maire and Robert Costello. Her birthdate of September fourth. She laid it aside and picked up the first of the pictures. A chubby-cheeked baby smiled a tooth-less grin at the camera. The writing on the back read: Alanna, age six months.

"The baby could be anyone," she said, though something about the sofa behind the child was familiar.

Maire leaned forward and jabbed a finger at the photo. "It's you, lass! Your hair and eyes. Don't be telling me you can't see that."

Alanna bit her lip and pulled out the other two photos. One was a picture she'd seen before. It had been snapped just before her father died and her mother took off. She was sitting on her daddy's lap, and his chin rested on the top of her red curls. Pressing her trembling lips together, she looked at the last picture.

Her three-year-old self held the hand of a young woman. The young woman could have been Alanna today. Curly red hair, vivid eyes, wide smile. The two of them stood in front of a basket stand much like the one she'd seen in the Travellers' community earlier today.

Air didn't want to fill her lungs no matter how fast she pulled it in. "Why did you leave me?" she managed to whisper. "You just left me at home and never came back."

Patricia took the pictures from Alanna's numb fingers. "I think we've heard quite enough of this scam. I'm going to ask you to leave. You people are well known for your con jobs. I'm sure you cobbled this picture together on one of those photo editing programs. You saw this picture in the paper and thought you'd seize an opportunity to ingratiate yourself here. It won't work."

Was Patricia right? But no. Alanna recognized the picture of her dad. That hadn't been altered. "I don't think she's lying." Her gaze locked with Maire's defiant one. "Where is my sister? Why you did it doesn't matter. Where is Neila?"

Patricia stood. "This has gone on long enough. I want you to leave." She grasped Maire's arm and yanked her from the chair. The other woman stumbled and nearly fell. She grabbed for her bag and succeeded in catching it by its handles.

Alanna sprang to her feet. "Don't touch her!" She wanted answers first.

Patricia continued to propel Maire toward the door. Alanna ran to block their path. "Let go of her! Barry!" she called over her shoulder to her husband, who had just shut the door to keep the rain out.

Barry came up behind her. "What's going on?"

"This . . . this *woman* is claiming to be Alanna's mother. She's here to try to con you out of money," Patricia panted.

"Let her go, Mother," Barry said. "*Now.*"

His mother released Maire's arm. "If you want to swallow her lies, be my guest." She stormed off to the stairs. A few moments later, the door to their suite slammed.

Barry glanced at Alanna. "I'd better go talk to her. I'll be right back." His quick steps went up the stairs.

Alanna clasped her trembling hands together. "Come back to the living room," she told Maire. She couldn't let herself even think the word *mum*.

Maire studied her face, then nodded. "But only because *you* asked me." She followed Alanna down the hall to the parlor.

Maire guzzled the tea, but Alanna couldn't have swallowed

a drop. She should sit, but her inner agitation made her pace the floor. "What do you want from me?"

"Why, child, I don't want anything other than to get to know my daughter."

Alanna eyed the woman's smile. "Why now, after all this time? You could have found me anytime."

Maire shook her head. "I tried. Social Services told me nothing. I think they were prejudiced against me. I overheard one of them calling me a 'bloody tinker' and then she came back and sent me on my way." She gave an indignant sniff. "I moved to America twenty-five years ago, but I never forgot my lass."

"Where is Neila? You took her with you." Neila was the one Alanna looked up to, the one who poured her cereal in the morning when Mum was too hung over to get out of bed. Neila had held her when she cried and wiped her runny nose. Alanna had missed her sister even more than their mother.

Maire shrugged. "I arranged a good marriage for her, the best, but she vanished one day. She eloped with another Traveller about five years ago and they went off to Texas. I lost track of her."

"Who did she marry?"

"Paddy Gorman."

"Did you never try to find her?"

"She was of age."

Alanna stared at the woman who said she was her mum. "You never really tried to find me, did you?"

"'Course I did, Alanna. I just said so, didn't I?" She raised the newspaper in her hand in triumph. "And I did."

"Why are you here?" she asked again.

Maire glanced around the room. "You married into high

society, lass. You done good for yourself. Lots of land here too. Me, I'm getting tired of being crammed together at the camp. You think your husband would let me park my trailer back in the clearing?"

"I doubt it." Alanna's eyes burned. This woman had never loved her. Even now she was here for some kind of handout. But at least she knew something about Neila. Alanna would ask Barry to help look for her.

Maire stuffed the newspaper back into her bag. "You come see us at the village. I want to stay in touch now that we've found each other."

"Do you know Patricia Kavanagh?" Alanna asked.

Maire glanced up, her gaze guarded. "Should I be knowing her?"

"You tell me why she was so upset to see you here."

"Women like that, who knows how they think?"

"I want to show you something." Alanna motioned for Maire to follow her. She led the way to the stair landing where the picture of Deirdre hung. "Who is she?"

"Deirdre O'Hara," Maire said, her voice full of reverence.

"Who was she?"

"My grandmother. Some say she had the second sight. But if she was having it, she should have known her own death. She disappeared right after Mum was born. Mum said a leprechaun spirited her away. Granddad always thought she ran off with a suitor. She was quite gorgeous, wasn't she?" Maire moved her gaze from the portrait to Alanna. "How did it get here?"

"I hoped you might tell me. Have you ever seen it before?"

Maire shook her head and turned her eyes back to the

picture. "Me mum's family wouldn't be having money for a portrait like this. But it's Deirdre, that's sure."

"What connection could there be between a Traveller family and the Kavanaghs?"

"She might have come to tell their fortune. She traveled around in a wagon from town to town, selling pots and telling the future."

"Where was she when she disappeared?"

"Down south of here, near Beaufort. My granddad came home from a construction job and found me mum wailing in the bedroom with Deirdre nowhere to be found."

Alanna shivered. "And he never found any sign of her?"

"Not a red hair from her head."

"Is your granddad still alive?"

Maire nodded. "He lives at the village, but he doesn't work much anymore. No one knows his age, but he's ninety-five if he's a day. Darby O'Hara. Everyone knows him."

"I'd like to talk to him." Alanna remembered Patricia's face when she'd seen Maire. Her expression had been one of fear, then warning, and Alanna wanted to know why. Besides, she found she wanted to connect to her family in some way. She'd been without a family so long. Now that she carried this baby, she wanted some roots. More than what Barry could offer.

Her gaze went back to her great-grandmother. Did Barry know of the connection between Deirdre and the Travellers? What she'd just discovered made her wonder why he'd married her.

Twenty-Four

Jesse craned his neck as the mansion came into view through the driving rain. He'd hoped to catch Alanna outside and reduce his chances of meeting Barry. Jesse's earlier certainty about his connection to her had faded, and he wondered . . . if he could touch her again, would he have another surge of memories?

Ciara sat beside him in the van's last bench seat. "You're being quiet today. Feeling all right?"

"Quite fine, thanks." He glanced at her. "You probably know Alanna better than anyone."

"We've been mates for five years."

"You knew Liam well too."

"So did you."

"I can't remember," he reminded her. "They were very much in love?"

"I never saw two people more attuned to one another," she

said. "Liam could start a sentence and Alanna could be finishing it."

"How did they meet?"

Her black eyes widened. "You introduced them. The two of you had been going out, but once Liam met her, that was it."

Just as Alanna had told him. "Was I in love with her?"

Ciara shook her head. "I never heard that you were. Both Liam and Alanna said you'd never even kissed her."

Then it wasn't his own memories that had surfaced when he remembered the softness of her lips, the scent of her breath. Unless he'd wanted more from their relationship than Alanna had? Maybe what he thought were memories were longings.

"Did I have feelings for her?"

Ciara bit her lip. "I often wondered about that very thing. You stared at her a lot."

That was the answer then. He'd carried a torch for his best friend's wife. One more thing to prove what a sleazeball he was.

The van stopped behind a beat-up truck. Probably a contractor. Ena slid open the van's side door and stepped out into the rain. She dashed for the porch followed by Fiona, who was driving the van. Ciara clambered around the seat and ran through puddles to the porch while Jesse pulled the van's door shut.

Rain pelted his face and ran in rivulets down his cheeks. He leaped over puddles and ducked under the shelter of the porch roof. Rain sluiced over the gutters in a stream that battered at the roses lining the house.

Ciara rang the bell. "Alanna, it's us."

Light steps came from inside, and the door opened. Alanna's smile was strained. "You're soaked. Let me get you some towels."

"We'll wait here," Ciara said. "Barry won't want all the water on his wood floors."

"I'll be right back," Alanna said.

"She looked upset," Fiona said, twisting her Celtic cross necklace between her fingers. "She knew we were coming, didn't she?"

"Only for practice."

"Maybe Barry doesn't want us here." Ena twisted a strand of her pink hair around her finger.

Jesse gritted his teeth to avoid saying what he thought of Barry. "Does she know we had to leave the hotel?"

"Not yet," Ciara murmured.

Alanna's steps signaled her arrival. She handed towels all around to her band members.

Ciara glanced at her. "What's wrong?"

"My mum is here," she blurted out. "At least she says she's my mum."

"I thought you hadn't seen her since you were three," Jesse said. "How do you know this woman is telling the truth?"

Alanna gasped, putting her hand over her mouth. Her green eyes nearly eclipsed her face. "Did Liam tell you that?"

Jesse laid down his towel. He hadn't known he knew about her mum until the words were on his tongue. "Does she look like a Traveller?"

Alanna's face went even whiter. The muscles in her throat worked, and tears filled her eyes. "How could Liam have told you?" she whispered. "He promised."

"Your mother is a tinker?" Fiona's lip curled.

"Fiona, you be watching your mouth," Ciara said, glancing at Alanna's face. She took Alanna's arm. "Introduce us. I'll be having a look at her."

The group followed Alanna down the hall to the parlor. Jesse took one glance at the woman seated by the window and knew she was Alanna's mother. Same bone structure, same shape of the mouth and hairline. He put his hands in his pockets and went to stand by the window. This wasn't his business.

"It's home I'd better be going," the woman said, rising from her chair. "You come see me, lass."

Alanna's eyes were wide and shocked as she nodded and went to show her mother out.

"She's up to no good," Ciara hissed. "I bet she wants money."

"Did you know Alanna was a tinker?" Fiona asked. "She doesn't look like one."

"Lass, you're so ignorant," Ciara said. "I didn't know, but it doesn't matter. Alanna is good and kind. Don't you be changing how you treat her."

"Of course not," Fiona said. "It's just—I hate tinkers. They'll steal you blind if you don't watch out."

"Then you'd better get over your prejudice," Ciara snapped.

Fiona shrugged and turned to glance out the window. Jesse didn't understand half of what had happened. Travellers? Tinkers? The words had spilled from his lips, but the meaning of it all eluded him.

Alanna returned and sank onto the sofa. "What did you think?"

"You have her bones," Ciara said. "You don't remember her?"

"Like Jesse said, I was only three when she left me. I remember my older sister better."

"Did she say anything about your sister?" Jesse asked. When Alanna turned her gaze on him, he let his breath out as if someone had kicked him. Memories flooded him again. They were sitting on a rock staring out at the Atlantic. Alanna's fingers laced through his as she told him about her sister.

"Her name is Neila," Jesse said. His face heated when the group turned to stare at him. "Your sister," he said. "Her name is Neila."

"How do you know these things?" Alanna demanded, her voice rising. "Liam would never betray my confidence. Never."

"I told you. I-I think Liam's feelings about you transferred to me somehow. Or he's possessed me."

The women took a step back when he said the word *possessed*, and he didn't blame them. It was a scary notion to think Liam was controlling things somehow. "I'm right though, aren't I?"

Alanna sagged against the back of the sofa. "Yes. Maire says Neila married a man and moved to Texas. I want to find her."

"I'll help you," he said, though he had no idea how. He could barely help himself. He caught the warning glance Ciara sent his way and hunched his shoulders against the censure in her eyes. They didn't understand. No one did.

Even he didn't.

"Look, this is getting wonky," Ciara said. "We have more problems than your mother. A big conference was arriving at the hotel today and they kicked us out. We brought our things with us. I hope you can find a place for us to stay or we'll be camping on the garden. We have a bloody huge amount of practice necessary before the tour."

Alanna's glazed eyes gradually took on more focus. "Threw you out? You mean you have no rooms?"

"Righto. Any ideas?"

"Barry had said you could stay in his condo. I thought he was going to give you the key. I'd rather be having you here though." Alanna glanced toward the staircase through the door to the hall. "There are plenty of bedrooms. We'll have to clean them up though. Barry says the mattresses are rotted, but I haven't checked all the rooms."

"None of us are above cleaning," Ciara said. "Except maybe Fiona, and she'll do it because she has to."

Fiona sniffed. "I always keep my own room clean. I don't like maids to touch my things."

"Righto, let's get to it then," Ciara said. "Where shall we start?"

Alanna rose. "This way."

The place felt creepy to Jesse. Even more so than the last time he was here and they practiced in the ballroom. He couldn't explain it, but walking down the wide upstairs hallway, he expected someone to grab him from the shadows. The air smelled musty too. Would Alanna expect him to go home at night? He wanted to be here to protect her. She might not realize she needed protection, but Jesse sensed it.

She reached a spot where the hall formed a T, then went left. The hallway went on forever with doorways interrupting the soft green plaster walls every so often. "Help yourself," she said. "I haven't checked these rooms yet. Maybe they're in better shape than the ones I saw in the wing where Barry and I have our rooms."

She'd said *rooms*. Jesse wondered if anyone else noticed. She must not be sharing a room with Barry, and Jesse hid a smile at that knowledge. He didn't want anyone else touching her, kissing her.

He opened the closest door. A double bed and dresser furnished the room. "It's not too bad." Thick dust lay on the floor. He stepped inside and sat on the edge of the mattress. The springs creaked, but the mattress held him. "It doesn't sag too much. A good vacuuming and it's doable."

"I'll get the vacuum," Alanna said. "It's in the other wing." She exited the room.

Jesse rose and followed Ciara to the next room. "This one isn't too bad either."

She wrinkled her nose. "Smells funny."

"Mold," Fiona pronounced. "Mold is dangerous to your health. I don't want to stay here."

"Good luck finding another place," Ena said. "We can wash it down with bleach water."

"Maybe." Fiona's voice held skepticism.

All the rooms were basic carbon copies. Double beds, a dresser, bare wood floors. The bed linens were rotted and so were the drapes, but the furniture was sound. Jesse knew Barry hadn't wanted them here. What was he going to say when he found them ensconced in his house without his permission? Jesse thought he wouldn't mind trading punches with Alanna's new husband.

Alanna came down the hall lugging a vacuum. "Here it is."

"You have bleach somewhere?" Fiona asked. "I'm not sleeping in mold."

"Oh yes, of course," Alanna said. "I'll get it. It's downstairs." She sounded distracted and kept glancing behind her.

"You worried about Barry?" Jesse asked. "What he'll say about us being here?"

She bit her lip. "I'm sure he'll be fine with it," she said, but her voice indicated the opposite.

Ciara crossed her arms over her chest. "He promised we'd have a place."

"I know he intended to have it all ready. His parents are here . . ." Her voice trailed off as if she wasn't quite sure how to explain.

"Let's get this place cleaned up," Jesse said, taking pity on Alanna. Her pained expression said it all.

He grabbed the vacuum from her and plugged it in. He yanked down the rotted curtains, and dust swirled into the air and up his nose. He coughed, then pulled the bedding from the mattress. The bare quilted cover was in decent shape with only a few stains. He switched on the vacuum. The sound of the motor drowned out his worry for her.

By the time he finished the room he was claiming as his, Alanna had returned with a bucket, rags, and bleach.

She'd just handed him the cleaning supplies when Barry's voice boomed out. "Alanna, where are you?"

She blanched. "Up here, in the back wing," she called.

Footsteps clacked along the wood floors, then Barry appeared around the corner. His smile died when his gaze settled on Jesse and the rest of Ceol peering out of their respective bedrooms. "What's going on here?"

"The hotel kicked them out," Alanna said, a plea in her voice. "They've nowhere else to go, and these bedrooms aren't as bad as you thought, Barry. A little cleaning and they're inhabitable."

"Kicked them out?" Barry reached his wife and took her arm in his hand. "I'll call and have a word with them."

"Too late. It's a convention, and we've already got our rooms started," Ciara said. "You promised we could stay here, and we're holding you to it. It will be much more convenient to practice when we're right here on the premises. Cheaper too."

"I'll not have you quartered in such mean spaces," Barry said. "Really, those mattresses aren't fit to sleep on."

"We'll get plastic covers for them," Ena put in. "Where's the bathroom?"

Like a man in a stupor, Barry pointed. "That room is the bathroom. It's a mess too."

How much of a mess? Jesse strode to the room he'd indicated and shoved open the door to reveal a utilitarian bathroom with an old toilet that had a tank at the ceiling. The clawfoot tub was in good shape and just needed cleaning. "It's not bad. Just dirty. We can clean it up."

"Why are you here?" Barry demanded. "You have a home to go to."

"We need him," Ciara said. "We'll be practicing all hours if we're to be ready in time. It's much more convenient to have us all together."

Barry shut his mouth with a snap, but his gaze lingered on Jesse. Jesse knew he'd just made an enemy.

Twenty-Five

By evening the rooms were as ready as they were going to be. Barry had grudgingly handed over his credit card, and Alanna had gone to town with the group to get bedding. Jesse drove. The group had made fast work of shopping at Target and stepped out to wet pavement and gray skies, but the rain had finally stopped.

The minute they got back to Blackwater Hall Jesse disappeared with his shopping bag. She wondered where he was going in such a hurry. An air of excitement surrounded him.

"Let's practice a bit before supper," Ena suggested later as Alanna smoothed the new sheets on Fiona's bed.

Ena had her camera in her hand, and Alanna had heard the clicking of it all afternoon as Ena snapped shots of them working. "Thanks for sticking up for me today," Alanna said. "About my family being Travellers."

Ena brought the camera to her face again. The only part of her head visible was her pink hair. "Righto. We can't choose our family, and it's not fair to be judged by our past either." The shutter whirred as she snapped a picture of Alanna.

Liam used to say the same when Alanna moaned about her past.

"Put the camera down and look at me, please." Alanna waited until the other woman lowered the camera and exposed her eyes. "I wish you'd quit hiding behind that thing, Ena. People love you, you know. You're the first one to try to bandage a hurt. You don't judge others."

"Been judged too many times meself," Ena mumbled under her breath.

Alanna was the only one in the group who knew Ena's full story, because it was so similar to her own: shuttled from one Traveller's home to another. The only difference was what Ena had had to do to survive and support a foster brother who'd ended up in the same abusive home. The shame of being forced into prostitution for a time had left her unable to look other people in the eye.

The story could easily have been Alanna's, so she had a special empathy for her friend. Barry had said nothing more about Thomas's accusation. She needed to ask him if he'd heard from his friend on the status of her citizenship.

Alanna put her hand on Ena's shoulder. "Thank you for not judging," she said. "What do you think of Jesse?"

Ena met Alanna's gaze briefly, then glanced back at her camera. "He reminds me of Liam. Something about the way he protects you."

Alanna inhaled sharply. "I thought it was my imagination. He really does think Liam has possessed him or that something from Liam transferred to him at the moment of death. It is a bit wonky though, don't you think?" Her hand rested on her belly, where she felt a small flutter.

"I like Jesse," Ena said. "He's real, just like Liam was. He cares about people."

"Liam didn't care as much as I thought," Alanna blurted out. "He told Jesse things I thought he'd never be sharing with another person."

Ena frowned. "I want to show you something." She flipped her camera over to the view mode and toggled back a few frames. "Look at this picture."

The photo was of Jesse. The way he stood with his hands in his pockets and his head tipped to the side was a carbon copy of Liam's usual stance. He even had one knee bent with the other one mostly supporting his weight, the same as Liam.

Alanna averted her eyes. "I can't look at it. It hurts too much to see him imitating Liam."

"What if he's not imitating him?" Ena whispered. "He was with Liam when he died. What if he's right? What if his soul moved to Jesse? Maybe a piece of Liam is in there."

"A soul doesn't transfer to another person. It goes one of two places," she said. "And I know Liam is in heaven waiting for me."

If she made it there. With the anger she felt, her destination was in doubt. A real Christian wouldn't be angry with God, would she?

"Watch him," Ena pleaded. "Don't discount a mystical connection."

"I'll be watching him. But that's all I can promise." Alanna smiled at her friend. "You want to call the others? I think they're down having tea in the kitchen. I'll be in the ballroom." She wanted to sweep up some debris before they started.

Ena shrugged and flicked her pink hair behind her ears. "Just think about what I said." She left the room.

Alanna followed her as far as the hallway, then turned right when Ena went left. She followed the hall to the rear stairs and climbed them to the ballroom. Grady was already there and had cleared away much of the debris. The wood floors shone from a polishing, and he'd arranged the instruments on the raised stage.

"Blimey, it looks fabulous, Grady," she said. "I was going to do it."

He leaned on the broom handle. "You got guts, little sister. Defying Barry like that."

Her pulse jumped. "He said something to you?"

Grady grimaced and began to sweep again. "He didn't have to. It was all over his face. He'd planned to have you all to himself, and your friends are spoiling his romantic interlude."

"You're here," she pointed out. "And his parents. We're hardly alone."

"We stay out of his way. I don't think your friends will be inclined to tiptoe around him."

"He was just gobsmacked. He's fine now." She hoped the words would reassure herself. Barry had been quiet ever since he found Ceol in the back wing. "We couldn't very well let them sleep in the van now, could we?"

Grady grinned. "It's your funeral, sis." He picked up the vacuum and went toward the door. "Hey, what about your friend, Ena?"

"What about her?"

"She have a boyfriend?"

Alanna hid a smile. "No. But don't you hurt her, Grady. She's too sweet and vulnerable."

He rolled his eyes. "And I'm some kind of Casanova? I like her. She's different."

"Her pink hair will clash with your orange hair," she said, smiling as she teased him.

He grinned. "I could dye mine to match. What do you think? Would I earn some points with her?"

"Maybe. Have you talked to her at all?" Ena could do worse than Grady. For all his mohawk and nose rings, he was empathetic and sweet. She counted him as an ally in a place where she wasn't sure who was out to hurt her.

"You could introduce me."

"I might do that at dinner. Who's cooking tonight?"

He wrinkled his nose. "You seen anyone else cooking around here? Grady Kavanagh, slave and cook."

She studied his crooked grin that hid more than she could decipher. "Why do you stay, Grady? You're so talented with landscaping. And cooking too. You could get another job."

"And leave all this?" He swept his hand around the room. "Where else can I be abused by family?"

Her heart clenched for him. He wanted to belong. She imagined his goal in sticking it through was to earn a place in the hearts of his brother and father. Poor guy might be chasing the wind.

He turned away as though he couldn't bear the pity in her eyes. "Dinner is at seven. Fix it so Ena sits beside me."

"I'll do just that," she called after him. She picked up her fiddle and tested the strings. It was still in tune. Closing her eyes, she dragged her bow over the strings in a plaintive tune.

When she heard footsteps in the hall, she thought Grady had forgotten something until she heard the whistled tune. Holding her breath, she turned as the whistler grew nearer. Liam! Whistling the song from the music box, the tune he'd set words to. Was his ghost here? She knew it was impossible—hadn't she just told Ena she knew her husband was in heaven?

The whistling stopped, and Jesse appeared in the doorway. He carried a basin of water in his hands. He glanced at her face. "You okay? You're a little pale."

"Tha-that song you were whistling. Did you remember the title? Do you know the words?"

He shook his head. "It's like they're just around the corner in my memory, but I can't quite catch hold of them. Just like all my other memories. Why do you ask?"

Had Liam played the song for Jesse, or was he just remembering the bit of it she'd played on the tape recorder? "Are you remembering more?"

His lids hooded his golden brown eyes. "Just bits and pieces. Nothing that makes any sense."

For a moment, she imagined stepping into the shelter of his arms. Her head would fit just right in the hollow of his shoulder, and she could almost feel the taste of his lips on hers. She took a step back. What was wrong with her? She had no business being drawn to him. This Jesse was so different from the one she knew before the explosion. His manner was calmer and his eyes were kinder. She didn't know what to make of it all.

She laced her fingers together. "What does the doctor say?"

"That my memory may come back in time, or that it might never come back."

She tried to imagine what that might be like. Stuck in a limbo where she didn't remember friends, her music, her time with Liam. A horrible situation. Pity stirred for this man she was determined not to like. She pushed it away.

"Is there anything you can do to speed the process?" she asked.

"Not that they've told me. The more I try to grab the memories, the faster they run away." His grin was wry. "I'm learning to live with it."

She listened to the sound of his voice, huskier than Liam's but with such a familiar inflection. Was it deliberate? Ena didn't think so. Guilt made people do funny things.

"You never said." His voice interrupted her thoughts.

"Never said what?"

"Why you're so fascinated with that tune that was on the music box."

"I . . . I heard it somewhere and was trying to figure out what it was." She could tell by the twist of his mouth that he didn't believe her.

"Do you know the words?" He sat the basin of water on the floor and pulled out a looped piece of plastic. "You asked me if I knew them. Did you forget them or something?"

She'd seen Liam do this a hundred times. He made up his own gigantic bubble blower with plastic. Her mouth gaped as she watched Jesse dip the folded loop in the basin, then step away and swing it in the air. A huge bubble emerged, glimmering with color from the light in the many windows.

The fascination on his face was an exact copy of Liam's when he played with his bubbles too. Alanna couldn't speak, couldn't breathe. This was more than coincidence. "Liam," she finally managed to whisper. The sound was too soft to reach Jesse's ears.

She stared at the man in front of her and tried to convince herself it was all her imagination. But she *knew* Liam. Knew him well and intimately. Though it was impossible, something of Liam had transferred to Jesse, but how? And would it last once his memory came back?

The rest of Ceol trooped into the ballroom. Laughing and talking, their presence made her gather her composure.

Ciara stopped when she saw the room. "Whoa, this looks fantastic! You did this?"

Alanna shook her head. "Grady did it."

"I'll have to be thanking him." Ena picked up the guitar on the stage and strummed it lightly.

Jesse put down his bubble loop and strode to the drums. He picked up his sticks. He ran through a few preliminary beats as the others got their instruments and filed into place. As they segued into the first song, Alanna could almost close her eyes and imagine they were back at Hibernian Hall playing together before everything changed.

"Sing, Alanna," Fiona urged. "We're just not the same group without your voice. I love it when you play your fiddle, but we need your voice too."

She lowered her fiddle to her left side. "I don't know, Fiona. Barry thinks you sound better without me."

"Barry is an *eejit*," Ciara said. "Give it a go, Alanna. See how your voice feels."

She did miss singing. "Let's try an easy song," she said. "'Scarborough Fair?'"

"I need to run to the loo," Ena said. "My coffee went right through me. I'll be back." She dashed for the door.

Jesse picked up her guitar. "Let me see what I can do with it while she's gone," he said. "I think I might be able to play it." He flipped it to his other hand so it was upside down and backward to the way Ena played.

Everything slowed as Alanna watched him play with the flattened tips of his fingers, just like Liam.

Just. Like. Liam.

Backward and with the tips of his fingers. Surely her mouth must be hanging open, but she couldn't control her reaction. She dimly heard Ciara's quick inhalation, Fiona's smothered exclamation.

Oblivious to the disbelieving stares around him, Jesse strummed the guitar in the chords of the song. Alanna couldn't have sung the words if someone held a gun to her head.

All she could do was watch in fascination as Jesse transformed into Liam right before her eyes.

Twenty-Six

J esse let the guitar music fade when he realized how the rest of the band was staring at him. "Why are you all looking at me?"

"Wh-where'd you learn to play like that?" Alanna asked. She swayed where she stood, and she licked colorless lips.

He shrugged. "I don't know. It's just when Ena put it down, I thought I might be able to play it. I guess I could." His fingers seemed to know just what to do the minute he'd picked up the guitar.

"Liam played the guitar backward like that," Fiona said. "And he flattened his fingertips just the way you did."

Jesse glanced down at his fingers, which throbbed a little from the unaccustomed pressure on the strings. "Liam probably showed me how. I don't remember, but we shared a room for four years." He gave a crooked grin. "And there's that whole possession thing."

His stomach plunged, and the tune he'd been humming filled

his head. The words from the song floated just out of reach again. Was Liam trying to take over his life? Maybe he should just let him. It would be the only way his best friend could live again.

"Who are you?" Alanna asked in a choked voice.

Did she expect his head to swivel like the possessed girl in *The Exorcist*? Or for Liam's voice to suddenly come out of his mouth? He started to say he was Jesse Hawthorne, but he wasn't sure anymore. Who was he, really? Little by little he seemed to be changing into Liam Connolly and losing his own identity. Maybe that was for the best.

He lowered the guitar to the floor and walked out, colliding with Ena in the doorway. Alanna called after him, but the words seemed far away and distorted. He couldn't face her now. He raced down the steps to the van. The keys were still in his pocket, and he fished them out. Someone had to know who he was. His mother.

He drove to his parents' home and parked the van at the curb. The aroma of gumbo filled the house, but his stomach was clenched too tightly to feel any hunger, though he hadn't eaten since eleven. He walked through the living room to the kitchen and found both of his parents at the table.

Dan and Alice. Even their names suddenly had a foreign ring to him, as if they were strangers. He stared from one to the other. Alice in jeans and a pink T-shirt. Dan in the gray suit he wore to the office.

His mother rose and came toward him with a welcoming smile. "Jesse, I wasn't expecting you."

His earlier certainty that Liam had taken him over faded with his mother's warm greeting. Surely she'd sense it if another spirit resided in her own son. He embraced her and inhaled the aroma of her perfume, some kind of flowery scent that was becoming familiar and dear. She'd stood by his side through every step of this nightmare. The love he felt for her intensified. He clutched her to his chest.

She returned his embrace until she finally struggled to pull away. "Son, what's wrong? Are you all right?"

He dropped his arms to his side. "I don't know, Mom. I keep having these weird memories." He ran his hand through his hair.

"Memories?" His dad stood and came close enough for Jesse to smell his cologne. "That's a good thing, Jess. We should call the doctor. Your memory must be coming back."

"But they're not *my* memories," he blurted out. "I'm remembering things that Liam knew."

His mother frowned. "What do you mean? I don't understand."

"I don't understand either." He faced them both, glancing from one to the other. "Did you wonder when I wanted to take drum lessons? When I insisted on buying that big bass drum? When I wanted to learn to play the bodhran?"

His mother stared up at his father, then glanced back at Jesse uncertainly. "Well, yes, it did seem odd. You'd never shown an interest in music, though we took you to piano lessons when you were five or so. I assumed the injury brought that latent talent to the surface."

"What else doesn't fit the Jesse you knew?" His life was like the beach by his house. Where his foot left an imprint, the sea left it distorted and unrecognizable.

"What's this all about, Jess?" His father's voice boomed with displeasure.

"I don't know who I am," Jesse said. "I hoped you might."

His mother cupped his face in her hands. "You're our own dear son. Jesse Hawthorne. Go to your room and look through your scrapbooks again. The doctors said that would help anchor you."

"Why am I so confused?" He wanted to beat his head against a wall. Maybe that would open up his memories.

"It will come back," his father said firmly. "You have to be patient, Jesse."

"Have you noticed anything else odd about me?" he asked. His parents exchanged glances. "What? Tell me!"

"You seem to be right-handed now instead of left-handed," his mother said.

He needed to sit down. Grabbing a chair, he sank onto it and put his head in his hands. "What's happening to me," he whispered. "Am I turning into someone else?" Had Liam been right-handed?

A knock sounded at the door and Jesse raised his head. His mother glanced at him with worry in her eyes, then went toward the living room. He heard the murmur of voices, then steps approaching the kitchen. His mother appeared in the doorway with Detective Adams in tow.

Jesse rose to face the officer. "Detective Adams."

"Sorry to bother you at suppertime, ma'am," Adams said to Jesse's mother.

Jesse stood. Was he about to be arrested? He realized he didn't care. Maybe in a jail cell he'd have time to think. He could find a way to get back to who he was.

"I need to get a DNA sample," Adams said.

Jesse wanted to roll his eyes. "You already got one, didn't you? Right after the bombing?"

Adams nodded. "We need a sterile sample this time. For a new test."

"I'm not sure our attorney would approve," Dan said.

"Is this about the bomb?" Jesse's mother asked.

"It's just routine."

Dan folded his arms over his chest. "I think you'd better get a court order."

Adams frowned. "Okay."

"Oh, let him have his DNA," Jesse said. "He had it once. I don't have anything to hide. He's not going to find anything from me on the bomb."

His father sent a glare his way. "Talk to your lawyer first, Jesse."

"It will only take a few minutes," Adams said.

Jesse didn't understand any of this, but he was tired of arguing about it. He stood. "Let's get it done."

He ignored his father's objections and followed the detective to the front yard, where he got in the van and followed the officer to the police station. An impassive female officer in the lab swabbed his mouth and had him sign a release form. He jogged back to the van and pointed it back toward Blackwater Hall. The thought of facing Alanna and the rest of them made his mouth go dry, but he was embarrassed about the way he had left.

Lights blazed from the mansion when he parked the van and got out. Something slithered by the pond, then he heard a splash. Probably a gator. The grass was wet and slick from the rain as he jogged across the yard to the porch. The peachy scent of the flowers by the steps contrasted with the fecund aroma of earth and leaf mold.

The air was alive with small sounds: the hoot of an owl, the cacophony from frogs and crickets, the splash of living things in the pond. And out beyond those sounds, the gentle swell of waves from the Atlantic as they played a melody on the sea grass.

The sounds should have been pleasant, but the place gave him the creeps. There was an air of desolation and danger about the estate. Did Alanna like it out here in the wilderness? She didn't seem the type to enjoy such isolation.

He rang the bell, and Grady let him in. He managed a smile when the other man welcomed him, then followed him to the dining room where the rest of the house's occupants were gathered. They hadn't filled their plates yet, and all of them turned to stare when he entered the room.

The light from the candles reflected off their eyes and made him feel he was surrounded by hostile glares. He blinked and the paranoid sensation went away. His steps clattered loudly on the wood floor until he reached the Oriental rug. He found Alanna's bright hair in what seemed a sea of people.

Maybe it had been a mistake to come back here. The more he was around Alanna, the more Liam seemed to take over. The smart thing to do might be to run from this place and forget all about Alanna. But when she turned those green eyes on him, his will to flee drained away.

She glanced up at him, then turned back to talk to Barry.

He'd hoped to exchange a glance with her. For something in her eyes to confirm their connection.

"You okay?" Ciara whispered. "We were worried."

He took a seat between her and Alanna. "Fine. I went by my parents' house for a few minutes."

How did he even try to explain what was happening to him? It sounded so crazy.

The aroma of fried chicken and gravy made him suddenly ravenous. He took some chicken from the plate that Alanna passed to him on his other side then handed it to Ciara. Both women were staring at him as if trying to see inside his soul.

He put down his fork. "What?"

Alanna's green eyes probed his face. "I've been pacing the floor since you left. I don't understand how you could know these things and do the things you're doing unless it's like you said. Is Liam in there with you?"

At last they weren't dismissing his fears. "I think he is. And I don't know what to do about it."

"Maybe an exorcism?" Ciara suggested. "This whole thing is brutal. And it scares me."

"I could talk to the priest." Jesse stared at Alanna. "But I don't much like what I've learned about myself. I don't want to go back to being the man I was before the explosion. You didn't like me, did you?

She shook her head. "But you were Liam's friend, so I wanted to."

He rubbed his forehead. "I have to fix this somehow."

Was exorcism the answer? And did he even want Liam gone?

At least the Jesse he was today made Alanna's eyes light up, just a little bit. He wasn't stupid, and he'd noticed the way she looked at him earlier. If there was a chance she might fall for him, he'd rather keep Liam's spirit around.

Twenty-Seven

a lanna's head throbbed, but she didn't dare take anything for it because of the baby. The evening couldn't be over too soon for her. Being around Jesse was torture. Everything in her was drawn to him now, and it felt off and strange when she'd disliked him for so long. But there were too many instances of Liam's influence to ignore now.

Exorcism. The very word brought a shudder down her spine. Wasn't that more about demons? Liam was no demon, so how could that help? Besides, she'd lost Liam once. She didn't want to lose the small piece of him that seemed to be residing in Jesse.

She rose and went outside to stand on the porch in the twilight. Bugs hummed in her ears, and the thick scent of the marsh swirled around her. The door creaked behind her, and she turned to see that Jesse had followed her.

"Are you all right?"

She shrugged. "I'm gobsmacked. I don't know what to make of all this."

He stepped close enough that his shoulders brushed hers. For an instant, she wanted to turn and bury her face in his shirt. Clenching her hands into fists, she stood her ground. "What are you going to do?"

"What do you want me to do?"

She turned her head and stared up at him. The porch light haloed his head with light. "You're so much like Liam now. It's like I can't stop looking."

"I don't want you to. I can be Liam. I don't have to try the whole exorcism thing. We can just get in my car and go away."

Her mouth went dry at the thought, and everything in her wanted to do as he said. But there was no going back, was there? "I'm married to Barry."

"The marriage hasn't even been consummated, has it?"

She shook her head and heat swept over her face. "You know why I married him."

"Liam is your real husband, and if he's here with me, then we belong together."

His persuasive words penetrated deep into her soul. She missed Liam so much. She stepped away. Before he could tempt her even more, she turned and rushed back into the house. Inside the foyer, she took a deep breath, squared her shoulders, then went to find her mates in the dining room.

She found Ena laughing and talking to Grady. At least they were having a good time. They brushed past her and went out to the front porch together. Fiona and Ciara headed to the parlor still talking to Barry about the schedule for the upcoming tour. Richard and Patricia strolled after them discussing protecting the seashore. Richard was doing most of the talking.

She glanced across the table and found Patricia staring at her. A shudder worked its way up her spine at the coldness of her mother-in-law's glare. Alanna recalled the expression of fear on Patricia's face when she saw Maire. Was there any connection between the women?

She was alone with Patricia so maybe she could get to the truth. "Patricia, I'd like to be friends. I know we got off to a bad start. Can we begin again?"

The woman stood to clear the table as if she hadn't heard, though the clink of tableware against china wasn't loud enough to drown out Alanna's words. "Patricia?" Alanna moved closer, then stopped when the woman raised narrowed eyes to lock with hers. "Why do you hate me?" she whispered.

"You will hurt my son," Patricia said. "Leave now before it's too late."

"I am not going to hurt Barry." But if she left with Jesse, there was no doubt it would hurt Barry.

Patricia put down the plates with a clatter. "Barry deserves better than you can give him. Let's drop the pretense. You know I hate you. I know you hate me. The most we can hope for is that you'll come to your senses and leave before Barry is hurt. I'm going to do all I can to see that happen. You're just like your sister."

"My sister?" Alanna put her hand over her mouth and stared at Patricia.

Patricia took a step back. "I meant your mother. It was obvious from meeting her that she has no morals. And neither do you, or you wouldn't have married a man you didn't love. You're using Barry, and I'm not going to allow it." She picked up the stack of plates and stormed off to the kitchen. "If you knew more about Barry and what he needed, you would never have married him."

But Alanna wasn't thinking about Barry. Had Patricia met Neila? Alanna believed that her mother-in-law feared something. What? How could Maire or Neila hurt her? She claimed not to have met Maire before today, but the fear had been obvious from the moment Patricia laid eyes on Maire. None of it was making any sense. Tomorrow she would go see her great-grandfather at the Travellers' village and see if she could understand this.

In no mood to talk to anyone, she went up the steps to her room though it was only eight o'clock. She paced the floor, then decided to go up to the ballroom and play her fiddle. The music would sooth her agitation and maybe even blunt her desire to go find Jesse.

The lights were off in the hall outside her bedroom door. She tried to turn them on, but nothing happened. Maybe the switch on the other end would work. The second floor was quiet except for the sound of her footsteps along the corridor. Running her hand along the plaster wall, she felt her way in the darkness until her fingers touched the light button. She pushed it, and light flooded the hall. She made her way through the labyrinth of hallways to the locked door where she paused.

It was so strange how Barry didn't want anyone in there. His mother had said if she knew him better, she wouldn't have married him. Staring at the door, she swallowed hard. Could there be information about all of this mess behind that door? She'd begun to fear Barry just a little, but it would take more information before she could turn her back on him. She twisted the knob, but the door was still locked. She took a bobby pin from the side of her hair where she'd pulled it back. After straightening it out, she leaned over and inserted it into the lock. Turning the pin this way and that, she tried to get the lock to open, but it held fast.

She was going to have to get the key. Maybe it was in Barry's room. She retraced her steps and stood at the top of the stairs. Barry's voice came from the living room. He was talking about the upcoming concert in Beaufort. She moved to his bedroom, pushed open the door, and turned on the lamp at the dresser. The austerity struck her again. It was like a monk's cell.

She glanced around. Every table was bare except for the lamp and medicine bottles. Her husband was the neatest guy she'd ever met. She stepped to the dresser and slid open the top drawer. Underwear lay in neat rows. She found socks in the next drawer and T-shirts in the bottom one. No keys.

Moving to the bedside stand, she checked the top drawer. A couple of books, nail clippers, some tie clips, and an old high school class ring lay inside. Still no keys. And there was no other easy place to look. No, wait, the closet. She stepped to the closet and opened the door. His clothing hung neatly inside.

A set of keys swung from a hook on the door, and Alanna lifted them. She'd have to move fast. He might come up any time. She turned off the light and hurried down the hall to the locked door. There were six keys on the ring. The first three didn't fit, but the fourth one clicked home. She checked the doorknob. It was unlocked.

Her pulse galloped in her chest. She didn't know what Barry would do if he found her inside. She wasn't even sure why she wanted to see what the room held, but her curiosity was strong.

She opened the door. Her hand felt the wall for the switch. Before she could turn on the light, she heard steps coming up the stairway. It was too late to go in. Pulling the door shut, she quickly locked it. She turned and started back to her room. When she rounded the corner, she saw Barry turning toward his room. He mustn't find out his keys were missing. She clasped them tightly in her fist.

"Barry," she called.

He turned with a smile. "What are you doing, sugar?"

"I thought I might play my fiddle, but I heard you coming up." Was she sweating? Her forehead felt damp, and she was sure he could see the guilt on her face. "Were you looking for me?"

"I was going to work for a while before I went to bed. Did you need me for something?"

"I'm fine." She hesitated. "Though it's kind of dark and I had trouble with the lights. Would you mind getting my fiddle for me from the ballroom?"

"Anything for you." He touched his lips to her forehead in a lingering caress. "I'll be right back."

Once his footsteps faded, she dashed to his room and hung the keys back on their hook without turning on the light. She returned to the hall and waited for Barry to return.

He came back with the fiddle and her bow in his hand. His smile brightened when he saw her, and she called herself every name she could think of for betraying his trust. What kind of wife sneaked around behind her husband's back? She should just ask him to let her go into the room with him.

"Thanks." She took the fiddle and bow. "I'd like to spend a little time with you. Can I come with you to your office?"

His smile faded. "I don't think so, sugar." His hand caressed her curls. "I don't have to work tonight. What would you like to do? We'd talked about dinner out, but your mother showing up messed up our plans." His eyes darkened.

Now she'd done it. He hoped for more than she was ready to give, especially after the things she'd seen and heard from Jesse today. And he wanted answers about her past. "How about a walk?" she suggested.

"You haven't had enough adventures in the dark yet? It's really not safe."

"You'll be with me." She couldn't bear to see his expression when she told him about her past.

"If you insist." He took her arm. "You'd better spray on insect repellant."

They went down the steps to the entry and past the voices in the parlor. Maybe this wasn't a good idea. A walk in the moonlight might give him romantic notions. They paused to apply repellant, then stepped out into the moist night air. The moon was bright tonight, glimmering on the waves across the sea grass. She smelled salt in the breeze blowing from the east.

"Careful of the potholes." He took her hand. "Oh, and I heard from the attorney I hired. He got the hearing in Ireland moved back three months, so Thomas will have no power over you by the time it comes. Your citizenship is coming through next week. It's over."

"Oh, Barry!" She reached up and kissed his cheek. "It's wonderful, you are!"

He pulled her closer, and his lips found hers. The intensity of his ardor repulsed her, and she pulled away with a laugh, then stepped into the swath of moonlight. "It's not as dark as I thought," she said. The attraction she'd felt for him was missing tonight. She wanted to be with Jesse, not her own husband. The realization was daunting.

"Want to see Pete?" he asked.

"Why do you like that gator? He scares me."

"We won't get close." He led her nearer to the pond.

She heard a low growl, then a splash, and stepped closer to Barry. "You be keeping him away from me." Her gaze probed the bushes for Prince. She hadn't seen him all day.

Barry laughed. "Just watch yourself around him, and it's okay. Stay back though. He's used to me bringing him something to eat, and he might get aggressive when he finds out I have nothing."

Off to her right, she heard a soft sound. Was that mewing? "I think I hear a kitten." She tugged her hand from his and started in that direction. If Barry had thrown another cat to the gator, she was leaving.

Barry called after her, but she continued on her mission. "Here, kitty kitty." The mewing intensified and led her to the tiny cat. Kneeling, she reached out and touched the kitten which immediately moved closer to her. She picked it up. "It's pure white."

"It probably has fleas." Barry's voice held distaste.

"I'll give her a bath."

"You can't possibly know its sex."

"It's so small, I just know." She glanced around in the dark. "Are there more? Where are your siblings, your mama?" The cat mewed in her arms, a plaintive sound as if it were answering her.

"You should let it go."

"I can feel her ribs. Poor little thing. I'm going to get her some milk."

"Alanna." Barry's voice was stern.

Her arms tightened around the kitten. "I'll keep her out of your way. She can stay in my room. I'll put her food and litter box in there too. You won't even know she's in the house."

She took off for the house without waiting for him to muster another argument. Whatever it took, she was keeping this kitten. She went up the porch and into the house. At least he wasn't coming after her.

Jesse's head turned as she went past the doorway into the parlor. "Is that a kitten?"

He was the only one in the parlor. The others must have gone on to bed. At least she didn't have to explain the cat's presence to Patricia. "Yes, she's starving. I was about to get her some food."

"She's cute." He followed her to the kitchen and went to the refrigerator. "How about some chicken? She'd like that."

"Cut it into small pieces." She watched him do as she asked. What would he do if she stepped closer and ran her fingers through the curls at the nape of his neck the way she used to with Liam? Would she see Liam in his eyes when he turned to look at her? She yanked her thoughts back.

He brought the chicken on a paper plate he found in the cupboard. "Here you go." He set it on the floor.

The kitten went to the food as soon as he put it down. "I'm saying it's a girl, but I don't know for sure."

"We can find out." He scooped up the kitten and turned it over. The cat howled in indignation as he probed. "It's a girl."

"How do you know?"

He shrugged. "I don't know. But it's a girl." He set the kitten on the floor and she went back to eating the chicken in dainty bites.

Alanna watched the hollow sides heave as the small cat ate. "She was starving. Barry thought she might belong to someone, but I think she's a stray. Hattie says they come and go."

Jesse knelt and stroked the cat. "What are you going to name her?"

"I don't know her personality yet. I'll have to think about it." Watching the man with the kitten, something lodged in her throat. She'd seen Liam sit like this with cats.

Her heart was knowing her Liam, but how was that possible? It was all too mystical to figure out.

He rose and his crooked smile came, the smile that was so like Liam's. Her gaze fastened on his mouth, and she couldn't look away. The curve of his lips straightened, and he stepped close enough to touch her. His hands came down on her shoulders. He bent his head toward hers.

She watched his lips grow nearer and she wanted to kiss him. Maybe a kiss would tell her the truth. She closed her eyes. "Liam," she murmured. The sound of his name awoke her from her stupor.

She stepped back. "I'm sorry," she choked out. "You can't be Liam." She scooped up the kitten and the food and ran for her bedroom. Even if Liam's spirit was there, it wasn't right.

Twenty-Eight

The kitten insisted on sleeping with Alanna. Every time she put the little rascal down, the cat clawed her way up the blankets to Alanna's chest. Alanna finally gave up and nestled the tiny white cat close. Sometime near midnight she fell asleep.

It seemed she'd just closed her eyes when a shriek awoke her. She lay in the bed with her heart pounding out of her chest. Was it a dream or something real? Struggling to sit up, she realized the cat was hunched with her ears back. She'd heard something too.

She swung her legs to the floor and went to the window. The wail came again. From outside. She snatched up her robe and went to the door. Barry's wide shoulders loomed in the hallway, and she clutched him with cold fingers.

"Did you hear that?" she asked.

"It's nothing to worry about," he said, his Southern drawl as soothing as his words. He draped his arm around her shoulders. "You should go back to bed, sugar."

"But what was it? Some kind of animal?" She shuddered and realized no animal sounded like that.

"We've never figured out what it is. I think it's a wildcat, but Mother is convinced it's a banshee."

"The banshee?" Alanna had never heard one. Shivers wracked her, and she clutched her robe more tightly. "Doesn't that mean someone in your family is going to die?" A thought gripped her. Was this happening because she'd disturbed the music box?

"Of course not. Go on back to bed." He guided her back to her door and pulled it shut behind him.

Alanna stood staring at the closed door. She didn't want to stay here alone. Not when her mates were just down the hall. It would be easier to deal with together. They had to have heard that unearthly shriek and would be wondering about it.

She opened the door. Barry was gone. Scooping up the cat, she raced in bare feet down the hall to the back wing. Turning the corner, she collided with a solid body. They both screamed before she recognized Ciara.

Ciara clutched Alanna's arm. "Lass, you'll be scaring me to my grave. What was that sound?"

"Barry said his mother thinks it's a banshee."

Ciara led her back toward her bedroom. "And I'll be believing it. If someone is dying tonight, it's not going to be one of us."

She pushed Alanna into the bedroom, where the rest of Ceol were sitting by the sides of the bed and on the floor. "Did all of you hear that?" Alanna asked.

"It would be waking the dead," Fiona grumbled. "I was having a lovely dream."

"We could tell ghost stories." Ena smiled.

"I'll not be listening," Fiona said with a shudder.

Alanna found herself looking for Jesse. She didn't want to even think about him, not after the way she'd nearly thrown herself at him in the kitchen. Still, she wanted him safe. "Where's Jesse?"

"He was here a minute ago, but he said something about looking for her, the banshee."

She hoped he wouldn't run into Barry. She clasped her arms around herself and wished she had just gone back to bed.

Until the wail came again.

"Maybe we can see the banshee," Ena said. "Anyone game to go with me?"

"I'll go," Alanna said. "It's better than sitting here wondering what's happening."

"I'll go too," Ciara said.

"You're all crazy!" Fiona grabbed a blanket from the bed and wrapped it around herself. "I'll be staying here."

"By yourself?" Ena whistled an eerie tune, and Fiona threw a pillow at her. "Come on. All for one and one for all."

"Oh, fine." Fiona tossed the blanket back on the bed. "Let's get this over. Who's going to be leading this brave party?"

"I want to," Ena said. "It's my idea, so I'll be deserving the best chance of seeing the banshee."

They trooped into the hallway after Ena. Alanna found the light switch and turned on the dim bulb. She wished Barry were with them. Or Jesse. What could four women do against a banshee? But if it was a banshee, what could anyone do?

She stayed close behind Ena as they wound through the halls to the stairway and down to the entry. Barry must have turned on the outside light, because its glow pushed back the shadows on the porch. But beyond the wash of light lurked total darkness.

"We'll be needing to rethink this," Fiona said. "It's dark out there. The moon must be behind clouds."

"Don't be such a ninny," Ena said. "Let's go." She opened the screen door, and it gave a shriek that made them all jump. "Sorry."

The door slammed shut behind them. Alanna stared around the dark yard where nothing moved that she could see. The gator grunted in its pond, and she heard a splash.

"Maybe the gator ate the banshee," Ena whispered.

The women giggled, and the oppression lifted from Alanna's shoulders. Whatever it was, it couldn't hurt them. She went past Ena to the steps.

"Wait a minute. We don't have shoes on," Fiona said. "What if there are poisonous snakes out there? Alanna has already been bitten."

Alanna drew back from the top step. "You're right. I got lucky once. We might not be so fortunate next time. We need to at least put on shoes."

Before they could all go back inside, an anguished scream pierced the night. Alanna's blood turned to ice, and she stared wildly around. This sound was different from the earlier one.

This one was human.

When it came again, she realized it was Patricia. The screams came from the window above their heads. "Stay here!" she told her friends. She ran back inside and up the stairs to the back stairway that led to the wing Richard and Patricia occupied. She found a light switch and turned on the bulb before plunging up the staircase.

She found Patricia standing at the top of the stairs in her nightgown. Screams poured from her throat. "Richard!" she screamed when she saw Alanna. She pointed back toward the door that stood open.

Alanna ran for the bedroom. Her steps slowed as she reached the open door. What would she find inside? She couldn't imagine what would cause the horror on Patricia's face or the keening pouring from her mouth.

A green lamp with a white shade illuminated the man lying on the floor. He'd vomited and his head lay in the bile. Alanna didn't have to touch him to know he was dead. No one living had gray color like that. Her steps slowed, and she knelt beside her father-in-law's body. Pressing her fingers to his throat, she checked his pulse. Nothing. His skin was cold too. Should she try CPR?

It couldn't hurt, she decided. She grabbed the edge of a sheet and cleaned the vomit from his mouth. Counting off the beats, she began to administer CPR.

Patricia was still screaming at the top of the stairs, only now she called Barry's name. Footsteps pounded up the stairs, and Barry's voice called out. "Mother, what's wrong?"

"In here!" Alanna shouted.

His shoes pounded across the landing, and he burst into the bedroom. "What's wrong?"

She paused the CPR, knowing the truth. "It's your dad." Her heart broke for what she was going to have to tell him. "I'm so sorry, Barry. I think he's dead."

He blanched and fell to his knees beside her. "You have to be wrong."

She wanted to catch his hand and pull him back but knew he had to see for himself. He made an inarticulate noise, then laid his hand on his dad's arm.

"Dad?" When he touched his father, he recoiled and a sob erupted from his throat.

Alanna embraced him, and he sank in her arms. "I'm so, so sorry," she whispered.

"He can't be dead." His stare didn't move from his father. He finally took a deep breath and straightened. "I have to pull myself together so I can help Mother." In another moment, his cell phone was in his hand and he punched in 9–1–1. In a choked voice he told the dispatcher he'd found his father dead on the floor.

While he was on the phone, Alanna went to see if she could help Patricia. She found her mother-in-law seated on the top step and rocking back and forth.

Alanna touched her shoulder. "I'm sorry, Patricia. Is there anything I can do?"

With her swollen face and blotchy skin, Patricia wasn't the put-together woman she'd been earlier in the day. "You've done enough." Her voice was low and vicious. "He hasn't been well— his heart. Worry over Barry caused this. It's all your fault. Leave me alone with my son."

Alanna's hand dropped back to her side, and she stepped away. There was no way she could combat such irrational hatred. Without answering her mother-in-law, she went past her down the stairs. Tears burned her eyes. Richard hadn't said much to her, and she didn't really know him, but she grieved for Barry.

Jesse was waiting at the bottom of the steps. "Richard's dead." She hugged herself and stepped away from him.

"Dead?"

She nodded. "I think it was a heart attack." In the distance, she heard a siren approaching. There was no need for the siren or for speed. No one could help Richard now. "I need to let in the paramedics." She brushed past him.

He trailed her. "I can do it."

She realized she'd dropped the kitten at some point. The feline wound herself around her ankles and mewed. Scooping her up, she headed for the front door without answering Jesse.

The ambulance came screaming up the drive. Her friends milled around the porch, obviously unaware of what had happened. Alanna stepped through the screen door and told them about Richard before the paramedics came rushing up the porch steps.

"I'll show them where to go," Jesse said.

Alanna let him. The thought of facing Patricia's hatred again made her shudder. She sank onto a rocker on the porch.

Ciara knelt beside her. "Are you okay?"

"Just shaken," she said, placing her hand over her belly.

"It was a banshee after all, you know," Ena said.

"You can't believe that," Alanna said. "It was a heart attack."

"Foretold by the banshee," Ena said. "The legends don't say the banshee causes the death. Just that it's a warning."

Alanna was too tired to make sense of her friend's superstitions. "Did you see anything when you went exploring?"

Ena shook her head. "We were afraid to go far after we heard Patricia screaming."

Jesse came back outside. "They'll be bringing him down."

From the upstairs window, she heard Patricia's sobs kick up again. In spite of the hostility between them, Alanna's heart ached for the woman. Alanna knew the pain of losing the man she loved.

Ciara stood. "I'm going inside. It's late. Call me if you need me."

Alanna nodded and said good night to her mates. Only Jesse stayed behind. He pulled another rocker over close. The mosquitoes whined in her ears, and the kitten kneaded her claws in her lap. She rubbed the tiny ears, and the rumble of the kitty's purr soothed her. Leaning her head back against the chair, she closed her eyes. The warm night was so beautiful, even with the trauma that had gone on.

She'd be resting for just a minute, then go inside.

With her eyes closed, she could imagine it was Liam rocking beside her. Her breathing eased, and her body relaxed. She drifted into slumber.

"Alanna."

The soft voice in her ear woke her. She kept her eyes closed. Liam would kiss her awake. He always did. She longed for his touch. For him to tuck her hair behind her ears so he could press his lips against her neck and make his way to her lips.

"Honey, it's time to go to bed." His fingers slipped her hair behind her ears. His lips left a warm trail on her neck and up to her lips.

Alanna inhaled the sweet aroma of his breath, relished the

warm pressure of his lips. Liam had always been her soulmate. She was so lucky.

Then she remembered. The love of her life was lying in a cold grave.

Her eyelids flew open and she stared into Jesse's face.

Twenty-Nine

J esse punched his pillow. Morning would be here all too soon, and he hadn't slept a wink. Every time he closed his eyes, memories flashed through his mind as if played on an old movie reel: Alanna's first attempt at cooking dinner and her tears when the bangers burned, watching her twist a curl around her finger while she read, her shriek when he threw her in the cold waves on their honeymoon.

No, not *their* honeymoon. Her honeymoon with Liam. Jesse was finding it harder and harder to keep track of reality. Maybe he didn't want to. The pleasure of kissing her last night had been exquisite, yet somehow so familiar. If this was what it meant to go crazy, maybe he didn't want to be sane.

Guilt rose from the depths of his belly. He'd kissed another man's wife. That was wrong. Even in his rattled state, he knew it was wrong, but he seemed unable to tame his obsession with Alanna. Maybe he needed an exorcism, but that didn't seem right either. If Liam's love for Alanna was strong enough to survive the grave, what right did his murderer have to sever it?

He ran his hand through his hair. The decision about what to do wasn't easy. Maybe he could pick up the pieces of who he was without being around her all the time. But still, he couldn't bring himself to leave, not when she'd been attacked twice. She needed his protection, didn't she? Or was he fooling himself about that too?

When he'd seen the detective at his parents' house yesterday, he thought Adams was there to arrest him. The more he discovered about himself and Liam, the more he despised himself for what he must have done. Maybe he should turn himself in and get it over with. Not only had he kissed a married woman, but he'd put the moves on the wife of his late best friend. He was scum of the earth.

He rolled over and closed his eyes. No more thinking. It hurt too much.

By the time the sun pushed streaks of light across his floor he'd gotten barely three hours of sleep. A racket outside roused him. He stumbled to the window and glanced into the yard to see workers tearing out windows in the old summerhouse. The contractor's crew had finally arrived.

Barry stood talking to a man in jeans. Jesse's gaze lingered on Barry. Dressed in khaki slacks and a pale blue oxford shirt taut across his wide shoulders, Barry dwarfed the worker. Jesse could see how he'd be attractive to women. Did Alanna love him? She must have some feelings for him or she wouldn't have married him. The realization stung, and Jesse glanced at his watch. Seven. Later than he thought.

He glanced at the scene outside again. Why hadn't Barry

sent the workers away? This was hardly the morning to be working on a construction project, not after Richard's death last night.

He quickly showered and dressed, then went downstairs. The group was eating cereal in the dining room. The heavy curtains were still pulled, and no one had turned on any lights. There was barely enough light to see their bowls.

"Good morning," he said.

His gaze found Alanna at the end of the table. She glanced at him, and a flush stained her cheeks before she looked away. Was she remembering last night's kiss too? He could think of little else.

Ena mumbled good morning, as did the other women. Grady nodded and shoveled another bite of cereal into his mouth. His skin was pale under the blotchiness on his cheeks. Jesse remembered Richard was his father, too, though he'd seen no evidence of a close relationship.

Jesse couldn't stand the gloom. He flipped on the chandelier over the table. Everyone blinked at the sudden illumination. Grady winced and hunched his shoulders. Jesse wanted to tell the man he was sorry for his loss, but he thought the attention would bother Grady.

"Are we practicing?" he asked.

"No practice today," Fiona said. "Out of respect."

"Of course. The family needs space." He glanced at Alanna and found her staring at him. She quickly averted her gaze. "So what are you all going to do today?"

"I thought I'd go shopping," Fiona said. "I need some supplies for my jewelry. Then Ciara and I thought we'd look for costumes for the tour."

Ena glanced at Grady. "I'll be hanging out here." She sent a comforting smile Grady's direction when he looked her way.

"I've got a-an errand to run," Alanna said. She rose and carried her bowl toward the back door. He could see her through the window feeding an old mutt. So like her.

Jesse wanted to follow her, but he didn't dare. She might order him to leave, and he wasn't ready to do that. "Can you drop me in the city?" he asked Ciara.

She nodded. "At your parents'?"

"Sure, that'd be great." He could borrow his mother's car today. He'd need to buy his own soon, but his savings was dwindling fast. The money from the tour would help replenish it.

Alanna avoided him, or so it seemed, until he climbed into the van with the other girls. He had to find out more information about who he was today, but he wasn't sure where to start. Ciara dropped him at the curb outside his parents' home. He waved good-bye and went inside, where he found his mother doing laundry.

She handed over her car keys without question, then poured him a glass of iced tea and forced some cookies on him in the kitchen.

"Who knew me best before the explosion?" he asked. "Other than you and dad."

Her brown eyes, so like his own, held worry as she studied him. "Jesse, you've got to quit pushing. Your memory will come back when it's ready to come back."

"I can't wait that long. I want to find out who Jesse Hawthorne really is. I didn't much care for the man who harassed a fellow worker. Is there more nasty stuff in my background I don't know about?"

"Of course not," she said, not meeting his gaze.

"Mom? What else is there?"

She rose and carried the pitcher of tea back to the fridge. "There's nothing else, Jesse. You're looking for trouble where none exists."

He'd have to find out the information from someone else. Many friends had stopped by to see him after the bomb incident, but their names and faces were a blur now, and the visits had stopped when they realized he didn't know them. He knew where to find the list though. His mother had kept a notebook with the names of all his visitors. It was in his room.

"Thanks for letting me borrow the car." He dropped a kiss on her forehead, then went upstairs to his room, a stranger's living space.

He'd once been at home in this room. Pictures of him at football games covered one wall. He didn't remember any of these scenes: prom with a girl he didn't know, football games where he laughed triumphantly into the camera, a party scene where he lifted high a mug of beer. He despised the expression of entitlement he wore in many of the pictures.

The bedroom decor was what one would expect in a college dorm. A twin bed with a Stingrays bedspread. Other hockey memorabilia covered the dresser. A Stingrays throw was over the easy chair in the corner. Hockey was a totally foreign sport to him now. Did he even like the game?

He sighed and went to the closet where he riffled through

the stack of photograph albums and scrapbooks his parents had collected for him from his condo after the explosion. The doctors thought looking through the stuff would help his memory, but it hadn't worked then. Maybe it would now.

The notebook he sought was about halfway down. He grabbed it and the address book under it, then went to the garage. If he stayed here to go through the books, his mother would want to know what he was doing.

He backed out of the garage, then drove to the Battery. He parked and walked along the grassy park area where the two rivers converged. The sunshine warmed his arms and lifted his spirits. The breeze brought the scent of water to his nose.

He sat on the seawall and listened to the cry of the gulls for a moment before he began to flip through the notebook. Two names appeared over and over in the early days: Mark Holmes and Ginny Smith.

When he cross-referenced their names, he discovered they lived at the same address. They must be a couple. And they didn't live very far from here. He strode back to the car and drove to the apartment complex. Since it was Saturday, they might be home. After pressing the doorbell, he heard footsteps.

The door opened, and an attractive brunette with her hair up in a ponytail smiled at him. She wore short-shorts and a skimpy tube top. "Jesse, what a surprise! Come on in." She stood away from the door to allow him entry. "Mark, you'll never guess who's here."

Jesse followed her toward the sound of a baseball game that blared from the TV. A man about his age, early thirties, removed his feet from the coffee table and leaped up, knocking off a stack of magazines perched on the end of the table.

"Jesse! Man, it's good to see you." Mark pumped Jesse's hand and studied his face. "You're getting your memory back?"

Jesse shrugged. "Bits and pieces."

"Great to hear." Mark pointed to the chair. "Have a seat. Bring me up to speed on what's going on with you."

Jesse forced a smile and perched on the edge of the armchair. "I'm still trying to put it all together. Could you tell me how long we've been friends, how we met?"

Mark exchanged a glance with Ginny, who had joined him on the sofa. "Man, you don't remember? We met at a strip club when I yanked you off a dancer. It took two of us to pin you down. You were totally trashed."

Jesse pinched the bridge of his nose. He couldn't imagine ever doing something like that. He must have had an issue with respecting women. Did that side of him still lurk somewhere? "Di-did we do that kind of thing a lot?"

Mark grinned. "Every weekend. That's where we met Ginny. She's an exotic dancer. The best!"

Ginny gave him a sultry smile and leaned against Mark. Her smile faded when she glanced at Jesse. "I thought you said you were getting your memory back, Jesse. You don't remember any of this?"

"Not really, no." And he didn't care if he never remembered this type of behavior.

"Want some she-crab soup? Ginny just finished making it."

Jesse smelled it then. "No thanks, I'm allergic to shellfish."

"Since when? Man, you can eat your weight in shellfish. Lobster, shrimp, crab. That's all you ever eat."

Jesse inhaled. Why had that initial reaction come out? He

had no memory of being allergic to shellfish, but he knew it was true. Or was it? "I'll have a little," he said. "Maybe I'm wrong."

Ginny frowned. "Shellfish allergy can kill you. Do you have an EpiPen on you?"

"What's that?" He shook his head. "Whatever it is, I don't have it."

Mark's stare intensified. "Man, what is with you? You don't even talk the same."

"The fire damaged my vocal chords," Jesse said. "My voice is huskier."

"It's not that. It's the way you string your sentences together. The head injury maybe? I've heard that kind of thing can change your personality."

"Maybe." Jesse hadn't been aware he spoke any differently. Was Liam taking over his speech too?

He rose. "I'd better be going. It was good to see you."

"Hey, man, what about the soup?" Mark asked, following him to the door.

"No thanks." He shook Mark's hand. "See you later." He waved good-bye to Ginny and escaped into the sunshine.

Jesse didn't want an exorcism anymore. Not if it meant he would turn back into the Jesse he used to be.

Thirty

Jesse hadn't left too soon for Alanna. She didn't want to see signs of Liam in his speech, his actions. And last night's kiss didn't bear thinking about. She'd been dreaming that she was kissing Liam. The dream was so real that she'd been unable to distinguish fantasy from reality when she woke up and realized it was Jesse. And even worse, she feared she was coming to care for this Jesse, the blend of Jesse Hawthorne and her Liam.

She was a married woman, even if in name only, and she'd been kissing him back. She sat at the dressing table and stared at herself. What kind of woman was she? A Christian woman, one who honored her vows? Or a woman who flung herself at any man who reminded her of her lost love?

She'd been a poor Christian lately, no denying that. Her anger toward God had made her tune out his leading. Self-hatred twisted her mouth. The fix was simple enough—all she had to do was let go of her bitterness. Easier said than done. She moved across the room and found her nearly forgotten Bible in the closet. Smoothing her hand over the cover, she inhaled the aroma of good leather and remembered how she used to look forward to her devotions every day. She and Liam read together every morning and discussed the passage.

It hurt to remember. Her hand touched her belly. She owed a Christian upbringing to her baby. "I'm sorry, God," she whispered. "Help me get past the bitterness." Being willing was the first step. God could take it the rest of the way.

She flipped open the Bible at random, and her gaze fell on the opening verses of Psalm 139.

> O Lord, You have searched me and known me. You know my sitting down and my rising up; You understand my thought afar off. You comprehend my path and my lying down, And are acquainted with all my ways.

All she'd gone through was no secret to God. He knew and understood everything about her. She read further.

> My frame was not hidden from You, When I was made in secret, And skillfully wrought in the lowest parts of the earth. Your eyes saw my substance, being yet unformed. And in Your book they all were written, The days fashioned for me, When as yet there were none of them.

The passage resonated through her, all the way to her marrow. Her child was unique, as was Liam himself. So where did that leave how she saw Liam in Jesse? Her heart *knew* her husband. Knew the imprint of his spirit, just as God had formed him. She knew him as she would know her child the instant she held the babe.

She thought back through the progression of the past few months. Her husband's mangled frame after he'd been thrown clear of the car after the bomb went off. There hadn't been anything left of his face, no distinguishing marks. The germ of an idea grew, and she gasped. Was it possible the men had been misidentified? That couldn't happen these days, could it? She thought the police had run a DNA test.

Her mouth went dry, and she swallowed. How had the two men even been identified? The police had said the man behind the wheel was the owner of the car, but what if Liam had asked to drive even though she didn't want him to? He'd been aching to get behind the wheel of that sports car. It was possible.

Would Detective Adams help her if she took a strand of Jesse's hair to him? Though this idea might be dotty, it wasn't as dotty as thinking Liam's spirit had transferred to Jesse. She slipped down the hall to the room where Jesse had slept. His hairbrush was on the stand. She pulled out the hair clumped in it and stuffed it in the pocket of her jeans.

She went outside to find Barry. He was telling the foreman all he wanted done on the summerhouse. Dark circles crouched under his bloodshot eyes. She doubted he'd gotten any sleep last night. It had been nearly four by the time he returned from the city. Without his mother. She'd gone to his condo near the Battery.

Just as well. Alanna wasn't sure what she could say to her. Patricia wouldn't want her condolences—not when she blamed Alanna for more stress on Richard.

Barry saw her coming and a smile lifted his mouth. "I didn't know you were up, sugar."

She reached his side and took his hand. "Did you go to bed at all?"

"No. Too much to do." He motioned to the clouds off to the east. "Heard there were hurricane warnings issued. I'm going to have them board the windows."

"A hurricane?"

He nodded. "So you stay close to the house."

She didn't nod and hoped he wouldn't notice. "Have you talked to your mother this morning?"

"I thought I'd let her sleep if she would. She'll call me when she awakens. We need to go to the funeral home to pick out the casket and make arrangements." He delivered the statement in a deadpan voice.

She winced, knowing his emotionless attitude was all that would get him through the day. "I'm so sorry, Barry."

He draped his arm around her shoulders. "I know you are. So am I. But we knew Father had a heart condition. It was only a matter of time." He dropped a kiss on her brow as his cell phone rang.

He turned away from her and answered it. "Hello, Mother, how are you this morning?" He listened a few moments. "I'll be there right away." He put his phone back into his shirt pocket and faced Alanna. "I've got to go. Mother is ready to go to the funeral home."

Alanna nodded, wanting to ask his permission to use one of the cars. But why bother him with such a petty request? She'd be back before he knew she was even gone. What she needed to do wouldn't take long.

She waited until the live oaks hid his car in the curve of the driveway, then went inside and sorted through the keys on the rack by the back door. Keys for a Lexus, a Ferrari, and a second Mercedes were hanging there. All more expensive than she wanted to drive.

She chose the keys for the Lexus and went out the back door. The six-car garage sat to the west side of the house. She had a right to drive one of the cars—after all, they were married. But she still felt like a car thief.

The side door was unlocked. He'd probably left it unlocked after getting out his Mercedes. Before she could lose her nerve, she hit the opener by the Lexus, then climbed inside and backed out. A garage-door opener was clipped to the visor, so she punched it and door went down.

She drove down the driveway to the street and pulled out, remembering almost too late that she was supposed to be driving on the right. She jerked the wheel to the proper side and just avoided the car in the left lane. The other car's horn blasted outrage at her idiocy.

She found her way to the police station and was ushered in to see the detective.

Adams rose from behind his desk. "I'm surprised to see you here. You have information?"

She pulled the hair from her pocket and held it out. "I'd like you test this."

His brows rose. "Why?" She told him her suspicions, and he frowned. "I'll have a DNA test run."

There was something in his manner she couldn't be putting her finger on. Lack of surprise, maybe?

"I didn't think you'd consider such a thing."

"We need to keep an open mind."

"Didn't you already run tests on Jesse and Liam? After the accident?"

"We did."

"And?"

"The results didn't come in until yesterday. They were"—he searched for a word—"inconclusive."

"So how did you identify them?"

Adams looked taken aback. "Jesse said he was Jesse. And as of this moment, we still have no reason to doubt him." He went to the door and opened it. "I'll be in touch."

Frowning, she left the office. If there'd been a misidentification, it would be the police's fault. Had he been suspicious of something like this already and didn't want to admit it?

Backing out of the parking space, she turned the car toward the Travellers' community. What was she going to say to her great-grandfather? Perspiration broke out on her forehead, and she flipped the air conditioning on high. He might have forgotten she even existed—if he ever knew. She had no memory of him. All she remembered was living hand-to-mouth at the camp, each month in a different family's house.

She drove to the Travellers' village without another incident. Children played in the yards and stared at the car as she slowly drove through. The clouds were dark out to the east. Did these children know a hurricane was coming?

Two little girls were close to the road. She rolled down her window. "Where can I find Darby Costello?"

The tallest girl, her light brown hair in pigtails, pointed down the street. "In the silver trailer at the end of the road."

"Thanks. Did you girls hear we have a hurricane warning?" They stared back at her. One nodded. "Watch the sky, okay?" She drove on slowly, taking in the expensive houses set amid others that were more modest. Mobile homes also added to the mix. She'd never seen anything quite like it. The Travellers here had done well for themselves.

This time of year, most of the men would be gone working their trade, some working their cons. That was the problem. The bad ones tarnished the good ones. And there *were* good ones. A majority really.

There it was. Her great-grandfather's trailer had seen better days. It was a steel travel trailer with more dents than smooth metal. The yard held flowers, so Alanna deduced someone cared enough to try to pretty it up. Maybe some of the neighborhood women.

She parked the car and got out, taking care to lock the vehicle. As she approached the trailer, she heard a TV blaring out the news. What would he say when he saw her? Would her mother have warned him she might be coming?

She wet her dry lips and rapped her knuckles on the door.

"I'm coming!" a tremulous voice shouted from inside.

She heard a bang as if he'd dropped something, then some

shuffling. The door opened and a wizened old man peered out at her. Darby Costello was bald except for tufts of white hair above each ear. He wore a flannel shirt and a pair of denim coveralls in spite of the heat. The rubber soles on his slippers nearly flopped off as he walked.

Bleary blue eyes regarded her. He spoke words she didn't understand at first. She listened closer and realized he was speaking Cant, the Gaelic-derived language of her childhood.

When he spoke again, she caught it. "Yes, I'm Alanna," she said in English. "How did you know who I was?"

"Yer mum was by." He turned his back on her. "Come in. I been expecting you." He shuffled away from the door.

Alanna followed him into a tiny living room crowded with worn furniture. The pungent odor of chewing tobacco wafted up from a chipped enamel spittoon. The smell of the tobacco brought back a dim memory of her sitting on a man's lap. This man's? She studied the angles and planes of his wrinkled face but couldn't dredge up the memory any better.

He pointed to the orange sofa. "Sit."

She sat on the sofa and waited until he shuffled to his recliner. "What did Maire tell you?"

"That you're looking for yer sister." He opened a pouch of Copenhagen and tucked a nip of it into his cheek.

Alanna leaned forward. "Have you heard from Neila since she left?"

He nodded. "She called every month for a while. Ain't heard from her in over three years though."

Her hope sputtered. "Do you have a phone number for her? Have you tried to call her?"

"Called once't. No one answered. Figured if she wanted to talk to me, she'd be calling."

Alanna's pulse began to race. What would it be like to hear her sister's voice after all this time? "Could I get her number?"

He regarded her with rheumy eyes. "Wouldn't gain you nothing. That horse is dead."

"She's my sister. I've never stopped missing her. Please, I *have* to find her."

He rolled the tobacco around in his mouth, then leaned over and spit in the spittoon. He rose and shuffled off. For a minute, Alanna thought he was going after Neila's phone number, but he went into the bathroom instead.

"You can let yerself out," he called from behind the closed door. "I'll be a while."

Why wouldn't he give it to her? What could it hurt? She was not leaving here without that number. Glancing around the room, she saw an old black phone on a coffee table. She lifted it up, but there was no phone book under it. She began to sort through the piles of magazines and books on the shelf under the stand. It had to be here somewhere.

But there was nothing that looked like a phone or address book. She rose from her knees and went into the tiny kitchen. A few glasses had been washed and placed on the dish drainer in the sink, but otherwise, the kitchen counter was empty. She began yanking open drawers until she found one containing miscellaneous items. She pawed through fuses, bottle openers, and lightbulbs down to some letters and notebooks.

And a published phone book. She lifted it out of the drawer and laid it on the counter. Most people jotted down phone numbers in the back, and she hoped he was one of those. Flipping open the back cover, she smiled when she saw the list of names and numbers.

The toilet flushed. Darby would be out any minute. She ran down the list. There it was. Neila's number. She ran back to the sofa and grabbed her purse. Feverishly, she dug out a pad and pen.

The bathroom door opened. "Yer still here?" Darby flipped off the bathroom light. His gaze took in the book in her hand. "Give me that!" He shuffled toward her.

Alanna finished jotting down the number and stuffed the pad back in her purse before her great-grandfather could reach her. "I'm sorry, Darby."

His face was red enough to illuminate the dark room. "Maybe Neila wants left alone."

She'd always wondered what it would be like to find her family—her mother, her sister, her grandparents. When she was a teenager, she daydreamed she'd open the door one day and her mother and sister would rush in with their arms open. They'd tell her they'd been looking incessantly for her, that her being left was a mistake. They loved her and would never have left her behind on purpose.

This family didn't miss her. None of them had been searching for her. They'd gone on with their lives and never thought about the little girl they'd left behind. They hadn't cried in the night for her the way she'd cried for them. Unless Neila still missed her, and Alanna had to know the truth about that too.

Alanna faced her great-grandfather with her purse clutched in her hands. "I have to find her."

He flapped a hand at her. "Get out of here and don't come back. Yer not one of us. Yer too big for yer britches."

She was one of them. She lifted her hand, wanting to mend the breech somehow, wanting him to know she wanted to be part of the family, that she'd never stopped being a Traveller. But the fierce glare he gave her from under his white, bunched brows made her drop her hand and go past him to the door. There was nothing more to be said.

She blinked at the first drops of rain that hit her face as she went to the car. Neila's phone number was all she could think about. She might be only minutes away from hearing her sister's laugh. That laugh she still heard in her dreams. Her memories of that laugh had helped her get through the years alone. She'd always known she'd someday find her sister.

Someday was here.

Alanna drove out of the village and back to Blackwater Hall. The rain intensified, and she flipped on the windshield washers.

Her sister's number was burned into her brain. She didn't even need to look at the piece of paper. Before she knew it, her cell phone was in her hand. She was almost out of power bars, but there should be enough for a short call. Moments later, she was punching in the number. Calling her sister couldn't wait any longer.

The phone rang three times on the other end before it was picked up. "Hello," said a male voice.

"Is . . . is this Paddy Gorman?"

"Yes, ma'am. Are you calling about having your driveway blacktopped?"

Paddy sounded more educated than she'd expected. She wet

her lips. "No, th-this is Alanna, Neila's sister." There was a long pause on the other end, and for a moment, she wondered if he'd hung up. "Hello? Paddy, are you there?"

"I'm here. Is Neila with you?"

"No, I'm calling to try to find her. Isn't she there?"

"I haven't seen the woman in three years. She ran off with the fancy lawyer."

Her hope crashed and burned before it had time to be born. "Three years?" she asked dismally. "You have no idea where she went?"

"Oh I know. But I'm not chasing after any skirt. She burned her bridges."

"Where is she then?"

"Back in Charleston, I'd guess. Where her fancy man lives."

Right here? So close by? Alanna began to smile. "What's his name?"

"I don't know his name. I only saw him once when he came to pick her up."

She exhaled. Maybe it wasn't going to be as easy as she thought. "Can you describe him?"

"I can do better than that. I have a picture of the two of them together that I can e-mail to you, though you might be better off if you don't find the selfish witch."

"Please send it, Paddy." She gave him her e-mail address.

"Just don't tell me if you found her, okay? I'd rather not know."

"Okay. Thanks, Paddy. I'm sorry she hurt you. Di-did she ever mention me?"

"Sure. She looked for you some too. Couldn't find out anything."

Joy colored the darkness with bright glimmers of light. Neila hadn't forgotten her. That reunion Alanna longed for might still happen. "Thank you, Paddy."

"Listen, I gotta go. Got a job I need to be at. Nice talking to you." The phone clicked off.

Alanna dropped her cell phone back into her purse. Neila was so close. She had to find her. Glancing at the clock on the dash, she realized she'd been gone longer than expected. Accelerating, she took the last curve to the estate. As she came out of the curve and into the final stretch before the drive, she realized she was on the left side of the road again. The rhythmic swish of the blades had hypnotized her. She veered into her own lane, then glanced into the rearview mirror.

And gulped. Barry was behind her. She hated to disappoint him. He would never understand the nature of the errands she had to run today.

She couldn't tell him either.

Thirty-One

a lanna turned into the driveway and drove to the garage, punching the button to open the door as she neared it. She pulled inside and turned off the engine, then closed the door again. Thunder rumbled overhead. Clouds roiled close and dark in a way she'd never seen, and she let out a sigh when she was safely in the garage.

When she got out, the building rumbled with the strength of the thunder. Barry pulled his Mercedes into the other bay. Through the window, she could see the muscle jumping in his jaw. Surely he couldn't be that angry about her taking the car. Something else had to be upsetting him. Taking a deep breath, she waited for him to get out.

He slammed the car door and came toward her, blocking the exit. His fists were clenched at his sides, and his brows were drawn together. "Where were you, Alanna? With Jesse?" There was no kindness in his tone.

She'd wondered if he sensed the connection between her

and Jesse. Now she knew. What would he say if he knew she suspected Jesse was Liam? He'd think she was quite dotty.

Her back stiffened at his tone. "No, I wasn't with Jesse. He went to his house." She started past him, and he grabbed her arm. His fingers bit into it. "Barry, you're hurting me."

Instead of releasing her as she'd expected, he pushed her up against the garage door. "Does he think I don't see the way he looks at you? I want him out of my house. Out of our lives—for good! You're not to see him again."

"I'm not a possession, Barry," she said, struggling to keep her voice even.

"You're *my wife!*" He pressed her harder against the wall. His head lowered, and he delivered a punishing kiss, grinding his mouth against hers in an embrace that grew more painful.

She couldn't breathe. Panic engulfed her, and she struggled to free herself. Her fists beat against his chest. He wedged his knee between her legs, and his fingers went to the waistband of her jeans. He began to pull her blouse free, and she heard the buttons give way.

No! She whipped her head from side to side and managed to free her mouth. "Let me go, Barry," she panted, trying to force his hand away as it crept under her blouse and up her skin. "You're too rough. You'll hurt the baby."

He wasn't listening to her protests and continued to pull at her blouse until it was off her shoulders. The glaze over his eyes horrified her. He didn't care what she wanted. He didn't see her as a person, just a body. He lowered his head again, and his lips nuzzled her neck. Revulsion shuddered through her.

She cast her gaze to her right. If she stretched, she could

just reach a hand shovel. Lunging for it, she wrapped her fingers around the handle and brought it toward his head. Before he saw what she had, she whacked the side of his forehead with it.

He reeled back with a groan. Blood spurted from a cut, but Alanna didn't spare any sympathy for him. She leaped for the door and escaped outside.

"Alanna!" Barry shouted. He staggered from the garage with blood pouring down his face.

"Leave me alone!" Shrugging her blouse back into place, she buttoned it as she ran for the back door of the house that opened to the sunroom. The door was locked, and she'd dropped her purse when Barry grabbed her in the garage. She ran around the side of the house to the front, checking the side door on the way. It was locked too. Where was Grady? Was anyone else here? Even if she made it inside, he'd come after her if they were alone.

Lightning lashed the sky, crackling into a nearby tree. The horrifying crash made her jump. She needed to get inside. Rain was coming down in buckets now, and every inch of her body was drenched. She reached the porch and went to the door. It was unlocked. She practically fell inside, cradling her stomach protectively.

Shivering, she slammed the door shut and considered locking it, but that would only slow Barry down. And anger him. But maybe he was in control of himself again. Maybe it was his father's death that had made him react so violently. She stood in the hallway and considered her options. She could talk to him calmly, sensibly. She could watch for him to come in, then go out the back door and leave. Or she could go to her room and lock the door.

None of the options was giving her any comfort. She needed thinking time. This was a big house. She could park herself somewhere until other people came back. It would give Barry time to cool off and herself time to think things through.

But where? Barry would look for her in her room right off. The ballroom was out for the same reason. There were other rooms in the house, but he'd be likely to search them all.

His locked room.

The thought came out of nowhere. What if he wasn't mad anymore and decided to go there to do some work? But no, he'd been up there last night. He usually only went in every two or three days. It might be safe. Besides, if she had the key, he couldn't get in anyway.

Rain thundered on the roof, sluiced over the windows, battered at the door. Through the window, Alanna saw Barry stumbling toward the front porch. No time to get to the second floor. She turned and raced for the kitchen door. Unlocking it, she locked it again before she stepped out into the rain. She ran for the garage but realized it was impossible to escape by car. The rain was coming down too hard, and even the driveway was flooding.

Her cell phone.

Rain dripped from her to the garage floor as soon as she stepped inside. She retrieved her purse from the floor. At least Barry would think she was inside. It was hard to think past the pounding rain. The sound of it filled her head, numbed her panic. She locked the garage door, then went to the car and got inside the backseat and locked it, then squeezed on the floor where she couldn't be seen if Barry looked inside.

She shivered from the cold rain that had soaked every inch of her clothes. If only she had a towel. She squeezed the water from her hair and hunkered down even tighter to warm up. Fishing out her cell phone, she checked it. No power bars. She punched in 9-1-1, but it didn't have enough juice to go through, so she dropped it back into her purse.

She peered up over the bottom of the window. The storm had intensified, and she heard nothing but thunder and rain. Easing open the door, she crawled out of the car and to the exterior door. She raised her head far enough to peek out into the yard. Through flashes of lightning, she saw mud puddles but no Barry.

The rain was coming down too hard to see to drive. Jesse sat in the car outside Mark's apartment and tried to decide what to do. The radio blared out the news that this wasn't just a spring rain but a hurricane moving in for a direct hit in the Charleston area.

The announcer's excited voice bellowed out. "This is a category two storm, but don't let that fool you. The rain bands in this storm are particularly bad, and we can expect heavy flooding. The outer edges will reach us in half an hour."

So it was going to get worse. He could go back inside and take refuge with Mark and Ginny, but the less time he spent with them, the better. His mother would be happy to have him home for the evening, but he wanted to be with Alanna. She was afraid of storms like this. And after the attacks, he didn't want her alone in that house.

He stopped and shook his head. These weird certainties

kept hitting with no warning. In spite of the intensifying storm, he wanted to try to make it back to the house. The small car hydroplaned along the streets, but he managed to keep the car on his side of the line. Headlamps barely pushed back the dark of the storm as he drove rain-swept streets in a line of traffic that intensified. Others were trying to get somewhere before the worst of it too.

He reached the road out of town and turned off where the road dipped before climbing a small hill. And found the basin flooded. An SUV was stalled in the middle of the water, but the occupants had already fled the vehicle. He'd never make it across in this small car.

His cell phone rang, and he saw Ciara's name flash across the screen. He answered it, "Ciara, is Alanna all right?"

"I've been trying to call her but can't raise her," Ciara said. "The road is flooded, and we can't get back. We found a couple of rooms at the Charleston Place Hotel. If you see her, can you be letting her know so she doesn't worry?"

"I'll tell her." He ended the call. His inner urgency to see Alanna kicked up. Why wasn't she answering her phone? This was the only road in or out, and though he couldn't drive it, he could walk. It was only two more miles. He'd make it there within an hour, even in the storm. A small cemetery was just to his right. He could park the car there and hoof it. Maybe there would be a better way on foot through the cemetery.

Angling the car through the open gate, he parked it in a pull-off area and got out. The rain immediately soaked through to his skin. It was hard to see in such a heavy downpour. The estate was to his right, north. He struck off in that direction.

Splashing through mud puddles, he ran for the slightly darker area where he knew the hillside was located. To his relief, he saw a small footbridge over the raging water that was quickly climbing to the bottom of the bridge. He lowered his head and ran for the other side. He reached it and leaped onto the grass.

His right sneaker hit mud, and his left one hit slick grass. He lost his balance and flung out his arms to try to regain it. The momentum threw him to the right, and he went down on one knee, still sliding toward the precipice into the water. He grabbed at tufts of grass, but they were too short and wet to allow him any purchase. Gaining momentum, he hurtled toward the water.

The next thing he knew, his head was underwater and the churning current tried to keep it there. His feet touched bottom and he pushed himself upward. He had to breathe! His lungs burned with the pressure to pull in oxygen. The churning water was too dark to see through, and he lost all sense of time and location. His vision darkened even more. Where was the surface?

His head broke through and he gulped in oxygen. The turbulent water pushed him along, and he saw a tree stump coming toward him like a deadly projectile. He dived for the bottom, and though the stump struck only a glancing blow on his head, it was enough to disorient him for a moment. When he gained his senses, he found himself clinging to a rock. Pushing himself up again, he greedily sucked in air. He had to find a way out of this swollen creek.

When he dived again, he felt along the bottom for tree roots— and found them. He wrapped his fingers around the roots, then managed to land his other hand on them as well. Hand over hand, he dragged his way toward the surface along the roots. When his head broke the water this time he was along the side of the bank, but the water hurtling past threatened to tear his grip from the tree roots.

The blow to his head still made him feel woozy—or maybe it was all the water he swallowed. It would be so much easier to just let go, quit fighting. Let the current tear the roots from his grasp and take him into oblivion. But he had to get to Alanna again, protect her. In that moment, Jesse realized he couldn't just give in. He had to fight.

Somewhere he found the strength to reach his right hand up and grasp the tangled mass of tree roots. He put the toe of his shoe into the roots along the wall of the creek and struggled against the current. Inch by inch he managed to climb his way out of the churning water until he lay gasping in the mud like a newborn turtle.

He groaned and rolled onto his back. The rain pelted him, filling his nose and mouth until he felt he was drowning again, but he was too weak to resist. The thud of the rain against the ground filled his ears, and he heard music. Coughing, he rolled to his side, and his head began to clear.

The music in his head continued to play, only this time he heard the words.

Two souls bound which none can sever. This nightsong is for you. Our love will last through fire and trouble. This nightsong is for you. Not even death can break our hearts. This nightsong is for you.

He recognized the tune now. The tune that played on the music box Alanna had played for them. The tune he'd been humming. In a moment it all flooded back. His life, the night of the explosion. He could hear the screaming metal in his head, Jesse's shout.

He was Liam Connolly, not Jesse Hawthorne.

Struggling to his feet, he knew he had to get to Alanna. Tell her who he was and get her out of that house.

In a loping run, he turned and plunged in the direction of the estate. The current had thrust him closer and he'd come up on the north side of the creek. He should be there within half an hour.

The wind blew the rain sideways, blinding him. He swiped the moisture from his eyes and peered through the darkness. The wind pushed against him, impeding his progress. It might take longer than he anticipated. The wise thing to do would be to take shelter in a closer house, but Alanna needed him. An inner urgency drove him on.

He had to save her.

Thirty-Two

Was he still looking for her? Alanna wished she knew when it would be safe to go inside. Where were her mates and Grady? Once other people were here, she would have nothing to fear. Maybe she had nothing to worry about even now. If Barry was still looking for her, he might be wanting to apologize.

She was overreacting.

She slung the strap to her purse over her shoulder and rose. This was quite wonky. The thing to do was to march in there and tell him she wouldn't tolerate behavior like that again. He was likely penitent. The incident in the garage wasn't like Barry. She pushed open the door, then ran for the house.

The rain drenched her again, pouring down her back, cloaking her vision. Her bare feet slipped in the mud, and she went down onto her knees. She struggled to her feet and staggered toward the door again. Running up the steps, she reached the back door. It was still locked, so she fished her key out and unlocked it before practically falling onto the kitchen floor.

The relief of being out of the rain made her inhale thankfully. In the mansion, the sound of the pounding rain was muted, too, and the sudden de-escalation of noise let her pulse resume a normal rhythm. Her present position was vulnerable, so she struggled to her hands and knees, then to her feet.

A towel was lying on the counter. She grabbed it and wiped her streaming face, soaked the water from her hair, and wiped the mud from her feet. She left the ruined towel on the floor by the door and went toward the living room.

There was no noise she could detect except the intensifying storm outside. Where was Barry? She opened her mouth to call for him, then closed it again when she heard him bellow her name. She thought he was up in the ballroom. The rage in his voice sent every nerve tingling. The sensible, gentle, kind Barry was still missing.

Or maybe she was seeing the real man for the first time.

She crept up the main stairs, careful to avoid the third step that squeaked. She didn't think he could hear her from the third floor, especially with the storm pounding the house, but she didn't want to risk it. She reached the hall and tiptoed to his bedroom.

The bed was unmade today, and his clothes from yesterday were in a pile on the floor. Very out of character from what she'd seen, but his behavior today had been out of character too. The death of his father must have profoundly affected him. The closet door stood open a crack. For a moment she imagined he was waiting in there and would grab her by the throat the moment she approached. She swallowed hard and told herself not to be a dope.

Aware she was holding her breath, she let it out and moved to the closet door. Her fingers gripped the doorknob. Her pulse was nearly as loud as the thunder crashing overhead. This was quite silly. Just open the door, she told herself.

She forced herself to yank open the door. Her shoulders sagged when she realized there was no one there. She grabbed the keys from the hook and retreated. Barry was still banging around in the ballroom. She had time to get to the locked room.

Her hand crept to her throat, and she jumped when she heard someone at the front door. At last, there were reinforcements. She ran down the steps to the front door and threw it open. The figure who stumbled through the opening wasn't recognizable at first. Blood poured from his head and his face was swollen with numerous cuts.

"Alanna?" he croaked.

Then she recognized him. "Jesse?"

He took her shoulders in his bleeding hands. "Alanna, it's Liam. I'm not Jesse. Jesse died in the explosion. I'm remembering everything now. Tell me you recognize me."

She stared up into his face. Did she dare believe what she so longed to without absolute proof? The grip on her shoulders hurt. "You're hurting me," she whispered.

He immediately released her. "Sorry, Lanna." he muttered, shaking the rain from his hair.

"You need a towel," she said. She went to the kitchen and found a clean dishtowel. What if he was right? The DNA would be proof, but her heart didn't need the results of the test. She let the notion carry her along, just for a minute. What if Liam was right there in the living room waiting for her? There was one way she could know for sure. She could kiss him when she was fully awake.

Her throat closed with longing for her husband, her Liam. Her eyes burned. She was setting herself up for crushing disappointment. Carrying the towel, she went back to the living room. "Here you go."

He took it and wiped the blood and rain from his face and hair. With his longish hair swept away from his ears, she saw something that made her gasp. A tiny scar on the tip of his right ear. Liam's puppy had nipped him and drawn blood, actually taking out a small bit of skin. Alanna stared at it now feeling everything she thought she knew shift under her feet.

"Liam?" she whispered.

He looked up. "I remembered the words to the song, Alanna." He sang in a low voice. "Two souls bound which none can sever. This nightsong is for you. Our love will last through fire and trouble. This nightsong is for you. Not even death can break our hearts. This nightsong is for you." His voice cracked on the last note of the song.

The words and the voice sank into her heart. It was her husband. How and by what means he was standing here, she couldn't be knowing. Nor did she care. She *knew* it was Liam. The verse in Psalm 139 about being fearfully and wonderfully made had resonated in her heart. Her husband was as unique and individual as the baby she carried, and every sense she owned recognized him.

She took a step nearer. "Liam," she whispered again. Then she was in his arms, and his lips were on hers. There was no question it was the man she loved. The scent of his sweet breath, the firm press of his lips against hers, the way he held her so tightly. She reveled in his embrace, burrowed against his chest, inhaled the essence of him.

She would never let him go again.

"What's going on here?"

When Liam's arms tightened around her at the sound, she began to swim up out of her joy-caused stupor. She murmured a protest when Liam's lips were withdrawn from hers, when his grip slackened. Wait, that voice. It was Barry. He was here.

She turned to face him. "Barry, you'll never believe it."

"Believe what? That you're a conniving, scheming whore who has taken my love and thrown it back in my face?" He screamed the words, spittle spraying from his mouth.

Advancing on them with his hands curled into claws, he bore no resemblance to the elegant, professional attorney she thought she knew. The kind man who had offered to help her and her mates had morphed into a monster she didn't recognize.

She held out a hand to him. "Barry, I'm sorry. But it's Liam. He's not dead. This is Liam, not Jesse."

He threw back his head and howled. "You betray me and then make up some kind of weird lie?" There was murder in his eyes.

Liam stepped in front of her with his hands outstretched. "C'mere, mate. Don't carry on like this. We'll sort it all out."

"We'll sort out nothing," Barry said, his voice devoid of anything but an icy cold. "I killed you once. I can do it again." From somewhere, he had a knife in his hand.

Before Alanna could shout a warning, Barry was hurtling toward Liam with the knife held high overhead. In one monstrous arc, he drove it into Liam's chest. There was a funny punching sound, then blood sprayed from Liam's chest and covered Barry's grinning face before he turned toward Alanna.

"Your turn, my cheating little wife," he said.

———

Blood poured from Liam's chest. Alanna stood frozen in place as the red stain mingled with the rain that soaked his shirt.

"Run, Alanna," he whispered. "Run!"

His words penetrated her stupor, and she realized Barry was advancing with the knife, its shaft still red with Liam's blood. She wanted to go to Liam, help him, but if she did, they would both die and so would their baby. She was no match for Barry's bulk and muscles. She needed a weapon.

She wheeled and ran for the stairs. He didn't know she had a key to the locked room. She could hide there until he ran past. Then she'd find a gun. Barry bellowed her name and started after her. She dared a glance back and saw him rushing to the steps. He reached the rug at the bottom and slipped, going down on one knee.

His fall gained her a few seconds. She ran down the hall and turned the corner, then raced to the end. Her hands shook as she jammed the key into the lock and turned it. She heard the click, then quickly opened the door and stepped inside. She locked the door, then realized there was a deadbolt so she threw it as well.

It was too dark in the room to see well. She would need to turn on the light, but would he see the glow of it from under the door? She realized she was standing on a throw rug. Kneeling, she bunched it up and wadded it along the bottom crack of the door.

Her mouth was dry and her blood roared in her ears as she put her head against the door and tried to listen. There. The sound of feet walking purposefully along the hall, then the squeak of a door opening. The sound continued, and she knew Barry was checking each room in a methodical way. What would he do when he reached *this* door? Surely he wouldn't be surprised it was locked.

She licked her lips and curled her hands into fists. Liam was bleeding in the hall and she was stuck up here unable to help him. How badly was he hurt? The stabbing had looked horrific. She prayed that Grady would come. Anyone who might help.

In the dim light, she stared as the doorknob turned and Barry tested the door. She held her breath, then let it out when his steps went on down the hall. He'd expected to find it locked. If she hadn't relocked it, he would have known she was inside. The strength ran out of her legs, and she sagged to her knees with her head against the door.

Get up! She had to find help for Liam. Using the desk beside the door for a prop, she struggled to her feet. It would be impossible to find anything in here without a light. She turned on the overhead light then turned to study the room.

She needed a phone to call for help. There was none in this room.

The walls were covered with photographs. Her gaze went from picture to picture. Every wall was covered with images of her. She approached the first wall. The pictures were from last year's concert. One of her favorite pictures was of her and

Liam together, but he'd been cut out of this print. Her hand went to her mouth to hold back the scream that struggled to be released.

Downstairs, Barry had said, "I killed you once. I can do it again." Had he planted the bomb under Jesse's car? She remembered that Liam had talked about his upcoming outing with Jesse for a couple of days beforehand. Could Barry really have been so diabolical?

The expression on his face downstairs slammed into her mind. Yes, the man could be that evil.

In a fog, she moved to the next wall. And found the woman she thought was herself was, in fact, another woman. Though they looked very much alike, this woman's hair was darker and her nose was different.

In fact, she reminded Alanna very much of her sister, Neila.

A sinking sensation swirled in her gut. She remembered what Paddy said about Neila running off with a "fancy lawyer." In the Charleston area. Yet she stopped contact with her great-grandfather and her mother. Could it be?

The music box. It had to be the one Alanna remembered as a child. It belonged to Neila.

She had to sit down a second. Everything was slamming into her. She sank onto the chair in front of the computer desk. The computer was on. She stared at the open web page. A search engine.

She had to get help. She rubbed her head. *Think, think.* There was no phone, but there was the computer. She quickly ran a search for the Charleston police department. There was no emergency e-mail link, so she clicked on the directory of personnel.

Detective Adams had a contact link there, so she dashed off a quick plea for help.

Who knew when he'd get it, though? And there was no link on the website for reporting a crime. She was on her own until help arrived.

Hattie. She'd said to come to her if she was in trouble. Maybe she could get outside and reach Hattie. The old woman might be able to talk to Barry.

She stared at the screen again. The truth about Barry and Neila might be here already. Her fingers typed in her webmail address, and she waited for the mail to arrive. There, the one from Paddy. She clicked it open, and an image filled the screen.

Barry stood on the left, his smiling face turned toward the woman next to him. The woman on the wall. Neila.

Alanna tried to wrap her mind around it. She'd known of Barry's obsession with her great-grandmother by the way he talked about her picture and the music box. Had he gone out and tried to find his own version of Deirdre through her and Neila?

Heavy steps came back down the hall and paused at the office door. She stared at the doorknob as it turned again. The steps went on past and around the corner. Was he going to get another key? He likely had a second key somewhere. The one she had couldn't be the only one. Barry was too organized, too methodical.

She swallowed hard and looked around for a weapon, any-thing to defend herself. The room held only a desk and chair, a few filing cabinets, and an armchair. Maybe there was something in the cabinets. Easing open each drawer quietly, she searched for a gun but found only files.

The closet. She moved to the other side of the room and opened the closet door. It was empty, but there was a panel in the back of it. A drawer pull was on the side of it. She yanked it open and realized she'd found a passage to a stairway leading up.

And a way out of a locked room. She rushed to the door and gently slid back the deadbolt so he would not know she'd been inside, then smoothed out the rug and flipped off the light before hurrying back to the hidden stairway.

Inside the old staircase, the air smelled dank and dusty. Alanna stifled a sneeze as she pulled the panel shut behind her, plunging the space into total darkness. Feeling her way, she crawled up the steps, counting them as she went. On the seventeenth stair, she came to a tiny landing. Her hands roamed the wood floor until she found the door.

She raised herself to her feet and fumbled for the doorknob. Turning it, she practically fell into the next room. She blinked in the dim light coming in through the many windows. The ballroom. She was in the ballroom.

Barry was below her. Could she find her way to Patricia's apartment and use the private entrance there? But that would leave Liam still here at Barry's mercy. She couldn't bear to think of what her love was going through two floors below. Was he still alive? She couldn't lose him again after she'd just found him.

Her hands covered her belly protectively. If only she could find a weapon. Lightning flashed outside the window, and thunder trailed it a second later. The room held only Ceol's instruments. She picked up her fiddle, taking comfort from the smooth wood.

Think. There had to be some way to reach help. If only there was a signal on her cell phone. Could she creep down the stairs and get to the house phone without being seen by Barry? If she made her way downstairs, she could hide in bedrooms along the way and eventually get to the entry. And Liam.

It was her only hope.

Lightning flashed again, and she heard a creak from behind her. She whirled in time to see Barry come up the secret stairway she'd just used. Dirt streaked his face and blond hair. His shirtsleeve was half torn off. His expression was calm and cold.

"There you are." The knife was still in his hand, but he held it loosely at his side.

He must have gotten his other key and gone into the locked room.

Alanna backed away a few feet. "Barry, I'm sorry I hurt you. Please don't hurt the baby."

He laughed. "I don't care about your brat." He took a step toward her. "You're all I care about, Alanna. You're mine, no one else's. I've done everything for you, but you still reject me."

Her mind spun like a hamster wheel. He said he didn't care about the baby. Could he have been the one who pushed her down the hill, who put the snake in her bed? "Did you try to make me lose the baby?" she asked.

He grinned and advanced another step. "Bingo, sugar."

The endearment was obscene on his lips. Alanna swallowed down the bile rising in her throat. "Love doesn't destroy what is important to the other person," she said softly.

"I didn't want you nursing another man's brat," he said. "I'll give you a baby of my own."

The very thought nearly made her gag. She retreated another step. "Where is my sister? Did you marry her too?"

"No."

"Where is Neila?"

His unblinking stare didn't change. "Part of nature. You have two choices, Alanna. You can join her, or you can let go of your childish devotion to that ridiculous man downstairs."

"You *killed* her?" Though she'd suspected it, hearing it confirmed filled her with grief. She would never have that reunion she'd dreamed of. Her eyes burned and she fought the tears. She had to keep it together to outwit him.

"She laughed at me," he said. "What is it with you tinkers? You jump from one man to the other. She said she wanted me, then she decided to go back to her husband. No one leaves a Kavanagh."

Over his shoulder, she saw lights sweep across the driveway. A truck on big tires pulled up outside. In the flashes of lightning, she saw a man jump out and help a woman down from the other side. Grady and Patricia. Would they help her? At least someone could tend to Liam.

Barry seemed oblivious of the truck and its occupants. His feet slid forward a few more inches. "We'll have a wonderful life, Alanna." His voice held a plaintive appeal. "I'll make sure Ceol is a household name. We will fill this house with laughing children. I'll give you everything a woman dreams of." He held out his arms. "Come to me, sugar."

Alanna could no more stop her head from shaking in a *no* movement than she could stop her retreat. His smile faltered, and his eyes narrowed to slits of gleaming malice. He dropped his left hand but held the knife up in his right.

"I see," he said slowly. "You've made your choice then." He began to walk toward her with clear intent.

Thirty-Three

The front of Liam's shirt was soaked with blood, and his vision swam as he regained consciousness. He managed to sit up with his hand plugging the knife hole in his chest.

He coughed and blood spurted from the wound. Not good. It might have nicked his lung because he found it difficult to breathe. He had to get to Alanna though. That madman would kill her. Struggling to his feet, he grabbed the towel Alanna had dropped and wadded it up, then pressed it over the hole in his chest.

His vision blurred, and he feared he might collapse again. He couldn't allow that. Gritting his teeth, he forced himself to move toward the living room. The phone was in there, and he could call for help. Staggering through the doorway into the parlor, he focused on his goal: the telephone that sat on the stand by the sofa.

When he reached it, he dialed 9–1–1 and got a message to hold. Probably the switchboard was lit up with calls relating to the storm that was raging outside. The wind hadn't reached its full fury yet, but it would soon.

He left the phone connected and staggered back toward the stairway. He had reached the entry when the front door opened and the wind blew two figures into the house. Patricia and Grady stood dripping in front of the door. Grady reached back and slammed the door shut.

Patricia was staring at him with horror. "What's happened?" she asked in a faltering voice.

"Quick, you've got to help Alanna. Barry will kill her!" Liam turned and pointed. "Up there."

Grady frowned, his expression doubtful. "We'd better call you an ambulance."

When Grady didn't move, Liam started for the stairs himself. "The phone is still connected to emergency dispatching. Get the police out here." He had to help Alanna. There was no time to waste.

Patricia put her hands to her face. "Not again," she moaned. She started after Liam. "Grady, call for help. I'll handle this." She grabbed Liam's arm and helped him up the steps.

Liam's chest burned, and he found it difficult to drag in enough oxygen. Aware he was slowing her down, he pulled his arm free. "Go on. Hurry! I'll catch up. You have to help her."

It was only as she nodded and hurried toward the stairs to the ballroom that he realized she might not be friendly to Alanna. He took a tighter grip on himself and forced his legs to move faster though his chest felt it would burst into flames at any minute. Grabbing the banister, he dragged himself up the final flight of stairs.

When he reached the ballroom, he heard Patricia cry out. "Barry, no!"

Liam stumbled over to where she stood and brushed past her. Alanna . . . Where was his wife? He spotted her to the left of the door. Barry was approaching her with the knife in his hand.

Barry glanced at his mother. "She is going to leave me, Mother."

Patricia's face was white, and she held out her hands to her son as she stepped between him and Alanna. "Not again, Barry. I can't protect you from this one. You have to put down the knife."

Barry's face twisted in a snarl that made him unrecognizable. "I'm your *son*! You don't even like her. Why would you protect her?"

"Let's go on a nice long vacation," Patricia said soothingly. She approached her son with her hand out. "Give me the knife, Barry." She was only a foot away from him.

"No!" he screamed. With his left hand, he shoved her out of the way and leaped toward Alanna. His mother stumbled back, then went down onto her knees.

Liam tried to tackle him, but the pain in his chest exploded. He tried to jump but only managed to leap three feet, so he flung out his hand and grabbed at Barry's arm. His fingers snagged Barry's shirt, and the man jerked it away.

Barry threw out his arms and pinwheeled. His stumble jerked him to the right of Alanna. Her frozen stance changed, and she blinked, dispelling Liam's notion that she couldn't move. Her eyes narrowed on Barry. She took a step back and swung her fiddle up in an arc that caught him under the chin.

His head snapped back and he reeled away. The knife spun out of his hand and clattered across the floor to where Liam lay.

Liam retrieved it. That was his blood on its tip. It could have been Alanna's next.

Liam wiped the knife on his jeans and stared at Barry, who was out cold. "Good aim, Lanna," he said. He regained his feet and stumbled toward Alanna. She threw herself against his chest, a painfully wonderful embrace. "Are you all right?" he whispered against her hair.

She nodded though she was sobbing. "We have to get you to the hospital."

"I wouldn't turn it down," he said, struggling to breathe. He was going to pass out again if he didn't sit. He stuck the knife in a belt loop.

Alanna guided him to a chair and helped lower him into it. He glanced up to see Patricia staring down at her son, her face white. "Thank you," he said to her.

She tore her gaze from Barry with obvious reluctance. "He's always been obsessed with Deirdre," she said. "Even when he was eight or nine, he'd sit for hours and look at her picture." She glanced at Alanna. "When he brought you home, I knew it was about to begin again. I wanted to drive you away, keep him safe. The police will take him away." She covered her face with her hands. "I can't stand it."

Liam had no sympathy to spare for the older woman. She'd aided and abetted her son's crimes. He drew in another agonizing breath and his vision blurred again. He put his head between his knees for a few moments, then straightened when Alanna spoke.

"He tried to kill you," she whispered.

"I know."

"I mean the bomb. Barry did that."

Liam closed his eyes and shook his head.

"What about my sister?" Alanna asked Patricia. "He told me he killed her when she was going to leave him."

Patricia's sobs tapered off, and she lowered her hands, then fished in the pocket of her slacks for a tissue. She wiped her eyes with it and slowly nodded. "I didn't realize he was dangerous until then. I came home and found them, much like today, only I was too late. Neila was already dead."

"He stabbed her?" Alanna gave a soft sob. "I'll never see her again."

Liam wanted to go to Alanna, comfort her, but the pain in his chest grew more agonizing. Spots danced in his eyes. He couldn't pass out. He couldn't leave his love. He pushed away the pain and managed to stay conscious.

———

The trembling wouldn't stop. Every time Alanna thought she had control of it, the shakes began again. She grabbed her battered fiddle, knowing that having it in her hand would calm her. "What did you do?" she asked Patricia.

"What could I do? I couldn't let the police take him away. Not my only child, my son."

Alanna studied the unrepentant face of the woman in front of her. Only a few lines at the corners of her eyes betrayed her age. Patricia had been pampered and coddled all her life. She was the type of woman who shielded her eyes from the brutality in the world, yet when she'd discovered her son was a murderer, she'd allowed it to go unpunished.

"Barry said Neila's body was with nature. What did he mean?" Alanna asked.

Patricia's coloring turned a little green, and she gave a delicate shudder. "He threw her in the pond."

The gator. The mental image overwhelmed Alanna. Her beautiful, laughing sister disposed of in such a brutal way. Neila would never laugh again, never feel the sun on her face.

She was going to be sick.

Alanna bent over and heaved. She coughed as the acid burned her mouth. Liam was there beside her, supporting her, wiping her mouth with the tail of his shirt and murmuring condolences.

Alanna clutched his hand for strength and kept hold of her fiddle in the other one. "You say you tried to drive me off. Why would you help me at all?"

"It wasn't for love of you, believe me." Patricia put her tissue back into her pocket. "I knew it would keep happening, over and over. I couldn't go through it again." She glanced at her unconscious son. "I thought the medication would control his fantasies, but it obviously didn't work. I shall have to tell his doctor."

"The prison doctor will be the one to tell," Liam said.

Patricia's abstract expression melted to horror. "Can't we come to an agreement? I'll pay you whatever you like to say nothing to the police. I'll put Barry into the hospital until he's well."

"I know why the medicine didn't work." Grady spoke from behind them. "It was Dad's fault."

Alanna turned to see him enter the ballroom. His orange hair was droopy and damp, and his blue eyes were tired.

Patricia stared him down. "What are you talking about, Grady?"

He swallowed, but his gaze held steady as he fixed her with a challenging stare. "I saw him changing out Barry's pills."

She gasped and took a step back. "That's a lie! Richard would never do such a thing."

"I asked him what he was doing." Grady looked down at the floor, then back up again. "He said he couldn't have Barry's mental illness passed on to any children. He thought he'd let Barry do what Barry always did, then be committed."

Her lip curled. "And you'd inherit. You were in on it, too, weren't you?"

He shook his head. "Of course you'd think that, but no. I told him it was wrong, and I wanted nothing to do with it. That if he kept it up, I'd walk away and never come back."

"And why would you do that? You're only here for what you can get," Patricia said.

His smile came Alanna's way. "Alanna, you're the only person in this house who has treated me like a real person. I was rooting for you to leave Barry and get out of this house of secrets."

Alanna caught a breath. He'd tried to help her in his own way. There was more depth to him than she'd thought.

"Are you the reason Richard died?" Patricia demanded of Grady. "You argued, didn't you? And he had a heart attack."

A flush washed over Grady's face, then faded away, leaving him pale. "We argued, yeah. I didn't want to hurt him, but I couldn't let him go forward with it."

"You killed your own father," she accused.

Tears stood in his eyes. "I didn't kill him. He had a bad heart. What kind of father would do what he did?"

Alanna heard a sound behind her and turned to see Barry lurch to his feet and pull a gun from a holster on his ankle. He waved the weapon in the air. "I heard all that. This place is mine and no one else's. You can die with the rest."

Alanna stared down the barrel of the gun as he brought it around toward her. His face was twisted with rage and hatred. How had she ever thought this man cared about her? "Please, Barry. Put the gun down."

He gestured to the door. "All of you, outside. We're going to make a visit to the pond. I can play the grieving widower well. The poor aristocrat who lost everything in the storm."

"Let us go, Barry. It's over. This will never work."

"Oh it will work beautifully." He gestured with the gun. "All of you, downstairs. Stay close together. Make one wrong move, and I'll shoot."

Patricia reached a hand toward her son. "You can't mean me, Barry."

His eyes were cold as he looked her way. "You drugged me all these years. I'm done being told what to do."

Grady stared at his half-brother. "Why would you want to kill me? I tried to keep Dad from hurting you. We can handle this together. I'll back up your story."

Barry laughed and waved the gun in the air. "I'm not stupid, Grady. Now go!" He stepped away from the steps. "Go slow, all of you." He caught at Alanna's arm as she started past. "Not you, Alanna."

For a moment, she thought he was going to let her go, but

he pushed the gun in her ribs. "If any of you run, I'll shoot her. Jesse, I know you don't want her hurt, so it's your job to keep everyone else in line. You go first."

The hard pressure of the metal barrel against her ribs made her wince. She glanced at Liam and wished she could help him. His face was pasty, and his breathing labored. She feared he'd never make it.

He gave her a thumbs-up and went slowly to the stairs. Holding onto the railing, he started down the steps. Patricia scowled at Barry but followed close behind Liam. Grady shuffled after them. The three were spaced a step apart. Alanna glanced at Liam. He still had the knife in his belt, but she wasn't sure he had enough strength to use it.

Barry marched Alanna to the stairs and followed his captives. She tried to think of how she could be disarming him. All she could do was sidle down the steps and watch for an opportunity to avert whatever he had planned.

The group reached the hallway. Liam stumbled once as he led them along the curving path to the staircase to the first floor. Alanna started to go to him, but Barry jerked her back against him. She put her hand on her belly. Somehow there would be a way out of this. Her baby was depending on her for life.

Liam reached the foyer, then leaned against the wall. Alanna expected him to go sliding to the floor any second. His face was paper white, and his eyes were glassy.

"Help him," Barry barked to his mother. He nodded at Liam who closed his eyes.

Patricia started to shake her head, then evidently reconsidered when Barry's eyes narrowed. Huffing, she grabbed Liam's arm before he could sink to the floor.

"What are you going to do to us?" Alanna asked. If she could keep him talking, maybe they could figure out how to be getting the gun away.

"Out there!" He nodded to the front door. "While the eye is going over."

Alanna hadn't noticed the quiet, but she heard it now: the sudden absence of wind, rain, and thunder.

Grady stumbled to the door and opened it. He held it open for his stepmother to help Liam out to the porch. Barry prodded Alanna forward with him. "I've got the door," he told Grady. "Go on out. But no funny stuff."

The scent of ozone and moisture rushed over her face when she stepped into the yard. Overhead the clouds swirled around the edges of a blue sky. The effect made her dizzy. The barometer would be low. Maybe that accounted for the way she struggled to breathe. Or maybe it was not knowing what Barry planned.

Barry motioned them toward the lake. "That way."

Having flooded their banks, the lake waters were only thirty feet from the mansion. The ground squished under Alanna's bare feet, and the cold and clammy mud chilled her. Moments later they stood at the edge of the water. Did he think they'd willingly walk into the water and drown? He must be daft.

The gun barrel in her ribs was beginning to bruise her skin. She pulled away slightly, and Barry shoved her away. She fell to her knees in the mud. Liam jerked away from Patricia and knelt by her side. He was shaking as if from a fever, but his skin chilled her when she touched him. She didn't like the breathless panting she heard from his chest.

He needed a doctor. And quickly.

"Get up," Barry said.

She was more than ready to obey, because she heard a splash in the water, followed by the now-familiar gator roar. Pete was nearby. Holding tight to Liam, she rose. Liam leaned heavily against her.

"Into the water with you." Barry sounded almost happy.

Patricia folded her arms across her chest. "Absolutely not."

"I could shoot you instead," Barry said. "The gator will dispose of any evidence. If you go in of your own will, at least you have a chance to swim to safety."

A false assurance. Alanna was quite certain Pete wasn't the only gator in this lake. She'd heard too many bellows. The lake churned with flotsam from the storm. She wasn't a strong swimmer. Liam was too weak to put up too much of a fight. Grady might make it, but she suspected Patricia couldn't swim at all. She was much too prissy to want to get her hair wet long enough to learn.

"How are you going to explain the fact that we all went into the water?" Alanna asked.

Barry shrugged. "I'll push the Mercedes in after you and tell the police that Patricia was suffering from chest pains so you tried to get her to the hospital. The driveway is flooded. The Mercedes would never get through."

Alanna glanced to her right. Everything he'd said was true. The police would believe him too. She could see a scenario like he'd stated playing out perfectly. The plan was too audacious.

No one would think he had planned and carried out a plot to kill all four of them. She saw Grady glance at the knife in Liam's belt, then his eyes flickered away.

She had to keep Barry's attention on her. Forcing a smile, she took a step toward him. "Barry, I'm your wife. We can work this out."

His expression went even colder. "A cheating wife. You've never once let me past the bedroom door."

She took a step closer. "That can change. We can begin again." Had Grady managed to get the knife? She couldn't look.

"Quit dallying. The eye will be past soon." His cold gaze settled on Grady. "You first, brother."

Grady smiled. "Let's talk about this. We're brothers, Barry. You won't want to have no family left at all."

"Some family I have. I'll be better off with you all dead. Then I can do what I want." He gestured with the knife again. "In you go, brother."

Grady started toward the water, then hesitated and half turned as if to say more to Barry. His hand came up out of his pocket.

Alanna saw the gleam of metal, then a knife sailed through the air and buried itself up to the hilt in Barry's chest.

Barry's eyes widened. His hand clutched the knife as if he meant to yank it out, then his mouth opened and blood poured out. He fell to his knees and pitched forward. He lay there only a moment, then got to his hands and knees and staggered to his feet. His arm wavered, and he started to raise the hand holding the gun.

Grady rushed his half-brother at the same time Alanna

leaped for the gun, but the gun went off, and a red spot bloomed on Patricia's blouse. She fell forward without a sound, and Grady stepped back when Barry swung the gun toward him.

Grady held up his hands. "Easy, brother."

Pete bellowed behind her and thrashed in the water as if smelling the coppery blood in the air.

Barry motioned with the gun. "You're next, Jesse, old man."

Behind her, Alanna heard a rustle in the bushes. A black nose peeked out, and she realized Prince was watching. She saw the dog creep out from under the bushes. The wind picked up the blood scent from Patricia and blew it toward him. He whined his distress.

"Distract Barry," Grady whispered to her.

Behind her back, she waggled her fingers at the dog. He crept out a few more inches, and his whining grew louder. Loud enough that Alanna thought Barry would hear it any second. She waggled her fingers again, and the whining went up a decibel.

Barry frowned and his gaze cut to the sound. He took a couple of steps in that direction.

"Prince, come!" Alanna called. The dog dashed from under the cover of the bushes surrounding the water. In reflex, Barry fired off a shot that went wild.

While his attention was on the dog, Liam stepped around Alanna and grabbed a downed branch. At the same time, Grady tackled Barry. Obviously nearly spent, Liam swung the branch, and it connected solidly with Barry's head. He reeled back and stepped into mud in the slope toward the water, then lost his balance and tumbled into the water onto his knees. The gun flew from his hands and landed at Liam's feet.

Barry bellowed and lurched from the water toward Liam. He grabbed the gun before Liam had time to react and seize it. Bringing up the barrel of the revolver, he narrowed his eyes. Before he pulled the trigger, a movement shot out from the bank. Prince! He ran past Barry, and the movement shifted his focus for a moment. In that instant, Liam leaped forward and wrested the gun from Barry's hand. In his weakness, he fell back as Barry turned to reclaim it. Fire barked from the barrel of the gun, and blood began to spread over Barry's shirt. His eyes wide and astonished, he fell back into the murky water and disappeared.

Thirty-Four

The fragrance of peaches from the crushed tea roses along the porch wafted to Alanna's nose. She sat on the porch holding Liam's hand as he lay on the swing. He was pale, but the bleeding had stopped. She could hear him struggle to breathe and prayed for help to arrive soon. The storm had blown for several more hours, and the flooded driveway cut them off from civilization.

Alanna had tried to comfort Grady, but he'd stalked away from her to grieve in private, and she saw his shadow under the trees as he paced back and forth.

Trees and limbs littered the saturated ground. Leaves and branches lay on the porch floor. Mud coated everything as well. The destroyed garden was a different place from the perfectly groomed space she'd first seen. The hot tea she'd made on the gas stove warmed them as the air was still cool. Their suitcases sat inside the door awaiting their departure once help arrived. She'd taken the music box too.

Alanna didn't intend to ever let it go.

The *whup-whup* of a helicopter overhead brought her to her feet. The chopper landed in the garden to the left of the manor where the least amount of limbs littered the yard. The door opened, and Detective Adams jumped out and ran with his head down toward the house. Paramedics jumped down and they all went to Patricia's body.

After several minutes, Adams left the body and walked toward Alanna and Liam. The bags under his eyes were even more pronounced than usual. Alanna decided he'd likely gotten no sleep last night. She rushed to the top of the steps to greet him.

Adams's gaze flickered from her to Liam on the swing. "I came as soon as I could. Your message said Kavanagh killed your sister and tried to kill you? What about Barry's mother? She appears to have been shot."

Alanna nodded and stepped aside to allow him onto the porch. "Liam needs to be getting to a hospital at once. I'll explain what happened on the way."

Adams stepped aside as the paramedics approached. "Let them stabilize him for the trip first. You got anything to eat? I haven't had a bite since lunch yesterday."

The last thing Alanna wanted to worry about was Adams's stomach. "I think there are bennes in the kitchen. You can help yourself."

"Much obliged." The screen door screeched when the detective stepped into the house. He returned a few minutes later with his cheeks puffed out. Two more bennes were in his hands. He chewed and swallowed. "There's a lot of explaining to do here."

Alanna kept her gaze on her husband. The paramedics had

inserted an IV line and were checking Liam's blood pressure. "How is he?"

"He's going to be fine, ma'am," one of the paramedics said. "Don't you worry."

"Did the blade get his lung?" she asked.

"Don't think so. We'll get some X-rays at the hospital though."

Alanna let out the breath she'd been holding. "When can we get going?"

"Just a few more minutes," the man said.

Grady appeared from under the trees and walked slowly toward them. "Everyone is dead. I can't quite wrap my head around it." He sank onto a step and buried his head in his hands.

She unclenched her fists. "Barry killed his mother, then tried to kill all of us. The gun went off in a struggle, and his body is in the water." She swallowed hard. "At least what's left after the gator was done."

Adams winced. "I checked some stuff after I got your message. Kavanagh has been treated for psychotic episodes ever since he was in his teens. His mother managed to hush it up when he was kicked out of school for attacking another boy when he was fifteen. He nearly killed the kid for speaking to a girl Kavanagh liked. His parents paid quite a sum of money to kill the story."

"Patricia covered up many things over the years," Grady said. "If she'd let him take the consequences, maybe he could have been helped."

Adams nodded and swallowed another benne. "There were at least two more incidents in college, I found, both over women."

"What about Neila?" Alanna's voice broke at the mention of

her sister. She would never have that reunion she had dreamed of for so long. Would Paddy care when he was told, or was he too bitter? She understood bitterness. It had nearly ruined her too.

"No sign of her, but we'll dredge the lagoon and see if we can find any trace of her body."

"Patricia said they fed her to the gator." Alanna shuddered and watched the paramedics work on her husband. They were loading him onto a stretcher.

"Then we'll likely never find the evidence." Adams's gaze lingered on Liam. "You've got your memory back?"

Liam nodded, his face pale. "I remember the crash, everything. Barry said he'd killed me once, so he must have planted the bomb."

Adams swallowed the last of his bennes. "The darkness that can lurk in the human soul still astounds me."

"You don't seem surprised that he's not Jesse," Alanna said.

"I was starting to have my doubts. If the second DNA test confirms the first, I'll be a convert. Too bad they take so long."

"Well, I don't need a test," she said.

The paramedics carried Liam past them. "We're ready," the blond one said.

"Where are your friends?" Adams asked.

The sooner she left this dark house, the better. "They got a hotel room last night when the storm started. They're at the Charleston Place." She hadn't told them the circumstances, just that they'd come through the hurricane all right. The full story could wait until they were together in person.

Adams grabbed the bags at the top of the steps. Alanna called to Prince, but the Irish Setter stayed hidden. She'd be coming back for him in the car. They boarded the helicopter and were soon airborne. She stared down at the mansion surrounded by live oak trees and black water. From up here, it appeared a beautiful home, free of the darkness that lived there.

She scooted as close to Liam as she could get. A bit of his color seemed to be coming back. The chopper lifted into the air, and she leaned over to the window. Debris littered the grand estate below. She caught a glimpse of the gator in the water, then a red streak as Prince raced to hide under the porch. Grady sat with his face pressed against the glass and stared down at the place.

Adams nodded to the estate spread out below them. "This is all yours now, Alanna."

"What?"

"The rest of them are dead. Your marriage to Barry was legal since Liam was officially declared dead."

Alanna didn't want anything of this dark place, only Prince. Maybe Hattie could be coaxed into taking some of it. "It should go to Grady, not me." Liam squeezed her hand, and she leaned down so she could hear his words above the *whup-whup* of the chopper blades.

"I have to talk to Jesse's parents yet," he said. "I'm dreading it more than you know. Especially Mom. She was good to me. I got to know who Jesse was much better by walking in his shoes."

"And your own parents. We'll call them." In spite of their differences, she smiled at the thought of their joy. Whatever their faults, they loved Liam. She hadn't told him what they'd tried to do.

Liam squeezed her hand. "Makes you wonder how much

upbringing has to do with evil, doesn't it?" he asked. "And how much is ingrained."

She nodded. "You were reading my mind."

"You might have grown up barefoot and motherless, but you overcame," he whispered. "The person God made you to be stood up under adversity. Maybe he knew you needed to have that stress to realize your full potential. You wouldn't be the same person if you'd grown up in a different environment." His other hand went to her belly. "Makes the responsibility for raising our child so important. He's put our baby with us for a specific reason. We have to do our part, then trust him with the rest."

Though Liam had tried to tell her this over the years, Alanna understood it now. She placed her hand over Liam's on her belly. "Feel him? He's moving."

Liam's smile was all she needed. They'd be getting him on his feet, then manage the next few days of explanations and trauma.

———

The audience rustled out beyond the heavy velvet curtains. This would be Alanna's last concert for a few months. Her belly hung low with the weight of their son, due in another three weeks.

Ena gave a test tweet on her pennywhistle. Liam picked up his bodhran and sticks. "Ready, my love?" he asked.

"Will you be nervous?" she asked. "Both sets of parents are out there tonight, meeting each other for the first time."

"It's not everyone who has two sets of parents," he said, smiling down at her. "I'm glad they were willing to get along."

The last few months hadn't been easy. Jesse's mum, in particular, had been devastated and still clung to Liam as if some part of her boy lived in him. And really, didn't it? Liam wore Jesse's face. It had taken Alanna a little while to get used to the change. They'd discussed having surgery to restore Liam's looks, but it hadn't seemed worth the pain and expense. The man she loved was more than his face—he was his character, his integrity, and his spirit.

Things were stiff between Liam and his father right now. She hoped tonight would help mend the breach. Life was too short to hold grudges.

The curtain opened to the stage band's strains of "Nightsong." The audience roared when they stepped to the stage. Alanna's eyes widened when Liam stepped to the mic. He usually had to be coaxed to sing.

"This is a song I wrote for my wife, Alanna, the love of my life," he said. "Many of you have heard the story of how even supposed death couldn't separate us. The song has never been more appropriate than this moment."

He held out his hand to her, and she took it in a daze. Her face could crack from the smile she wore. Liam picked up the mic and began to croon the lyrics to "Nightsong" to her.

"Two souls bound and none can sever. This nightsong is for you. Our love will last through fire and trouble. This nightsong is for you. Though death may try to break our hearts, I'll find you where'ere you go. This nightsong is for you."

God had been so faithful, she realized in a rush of emotion

that choked any possibility of joining Liam in the song. Even when she had doubted, God had performed the miraculous. She held her husband's hand and faced the crowd, which was on its feet roaring its approval.

Tears filled her eyes and spilled to her cheeks. Love was the greatest gift of all and transcended death. Her heart full, she managed to sing the final chorus of the song with Liam. He swept her into his arms, and his lips met hers as the crowd nearly lifted the roof from the rafters.

Discussion Questions

1. Have you ever been ashamed of your heritage and upbringing or did you grow up in the perfect family? How did it affect you?

2. Do you think Alanna handled the situation with Liam's parents correctly? Why or why not?

3. Have you ever been angry with God? If so, how did you handle it?

4. Evil can lurk behind the most handsome face. How can we recognize it?

5. Prejudice can exist against many different ethnic groups. Alanna experienced it from being a Traveler. How do we combat prejudice?

6. Jesse wanted the accident to be a chance for him to be a better person. Do you think it's possible for a person to change that much?

7. Patricia went to great lengths to protect her son. Do you think she could have changed anything if she'd acted differently?

8. Alanna realized God created every person uniquely. Have you seen that in your life and the lives of others?

Acknowledgments

J'm so blessed to belong to the terrific HarperCollins Christian Publishing dream team! I've been with my great fiction team for fourteen years, and they are like family to me. I learn something new with every book, which makes writing so much fun for me!

Our fiction publisher, Daisy Hutton, is a gale-force wind of fresh air. She thinks outside the box, and I love the way she empowers me and my team. The last two books have been with my terrific editor, Amanda Bostic, who really gets suspense and has been my friend from the moment I met her all those years ago. Fabulous cover guru Kristen Ingebretson works hard to create the perfect cover—and does. And, of course, I can't forget the other friends in my amazing fiction family: Becky Monds, Kristen Golden, Karli Jackson, Jodi Hughes, Paul Fisher, and Kayleigh Hines. You are all such a big part of my life. I wish I could name all the great folks at HCCP who work on selling my books through different venues. I'm truly blessed!

Julee Schwarzburg is a dream editor to work with. She totally gets romantic suspense, and our partnership is pure joy. She brought some terrific ideas to the table with this book—as always!

ACKNOWLEDGMENTS

My agent, Karen Solem, has helped shape my career in many ways, and that includes kicking an idea to the curb when necessary. We are about to celebrate fifteen years together! And my critique partner of seventeen years, Denise Hunter, is the best sounding board ever. Thanks, friends!

I'm so grateful for my husband, Dave, who carts me around from city to city, washes towels, and chases down dinner without complaint. My kids—Dave, Kara (and now Donna and Mark)— love and support me in every way possible, and my little granddaughter Alexa makes every day a joy. She's talking like a grown-up now, and having her spend the night is more fun than I can tell you. And as I write this, my little grandson, Elijah, is due to arrive in two weeks. Exciting times!

Most important, I give my thanks to God, who has opened such amazing doors for me and makes the journey a golden one.

About the Author

Photo by Clik Chick Photography

C olleen Coble is a *USA Today* bestselling author and RITA finalist best known for her romantic suspense novels, including *Tidewater Inn*, *Rosemary Cottage*, and the Mercy Falls, Lonestar, and Rock Harbor series.

Visit her website at www.colleencoble.com.

Twitter: @colleencoble

Facebook: colleencoblebooks

THE
SUNSET COVE
series

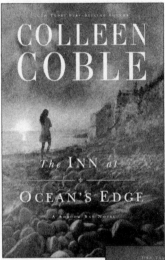

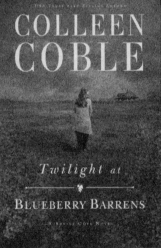

AVAILABLE IN PRINT,
E-BOOK, AND AUDIO

AVAILABLE IN PRINT,
E-BOOK, AND AUDIO

AVAILABLE IN PRINT,
E-BOOK, AND AUDIO

THOMAS NELSON
Since 1798